I0524366

Coven of Desire

WHISPER

ELLEN MINT

Whisper
ISBN # 978-1-83943-745-8
©Copyright Ellen Mint 2021
Cover Art by Claire Siemaszkiewicz ©Copyright October 2021
Interior text design by Claire Siemaszkiewicz
Totally Bound Publishing

WHISPER

Dedication

My endless gratitude to you, yes you, for picking up this book and reading it. For every book sold, my dog gets one treat…and she loves anyone who gives her treats.

Thank you to my all-mighty alpha reader Kristi, my word-whipping new editor Anna, and my ARC team. This book would be a pile of brain goo with an incubus running amok.

Chapter One

A cross March wind sheered through the air and straight up my skirt. I latched onto the hemline to keep from flashing the world and stumbled. The back of my ankle twisted, causing the side of my foot to touch the frozen, drink-splattered cement. Disgust crawled up my spine from who knew what was sprayed outside the club buzzing with college students about to flee town on spring break. I tried to contort my body to gain my balance, yank my foot off the ground, and somehow keep my foot as far from me as possible.

The neon lights of a dancing horse outside the Gallon Stallion blurred into warp lines. That vomit and urine-soaked ground I'd tried to avoid rushed up to meet me. I foresaw a broken nose in my future. Hands unnaturally warm in this unforgiving night's chill wrapped around my waist.

I didn't just stop falling — I righted onto my stilettos while blinking in surprise. The hands became arms winding around me and hot breath curled around my ear. "Beware the terrain, there is treachery in the air."

My skin shivered from the heat of his body caressing mine. March's unforgiving cold tried to break in between us but he rarely left any room. Shaking my head, I tried to fight off the sexual hunger of my personal incubus. It was like attempting to battle a ten-story lizard with a French fry.

Falling into a warm, clean bed with Ink brushing his fingertips over every inch of my skin sounded better with every frost-tipped breath. Heat finally wound its way down my thighs, and I turned to face him…when a car turned and slowed.

The jet-black Mustang was a few decades out of date but kept in great condition. It shone like an oil river as it stopped right beside me. The dancing neon horse galloped on the hood while the driver rolled down his window. A face eclipsed by shadow called out, "Layla Leeland?"

"That's me," I said, my heart racing. Was this one it? I glanced back at Ink, my partner in more than one sense.

While I was freezing in my dress that was too tight thanks to lots of study nights plus pizza, Ink showed no signs of the cold. He'd dressed in his usual crimson shirt and black slacks, but left the top three buttons undone. On his shirt. Not that it'd take much to get his pants opened.

As I leaned closer to Ink, the driver suddenly called out, "I only take one passenger!"

I nodded hard to my incubus. He clasped his hands around mine and tugged me closer to whisper, "Are you certain?"

Only one way to know. Taking my purse from Ink, I said to the driver, "No problem." To Ink I added, "I'm certain you can find your own way."

"I have been known to improvise a time or two." His wavy black hair caught in the wind, aiding in the nonchalant air projecting off him. But in his eyes, fire flickered against the amber irises.

With a set in my shoulders, I opened the backdoor of the Mustang. Water dribbled from the upholstery, drops striking the dry blacktop. I slipped into the car and closed the door. It surprised me to find the dry leather caught my nearly exposed ass, but I was grateful to be out of the cold.

The Mustang roared to life. With the edge of my vision, I watched Ink pass by. For a moment, black wings of shadow trailed behind him.

Stop worrying, Layla. You've been through worse. Standing outside clubs until two in the morning for starters. I rubbed my legs to try to get some life back.

"Any chance you could turn the heat on back here?" I asked.

"Sorry, lass. Heater doesn't work," the driver called. In the rearview mirror, I could only see the lip of a cap tugged tight over his eyes. The rest of his face hugged the shadows even as streetlights buzzed past. "You use DriveDrop a lot?"

I checked my phone. The screen was fully cracked, not from attacking witch hunters or even werewolf claws but from my keys rattling around in the same pocket. A dozen other ride-share apps were open, all waiting for pickup. I quickly closed each one while smiling. "No. This is my first time."

"Good. Good. You go to university?"

His accent flitted in and out like a brush fire he couldn't quite stomp down. I moved to put my phone in my purse when a text message popped up from Calvin. He was worried. "Huh? Uh, yeah. I'm a nursing student."

"Oh, so you like saving people?"

"As many as I can." There wasn't time to soothe my beast boyfriend. Slipping the phone into my purse, I glanced out of the window. I hadn't been this far downtown in months, maybe years. In my younger days, I'd have thought nothing of staying up till two, four, even six in the morning.

God, I sounded like a decrepit crone at twenty-five.

A hair caught against my neck and I absently moved to scratch it, when the driver's head snapped up. In an instant, I remembered what I'd hidden under my full hair and dropped my hands to my lap. Nothing pierced the shadows of his face but a tongue the driver drew across his open lips. They didn't move as he asked, "You from here? Got a lot of family?"

The only family I knew of was six feet under in a random cemetery. I wound up in this city because it was where my life stopped, thanks to a reckless driver. Biting my lip to keep the roiling thoughts at bay, I glanced up at the shadows in the mirror. "No."

Only the salivating tongue lashed through the air as an answer. A force rocketed me up out of my seat, the wheels striking something hard. It sent my purse tumbling, and the edge of my book poked from the folds. My spell book. Shit.

I raced to cram it back in to try to hide it. The hairs on the back of my neck rose. Piercing through the shadows of the drawn hat, the driver's eyes focused on me. Did he see the proof I'm a witch?

A low chuckle rose, his laugh matching the rumbling of the road under the tires. When did the car speed up? The city's streetlights were a myopic blur. Instinctively, I locked my hand around my purse and held my breath.

"Wh…?" *The architecture's all wrong.* My brain screamed that fact at me as I stared up not at the seventies cement apartment buildings that made up my neighborhood but at warehouses. The driver rammed the Mustang up a ramp. It sent me flying skyward again. "Where are we?"

"Packing district, I think. Lots of unloading and the like. Not an easy place to find," the driver said.

Only the stretch of the half-moon reached through the cold March sky. The city lights faded to a blotchy gray behind us. A pounding began in my heart, one I'd come to recognize as my innate warning system. I had to get out of here. This was stupid. What was I thinking? I wasn't ready to…

The car swung a turn and ahead of us rested the choppy, endless depths of blackest ink. A single buoy cast a red light from the tip, revealing the rolling waves of the great lake we were driving straight for. "What are you doing?" I shrieked, clamping onto my purse.

His laugh shifted into an unholy whinny. The engine roared, shooting us up a pile of pallets at fifty miles an hour. They crunched under the wheels like the bones of children in a cauldron. I gritted my teeth, my soul wrenching at the sound. A steel barrier wrapped around the dock, trying to keep the lake life away from dry land.

It didn't even give the madman pause. Giggling in glee, he rammed straight into the barrier. The iron ripped in half as we flew into the air. I lashed a hand out to try to catch myself. The palm planted onto the back of his seat, my nails digging into the headrest, when the whole car splattered into the freezing water.

"What the fuck are you doing?" I screamed and reached for the door handle. I heard the sound of the car being put into park, as if it mattered while we sank into the lake. Water seeped up through the floorboards, its icy grip stabbing into my bare toes. I tried to pull away, when I realized my feet were trapped. The soles of my shoes were glued to the floor. Every time I tugged, nothing happened. Not even the carpet would come up.

"Sit back, don't struggle," the madman said calmly.

No fucking way was I going to let him drown me. I moved to yank my foot out of my shoe when I realized the hand on his headrest was glued down too. An unnerving warmth pulsed against it, like a heartbeat inside a whale.

With only one hand left to me, I wrapped it around my wrist and tried to pull. All it got me was a slow laugh from the maniac. "I got a bad feeling about you. If'n we'd met in person, I'd ha'e sensed it. Technology. The great equalizer, eh?" He waved his phone in the rearview—which was when I realized the mirror dripped green slime. My reflection faded to a bubbling mass of mucus.

"Oh, god!" Water washed up to my knees. My skin ached from the cold, but I couldn't do anything. My legs were trapped, my hand stuck, and freezing cold water was going to drown me.

"Told ya not to fight it. Makes the meat all tough." He smiled, this time revealing his teeth below the hat. They were serrated like a shark's. "Just let it go. Sit back and wait for the inevitable."

"Fuck you!" I shouted and reached for my purse. Damn it. It too was glued to the sinking car. Water seeped up over the seat, waves rushing into my purse. I didn't care about my phone, but focused on the only means of escape—my book.

"Whatcha doing there?"

"Ending you." It wasn't that great of a line, rendered toothless as the car buckled to the right. My book tumbled from my bag, the front page stuck to the gooey seat. Now I could feel the tendrils of the creature suckering to the whole of my back. Why did I wear a backless dress?

Straining, I tried to reach for my book even with my hand and feet trapped. The creature laughed, all semblance of his human shell fading away. A full whinny, high-pitched and squealing like nails on a chalkboard, erupted from the monster.

"What are you up to now, witch?"

What was I? I needed my book. It was the only way to… Water swept up my chest, the cold punching into me harder than a fist to my ribs. All breath fled my lungs in an instant and I blanched. *Hold it. Hold it for as long as possible.*

Sucking in air, I glared at the creature taunting me. It'd reformed to nothing more than a swiveling pillar of green goo, but that jaunty newsboy cap remained. "Do not fight the inevitable."

"Why are you doing this?" I shouted, as if knowing why the monster wanted to kill me would help stop it.

The green blob split apart and elongated to a horse's mouth. It opened wider, drawing me to the razor teeth bursting from inside. "To survive. You humans have such delectable organs. It's cruel of you to keep them all to yourself."

"I think my liver's quite happy where it is," I said, only for water to rush into my mouth. Straining, I tried to tip my head back, but it sent more waves up my nose. A choke burst from my lungs, spraying the swallowed lake water at the monster.

It shook its deformed horse head but didn't let me go. Why couldn't all these damn creatures die from the common cold? Not about to give up, I tugged on my seat one last time. But there was no escape.

Tipping my head back, I pulled in the last of the air I could and sank under. Sound dulled. The beating of my panicking heart overtook me. I'd hoped—once under—he'd let go, or his glue would dissolve, but no luck.

"Abandon your struggles, witch," the creature taunted. His words didn't slip from the horse's mouth now submerged, but reverberated up my skin attached to the seat and into my brain. "The water will cascade down your lungs and I shall feast on your corpse."

No!

Chapter Two

Pain seized through my body, my mouth screaming for me to open it and pull in fresh air. But there wasn't any to be found. *Just hang on a little longer.* I tried to peer through the murky depths, hoping to find my chance of escape, but only an indigo death awaited me.

"Sleep, witch. Rest in the waters, return to them your life. I'm ever so hungry!"

Damn it. I didn't have a choice.

I slammed my head to the left, jarring my shoulder against my neck. Oxygen filled my body, the ward I'd drawn there pumping magic through my body. Without the panic of drowning flooding my brain, I was able to focus. My purse rested just out of reach.

My skin screamed in rage as I strained for my bag, but I didn't have a choice. Fuck! Bubbles rose from my lips, each one popping on the fading ceiling of the car.

The creature was rearranging itself. Horses didn't work to ensnare people anymore, so it had to find a new way. It had to evolve.

Above the surface of the water, the half-moon bobbed, drifting ever farther away from my reach. If I didn't get out of here soon, the magic would wash away.

"Why aren't you gurgling yet? Don't tell me that *witches can't drown* fairytale is real."

Who needs skin anyway?

Digging my heel into the pulsing floorboards for leverage, I ripped my back a half inch off the monster. It shrieked, hopefully feeling at least a quarter of the pain I did. Shaking it away, I launched for my purse. The creature shifted, dragging my spell book even farther.

"Ah, ah. That's not very nice."

No! The floorboards melted away, revealing the sandy and rocky lake bottom. We kept drifting from the shore, weeds and debris scraping at my feet. I tried to kick them, but the rest of my legs were trapped.

There. In a blink, I ripped my hand free of my purse, revealing the kitchen knife I'd kept hidden. It was only supposed to be used for peeling apples, but it could be used on sea life in a pinch. A low laugh bubbled around me, obscuring my vision.

"Does the witch think it can prick me with that?"

Twisting my arm around, I stabbed my knife straight into the mucus-soaked upholstery and dragged the blade down. Instead of springs and fluff, quivering green tendrils burst free and the monster screamed.

Silver-tipped, asshole. Just as Ink had promised, the sticky trap let loose and I floated free. The surface taunted me, a single strip of red light managing to reach this deep under. But I couldn't abandon my spell book.

Good thing Auntie Didi had insisted on those swimming lessons. While I spun around inside the monster flailing its dripping guts, my book slipped off the melting seat and fell for the bottom of the lake. I folded my arms tight to my chest to swim, when a tendril snapped from the melting creature and struck my neck.

Fuck! Water gurgled into my mouth, my ward severed. The oxygen I'd taken for granted drained to nothing.

"You wretch!" the monster roared. A second tendril shot for me. I slashed wildly, mostly missing. Another wrapped around my ankle to tug me away. "Do you have any idea what you've done?"

No! I couldn't let it pull me away from my purse. Lashing back with my foot, hoping to at least sting it with my heels, I struggled to reach. My bag drifted with the waves, just out of reach of my fingers.

"He promised me," the creature kept on crying.

Slamming the knife to the hilt into the back of the monster's seat, I used the leverage to reach forward. I blindly groped into my bag but found the bottle in an instant. Giving it a shake, a soft blue light rose. With all of my strength, I hurled it against the windshield. The monster phased away the green glass, letting the plastic bottle tumble through the water to fall where it'd been dragging me.

So far, so good.

Pain seared through my head, my lungs screaming at me to get oxygen.

Not so good. My spell book. It was the only hope I had left.

Darkness danced in my vision, my fingers and feet numb. The knife slipped as I lost all feeling, leaving me at the mercy of this monster I'd only wounded. "If you're the one I was told about, then Mr. White—AH!"

Black ichor bloomed in the water and my leg swung free. I turned and eyes of a full moon met mine. A tendril shot for the wolf, but a full spread of claws slashed against it. The flesh of the monster roiled in agony, the last cut enough to finish this.

I had to get to the surface. Straining my arms, I began to stroke, when pain of a different kind thundered through me. Even though my heart was straining and my lungs burning, I felt an awful flush of abandonment and shamefully turned to my book. I couldn't leave it behind.

While the swimming werewolf opened its mouth to sink his teeth into the skin of the monster, I dove for my book. A calm overwhelmed me once it was in my hands, which was quickly replaced by a warning of dread. I'd been under too long.

How far is the surface?

Terror bubbled inside of me and my limbs began to flail. My body needed air and was going to do all it could to get it. Above me, I could only see light flickering on the ethereal surface.

The darkness pressing around me sensed its opening. Swirling in a vortex, it stilled my legs and froze my arms. Slowly, it plucked away my vision, winnowing down my field of view until I could only see a single prick of red light.

Give in to the shadows. Why must you fight so?

A hand pierced through the impenetrable clouds and locked around my wrist. Without a second's pause, it lifted me through the darkness and out into the frozen air. I kept flying until I landed in the arms of my incubus standing on the water.

"Ink...?" sputtered from my lips along with a lungful of lake.

By the crimson light of the buoy, his strikingly harsh features grew more demonic than usual. "Is the deed done?" he asked calmly, as if we weren't floating right above the surface of a great water battle.

More water splattered from my lips, coming in spurts. All I could do was nod my head, when panic seized me. "Cal!" I shouted, spinning in his arms and trying to reach for my savior wolf. It nearly sent me falling back into the freezing water. Ink redoubled his hold and a wolf's black nose burst through the surface of the water.

"Thank god," I sighed, collapsing back into Ink's arms. A soft exhalation escaped from the incubus and he carried me across the waves back to the shore. Cal paddled along. When I touched down on cement, I thought I'd collapse to my knees and kiss solid ground. My bare toes bounced against the frozen dock and all I wanted to do was leap back into the water.

Shivering, I turned to Ink and snarled. "Wh-wh-why didn't y-y-you help?"

The demon untouched by cold shrugged. "You seemed to have it under control."

Under control? There were a good ten times I could have died. And if it wasn't for Cal... He'd reached the dock but was unable to leap up. With a sigh, Ink bent over and hoisted the four-hundred-pound wolf up into the air to join us on dry land. The second his paws hit ground, Cal shook, spraying Ink with the water the demon tried to avoid.

"This is what I get for assisting," he groaned.

I reached for Cal's head, needing to feel his warm body to prove he was still alive, when he turned. Carried in his jaws was my purse. I'd fully forgotten about it. I caressed the tips of my fingers over the top of his head and around an ear. "Thank you."

His tail wagged even as the wolf melted away to a breathtakingly gorgeous and completely naked man. I glanced at my bare toes rippling on the ground instead of watching Cal's transformation, but Ink stared as if he had a box of popcorn handy. As Cal rose to his full six-foot height, he shook his golden hair, then rushed forward for me. "Are you okay?"

Despite being in the same arctic waters, his arms were warm. I reached for them, wanting to nestle my head on his chest...which was naked. *Because all of him is very naked. Not the time, Layla.*

"Yeah, yes, not that Ink here was any help."

The incubus slammed a hand to his chest in mock outrage. "Were you not the one to insist that you 'had it'? And my assistance would be a nuisance at best?"

I wanted to throw back at him that he'd be cast back to hell if I died. But there wasn't any reason to bring that up. We'd won. The monster was dead. It all worked out.

"Besides, your faithful companion was more than happy to risk frostbite on your behalf. Hoping to sleep at the foot of her bed tonight?" he whispered at Cal who folded his arms together and sighed.

"Why didn't you call me?" Cal turned this mess back on me. "I thought that was the plan. One of us gets a ride, then we all converge."

"He was too crafty and wouldn't allow passengers." And it wasn't because I thought I could do it all on my own. Nope. That'd be stupid and I wasn't stupid.

"Surprising from a kelpie," Ink said, staring into the dreary water stained with the monster's ichor. "Stranger still for one to be in this part of the world."

What'd it say about being warned? And there was that name again, Mr. White. The mystery pounded at the back of my skull, but the headache from my entire body turning into a popsicle was louder. "All I care about is no more drowned college students."

"Minus a liver, spleen, or pancreas," Ink added, causing me to shiver from my macabre new life. Blood, organs, every possible bodily secretion—I knew I'd be dealing with them when I became a nurse. I just didn't think I'd spend my nights fighting creatures that ate them.

The fire in Ink's eyes dampened to little more than an amber flicker. He stared long at me and asked, "If the entire nest is not flushed clean, then they will reconvene. Did you, in the midst of your underwater drama, manage that?"

A great burst of water shot from where I'd thrown the bottle. The combination of magic and chemistry created the perfect kelpie bomb. "Yeah," I said, watching bits of kelpie egg rain down against the water's surface. "I'd say so."

I wanted to revel in the rush of winning, to shake my fist at the water and shout how I'd beat the monster, but in one fell swoop, the endorphins keeping me running dissolved. The freezing cold water clinging to my skin hardened into tiny icicles. My entire body began to shake violently, exhaustion and fear collapsing me into a quivering heap.

It was Ink who caught and enveloped me. He drew his chin across the top of my head and nestled me safe against his hellfire-like chest. "You require a warm bed, my bond," he whispered, his voice dropping straight to my loins.

"That sounds…" I started before remembering there was no need to tell him what I wanted. He always knew.

Ink lifted and carried me in his arms. "I will take her to the apartment," he declared aloud, then glanced to the naked werewolf who'd saved me from a watery grave.

"What about me?" Cal asked.

"Call a ride."

Before I could object, Ink did his demon magic and whisked us away from the frozen shoreline back to my messy but heated apartment. I might have killed one monster, but there always seemed to be more on the horizon. How many were working at the behest of someone else? Instead of my warm bed, the two men who shared it, or the monster I left rotting in the lake, all I kept thinking about was Mr. White.

Chapter Three

I should have been so deep into a coma only the kiss of a forward and sketchy prince would wake me up. But despite being gifted powers I didn't even know existed six months ago, I could do nothing to stop the incessant racket of dawn's garbage collection.

A chill raced up my naked leg and I jerked back, hoping to hide it under my blankets. Instead, I found the furnace body of my werewolf boyfriend. In his sleep, he'd locked his arm around my belly, though the safe embrace had loosened to a vague hug overnight. Now, he jerked in response to my shuffling, holding me tighter than ever before.

I held my breath, waiting to hear a smacking of waking lips, or a low chuckle. Perhaps even a cough as he accidentally inhaled my hair. But Cal was off in his dream world. I didn't want to wake him. He so rarely slept this well.

Another cold wind piercing through my apartment walls sent me scurrying deeper into Cal's snare. As I did so, a stiff morning surprise didn't so much brush my ass as try to burrow inside. Even with my cotton sleep shorts on, Cal moaned like I'd taken his cock in my mouth. I arched my back, tempted to see if I could wake him with just a shake of my ass.

Closing my eyes, I tried to will back that flush of desire. Sleep was far more important than...

Fingers brushed through my hair and the whole of the bed buckled. I started to fall face forward and opened my eyes in shock, only for a smirk and a fiery gaze to greet me. "Morning, my bond," Ink whispered.

The demon lay on the last scrap of my queen-sized bed, sandwiching me between him and Cal. I started to rear back in shock at a man randomly appearing, only for Ink to hook his palm behind the back of my head and wrap the other around my hip. He pinned me in place. "Your heart's gone aflutter," he said with his intoxicating lips.

It wasn't only the dripping words that did me in, though he could spin the charm when he wanted. When I watched consonants wrap around his lips, the bottom puckering into an almost-kiss, my mind numbed. With the vowels, his cupid's bow sculpting to a point, my body lit on fire. I ached for him to cover my body in his words.

Ink's lips lifted into his trademark knowing smirk. Clasping his fingers to my hair, the demon pulled me to him for a kiss that struck a match down the entire length of me. "I do believe," he whispered, forming every word so his lips caressed and swept over my mouth. Slowly, he worked his way along my jaw, adding a flick of his tongue to punctuate his sentence. "It is my duty."

With the tip of his tongue, Ink licked back down the hollow of my ear. "To set your heart ablaze."

He raised the hand on my hip to bunch the failing elastic on my shorts. It let his fingers fall down the curve, Ink tracing the line that went from thigh to... *Oh my!* I strained higher, trying to encourage his fingers. Instead of Ink gasping in delight, the moan came from behind.

Damn it. How did I forget Cal was right there? Because Ink knew how to push every button inside of me, and all of them led to sex. "Wait." I reached to catch his wrist before he tugged down my shorts.

"Whatever for?" A laugh trilled with his baritone words in an erotic harmony.

I had to take a breath to calm the buzzing in my veins before I could respond. "Cal's back there."

"And?" He caught my chin in his hand and pulled me to his lips. Another wave of blinding lust swept over me. What if I left the bed? There was the couch in the living room. Ink and I could...

A hand curled under my breast that couldn't belong to Ink's as the demon was busy elsewhere. It kneaded through the worn camisole, fingers pinching my nipple until I arched my spine. Cal moaned, his toying with my breast increasing as he started to grind his hips.

"The beast awakens," Ink said.

Teeth bit down on my shoulder, the seal pinching tight and radiating a cascade of pain quickly surpassed by pleasure. I pointed my toes, marinating in the rush as Cal opened his mouth wide and clamped down again. Ink caught my wayward leg by wrapping his palm around my thigh.

Flames sparkled in his eyes and he waggled his brows. Worrying his grip back and forth over my thigh, Ink shifted his hand toward my knee. "I believe we no longer need suffer the impunity of these pantaloons. What say you, dog?"

Cal licked his tongue up the full length of my neck. He burrowed his nose in the hollow of my ear and gripped the wayward 'pantaloons.' While running his wet lips along my ear, he latched strong fingers onto the waistband and tugged down. I wiggled to help, but Cal propped my hip up off the bed with his knee.

He abandoned the shorts to Ink when they only reached my lower thigh. Cal was too busy dragging the full spread of his nails up my skin. Goosebumps trailed his touch, causing a moan to rise in my throat. My mouth opened, needing to release it, when Cal simultaneously lunged forward with both tongue and finger. The first twirled in my mouth while the second plunged deep inside.

Even with my werewolf boyfriend's tongue sweeping over mine, I let loose a cry of feral hunger. He crooked his finger inside me, not thrusting, but searching, sweeping for that little inner nub that made me go delirious. All the while, Ink tossed away my shorts and gripped my ankle.

Before I could breathe, he lifted my leg high, spreading me half-eagle while pinning me on my side. With a gleam, he passed my leg back to Cal, who bent it toward him. I wanted to yelp in shock at the strain, but the incubus suddenly appeared before me. Tipping me to face him, Ink smiled wickedly.

Cal's finger solo became a duet, his thumb taking the lead on my clit. Another moan rose and Ink drew his impressive cock down my belly. He nipped along my jaw, increasing the pressure with every thrust of his hips. I reached out with my only free hand, cupping and kneading the bubbly ass cheek of my incubus.

"How badly you want to bite it," Ink whispered, his hot, brimstone breath caressing down my ear. It wasn't a question. He never had to ask me anything. "But I believe"—his smile twisted to a devious grin—"you desire an impaling more."

Cal shoved my thigh into the air, and the tip of Ink's cock reverberated through me. He met me eye to eye, one hand rolling back to catch as many of my curls in his fist as he could. When he had them, Ink thrust all of himself inside. Electricity snapped through me and I leaned for him, to bite on his shoulder, to moan against his pristine tan skin.

But Ink yanked me back by my hair. "Tut tut," he said, shifting his hair hold from the free hand to the one pinned against the bed. Tugging once again, he thrust deeper than before. "We deserve to hear the fullness of your song, my bond."

Moaning, Cal lifted me off the bed enough to sweep both his hands over my breasts. His hulk of a cock kept toying with my ass, the crown sweeping from one butt cheek to another while he licked the back of my ear. Ink kissed me hard, his hips swerving and jerking to thrust all of him inside of me. Then he tugged on my hair and tipped my head back until Cal could press his lips to mine.

Instead of the usual sweet and sensual kiss of my boyfriend, this one stung of claiming his territory. Of how he'd prove in this moment that he was worthy of me. Even with Ink pounding away inside my cunt, I reached for Cal, threaded my fingers through his short blond hair, tugged him closer and bit his cheek.

A growl rippled from the kiss-soaked lips beside mine. I radiated in the heat rising from his throat, in the glint off his human fangs. Nudging my head with his, Cal clamped his teeth to my shoulder and jerked the whole of his body against me.

"Layla…" he gasped, his voice wild and rippling with the call of the wolf. Panting, his teeth pressing against my cheek, Cal said, "I need you."

Abandoning my breasts, he drew his palms down my body, traced the inward pull of my waist, spread the fullness of his fingers over my hips, and latched onto my upper thigh. "Please…please need me."

"Ink?"

The demon smiled and slipped free. A small regret went with him, my body well aware what Ink could do with just his pinkie finger. But Ink showed no sign of remorse. "My bond," he said, fluttering his fingers over the top of Cal's until the both of them spread me open, "you needn't ask."

"Fuck!" Cal was an RV to Ink's sports car. I'd thought myself ready, my inner thighs soaked from arousal, but Cal only managed his crown in before I wanted to scream.

"Layla, are you…?" Cal asked, catching on quickly that something wasn't right. I had lube. I had to have lube. I'd been dating a man whose penis could be confused for a Coke can for four months. *Where the fuck did I put it?*

"Please," Ink purred. The force from before broke into a strange tenderness. He brushed back my hair and gently caressed his knuckles over my cheek. "Allow me."

Without another word, Ink flipped positions and nestled his head right against my splayed-open cunt. He couldn't be…? "Holy fucker nuts!" Ink's wicked tongue lapped over the fullness of my clit. I bucked against him, causing Cal to slip out of me.

That wouldn't do. With one hand behind me, I pressed to Cal's back and attempted to tell him to try again. I couldn't do it with words—Ink's sliding and vibrating tongue, lips, and edge of his teeth melted the verbal parts of my brain. All I knew was I needed Cal's cock inside of me.

Ink dug his chin against my inner thigh, his thick black waves caressing my sensitive skin. "Come, my moon friend," he whispered, punctuating every word with a flick of my clit. "Join in the bounty."

Pausing a moment, Cal worried his hand over my arm. I tried to pat it reassuringly, when Ink clamped his lips around my clit and began to suck.

"Get the fuck inside of me!" I shouted, digging my nails into him.

Cal bucked hard. No half an inch, not even just the head. He pierced the whole of his mountainous cock through me and a dizziness overcame me. A strange lightness filled my being, as if every pain from the world in my body vanished in a single moment.

Then the werewolf bit my shoulder and I came so hard my vagina clamped onto his cock like a python. Cal trembled behind me, a whimper rising. Or was that me? I couldn't tell, my ears muffled from the rush of my soul trying to leave my body.

"A good first try," Ink said, drawing the sharp point of his chin against my labia. "But we can do better, wolf."

"Yes," Cal said, and he began to thrust.

Fuck me! I scrambled to find anything to hold, sheets to dig my claws into, a mattress to rip to shreds. But it brought me face to face with Ink's hypnotically swaying cock. I licked my lips and pressed a kiss to the crown. He answered by flicking my throbbing clit with his tongue.

A tremble of reverberations danced up my spine, too small to be an orgasm, but enough to drive me forward. I licked his cock into my mouth and Ink answered in kind. My clit cried in joy as he sucked the whole nub between his pursed lips. Meanwhile, the rest of my inner pleasure center erupted in joy from Cal's rhythmic thrusting.

He kept pushing my leg forward, then back, my thigh brushing over Ink's head and abandoning it. Was he trying to get me to kick Ink in the face?

Oh! Oh, god!

Cal yanked my leg all the way back until it rested across his hips. Every reverberation from his wild thrusting carried through my muscles. It drove me mad and I twisted even farther, opening myself as wide as I thought possible.

The tiny orgasms grew to medium, then large, then I feared I might die if they didn't stop. Cal's warm palms cupped to my breasts, his chest knocking against my back as he cried out for me. Ink's wayward fingers kept gliding just outside my labia, pressing the lips tighter then looser around Cal's cock. He didn't stop sucking me off for a second, and neither did I stop licking him.

A baritone groan rumbled in Ink's chest, his hips flexing in a wave to match my furious licking. I took his balls in my hand, ready to cup and tug them to his delight, when a howl broke directly behind my ear.

It rattled against the windows and shook my water glass until the plastic cup struck the floorboards. I didn't hear Cal flop to the bed behind me, nor the slick noise of his spent cock gliding out. But I knew his arms encircling me, his face tucking tight to my back as he held me in an embrace of wonder and exhaustion.

"I love you," he mouthed against my skin, following it up with a kiss, then another on my shoulders.

I finally flipped over to face my werewolf. His usually tucked-up hair was flattened and smattered over his forehead. Sweat glistened down the whole of his torso, beads rising in his fine blond chest hair. His pink lips glowed a bright red and so too did his ears. That happened every time he'd come hard, and I adored seeing the scarlet poking among his gold.

Brushing back his locks, I said, "I love you, too," and moved to kiss him sweetly on the lips.

A hand cupped to my arm and Ink's head suddenly appeared on my shoulder. "Well," he said, his naked body shaking back and forth like an eager puppy, "shall we go for round two?"

My answer came in the form of an alarm beeping from the floor. Even while holding tight to my stomach, Cal reached behind to check his phone. "It's nearly eight," he groaned and I repeated it.

I plucked up my clothing, not caring what I wore to sit in a dark lecture hall while putting my knowledge of acute and chronic illnesses to the test. Absently, I brushed a palm over my neck where I'd replaced the air ward with my healing one. The ink had fully faded along with the spell. It'd sure be nice if I could just draw that symbol as every answer for my midterm.

"Do you think I can get an extension if I say I stopped a murderous horse from drowning people?"

Cal's cello-like laugh punctuated behind my head. I turned to find him adorably rubbing the sleep from his eyes. He raised his arms in a massive stretch, alighting every imposing muscle in his naked body. Something about his being a werewolf meant he got the physique of an actor paid a million dollars to devote his every second of life to working out while he ate meals of candy bars.

"I rather doubt he'd excuse us from the test even if we were bleeding and on fire. Though, if you're concerned..."

I'd been trying to cram as best I could while staring at my tiny phone screen with club EDM screaming in my ear. The chances of passing this test felt next to impossible and I needed to at least get a C.

The unending heat of Cal's body caressed down my side. He brushed away my hair and whispered, "We could do a quick cram session."

"Oh?"

He licked his lips nearly pressing to my ear. "In the shower."

I wrapped my arms around Cal's neck and he lifted me off my feet. Leaning closer, I was about to kiss him, when I glanced back to my incubus. "Are you coming?"

Ink's crackling fire of a laugh shivered up my spine. "My bond, you always know the answer."

Chapter Four

"This place stinks of dented cans of corn!"

It was a whisper, but whenever Dana spoke, it amplified a hundredfold like she screamed into a bullhorn. A slow stink-eye from the librarian rolled over us college students forced to seek refuge in the public library.

Every table, chair and nook had been claimed thanks to midterms. Only one day remained before the proper college teenagers could flee to a beach and us older students would trudge to our night jobs for overtime. Rather than fight for a space, we'd traveled deeper into the city.

The library building felt older than it was, decked out in that Greco-Roman style to impose upon the little people and keep them at bay. Though, that was undone by the display of pooping books at the front complete with a multi-colored plush scat pile.

"Why didn't we head to Grizzly's?" Dana complained as she claimed a table between the circle of computers and the biography stacks.

"Because the cramming art students would have bitten our heads off and used the blood for a crimson sunset," I said, pulling out the chair beside her and buckling down. To say the test kicked my ass would be about on par with saying Cal got a little hairy at night.

"I prefer it here," Fariah said, already laying out her spread of organized study materials. I swear, in another life she had to be some decorated general, up every morning at dawn moving the tiny pieces that represented battalions of men over the battlefield.

"Hello, everyone." The voice snapped me from envisioning my quietest friend in a suit of armor. I stared up at jovial, crystal-blue eyes and found myself reaching for his hand. Cal met me halfway, but didn't take my fingers. "Found a good spot?" he whispered, his face drifting ever closer to mine.

A silly laugh bubbled in my throat and I nodded. "Least we think so. There could be monsters lurking under the table."

"Well..." His lips nearly caressed against the nape of my neck, Cal gliding behind me as he said, "Then you need someone to protect you by checking."

I shifted to follow him. "Know any good options?"

"Men who'd lay down their life for you?" Cal's voice dropped to being barely audible as he said, "Or men who want to slip between your legs?"

"Why not both?" I whispered, leaning so close my lips nearly pressed to his.

An ear-piercing squee erupted, ripping me from Cal to...the reminder that this was a study session. And not like the one we had in the shower, which was very unhelpful in retrospect.

Dana's eyes opened wide, her lips parted to aid in another squeal. Embarrassment climbed up my spine and I wanted to sink deeper into my jacket. Instead of Cal, or me, it was Fariah who sighed, "Could you stop that?"

"What?" Dana said back. "They're so damn cute it makes my teeth hurt."

"We're really…" I tried to counter.

The friend who'd been pushing our romance for over a year shot back, "You were making goo-goo eyes at each other while the professor was passing out the test. I saw it."

Okay, no shower sex before a test.

"Layls…" Dana dragged her chair over the tiled floor, causing it to whine in agony. "Tell me you're using protection."

Oh sure, I damn near drew a magical ward every day now. Wait, she meant… Damn it. I knew how Dana was, but I couldn't stop the blush burning over my cheek. My friend who'd probably ask Jesus about his sex life caught my hand. "Are we going to have a little baby Layla with blue eyes soon?"

"What? No!" I yanked from her grip, my mind roiling not just because I sure as shit did not have room in my life for kids. See, the nice thing about werewolves was they couldn't breed with humans. So no need to worry about birth control. And the bad thing about werewolves who seemed to be obsessed with family was…I couldn't give him a kid. I swiveled to Cal, hoping for him to rescue me.

"Scott, Jared!" my werewolf protector shouted, waved a hand at the only other two men in our nursing class, and ran to their sides.

Raising my head—the mantra of my mom insisting I didn't need a man ringing through my ears—I buckled down to work. I re-read the same paragraph about lupus four times before I said from the side of my lips, "Do you have to do that?"

"After we've had to suffer you two awkwardly flirting for a year? Yes. Yes, I do." Dana said it so definitively I couldn't even argue with her. Resigned to my fate of burning hot whenever they caught me near Cal, I tried to focus, but my friend wasn't done.

"Look, I love you, you know that, right? And we like Cal too. Right, Fariah?"

For her part, Fariah tipped her pen in agreement but didn't glance up from her studies.

"You're really cute together. Can't stop being mushy or playing grab ass when you think we ain't looking. Just…promise me one thing, Leeland."

That I didn't suddenly give birth to a litter of werewolves? Shouldn't be too hard. I crossed my arms and waited for the request.

"Wait until we're graduated before you fuck it up."

What? "I don't—"

Dana talked right over me. "Maybe you're, I dunno, cursed or something. But I don't think I've seen a guy last more than, what, a month?"

"Two," my other backstabbing friend added.

"So you think you can, maybe, stick it out with this one? At least so we don't have to deal with the hella awkward fallout?" She held her hand out to me like we needed to seal a deal.

What did they take me for? Fine, I hadn't had a lot of long-term boyfriends. But the last two were, frankly, dicks with assholes attached and little more. Even Dana agreed I did the right thing in exorcising them. Now I'm suddenly this evil heartbreaker leaping from bed to bed just because I'm with Cal?

Snarling, I batted her hand away. "You're the fucking worst, you know that? Both of you. My love life is…" I paused in saying it was none of their business. I couldn't tell them about the monster tumors trying to kill me, the demon bound to my soul, the witch hunters who nearly took me. Not even that I nearly drowned last night.

All I had left to share with them was my love life. "Not that dramatic," I limply ended with.

"Uh-huh," Dana said, and leaned over her chair to stare in Cal's direction. "I've seen him in gray sweatpants."

"For fuck's sake," I groaned, my body melting into the chair. Though, I did glance back to my werewolf with a cock that'd throttle the competition in any gray sweatpants' competition. "Can we get back to work? These Crohn's sufferers aren't going to care for themselves."

Fariah snorted in agreement and Dana realized she wouldn't get more out of me. But I couldn't stop drifting back to Cal. The dangerously hot, stupidly sweet guy who'd walk a mile in snow to get me the good eggrolls. Exactly the kind of guy who'd grow tired of me in time.

* * * *

"What are you working on?"

I jumped in my chair, scattering my pens across the table. Cal caught the Sharpie that bounced against his book and, for a moment, we shared a look. It was the same marker I used to cast my spells. What was it doing out of my pocket? I reached for it while ignoring the breath brushing down my neck.

And the fingers drumming on the back of my chair. He either wanted a damn answer or popped by to torture me.

I wanted to ignore him, already covering over my obsession with my textbooks, but my friend and drama-bloodhound whipped her head up. Dana's eyes narrowed like a falcon's prepared to spear its talons into prey. "Who invited him?" She practically snarled at the appearance of the man they knew as my random fuck-buddy from November.

Her half-threat rang in my ears, and I whipped around in feigned shock at Ink butting into my business. "What are you doing here?" I tried to gasp in surprise, but it sounded shallow and rehearsed.

"Wondering what has ensnared your intentions so from this muckraking periodical." Ink pushed aside my textbooks with his pinkie to reveal the newspaper I'd snatched up from the front desk. It was a few days old, the main headline about the councilman's disappearance. What caught my attention was the smaller article under the fold, which was exactly what Ink narrowed in on.

"Nothing," I said, trying to cover up my little crime by shoving the paper to the floor.

With a sigh, Ink said to the whole table, "You're not reading about this White character and his recent acquisition of an abandoned building in the downtown area."

Damn it. Cal's head snapped from the mercifully dressed incubus straight to me. I leaped to my feet and caught Ink by the arm. He leaned into it, for a moment pressing my breasts against him, and flames leapt off the sides of Dana's face. I leaned back and said loudly, "Let's talk elsewhere."

Before the demon could answer, I tugged him deeper into the stacks, past the biographies and poetry books. I took a hard left at the poster of a leprechaun asking kids to read and hurled Ink into the middle of the shelves. For some stupid reason, I expected him to tug on his cuffs, adjust his hair, do basically anything other than press his hips to mine and guide me back until my spine jostled the books.

The hardbacks bounced against the metal shelves and a fiery shiver danced up my legs. Ink widened his stance and gripped one hand to the shelf beside my head. "I cannot help but recall the last time we found ourselves entwined in this tomb of knowledge. Do you wish to repeat the festivities..."

"Layla?" Cal's voice called from outside the aisle and, for a moment, I could breathe through the heady lust radiating off of Ink.

The incubus didn't even miss a beat, slyly asking, "...or perhaps add a third?"

"Is that what you're up to? A little..." Cal stared at Ink while walking closer until all three of us whispered together, "fun in the stacks?"

"Oh, we've already quite enjoyed each other's tempestuous bodies while balanced upon a buckling shelf," Ink said like he was describing the weather outside.

"Cool," Cal responded slowly, scratching along his ear. He repeated that one word three more times and I winced. Was it better to let him stew in a touch of jealousy thinking I got horny during studying and desired Ink while he was right there than tell him the truth? Probably.

"Sorry," I said, hoping that'd smooth over the frayed nerves.

A momentary redness tinted Cal's pale cheeks as if he was battling the demon of jealousy, and also shame for being jealous. He dipped his head, his gaze on the floor. It might work, a good excuse to get him...

"She had no desire for me."

Damn it, Ink!

That fucking demon code of being unable to lie meant he used the truth like a sword. Cal's awkward shuffling froze and he snapped rigid. Ink said, "She was pontificating upon an article regarding Mr. White."

"Not this again."

I bunched my fists up and hunched tighter into my shoulders. "I'm doing my damn job. My other damn job. The one you" —I jabbed a finger at Ink—"keep telling me I have to do."

The incubus parted his hands wide. "I tell you nothing, merely share my knowledge obtained over the centuries. What you do with it is at your command."

"Layla, babe. You've got to let this go."

His pet name set my obstinate meter higher. Cal tried to catch my hand, but I yanked it away and shoved Ink from me. "There's something there, all right. This White guy keeps coming up. First with your fa—" I blanched at Cal's face crumpling and switched from mentioning the father that killed Cal's brother to, "the asshole claiming a Mr. White was coming for the pack."

"And Mark said it was all a delusion. Which often happens with megalomaniac cult leaders seeing traitors everywhere." He said it calmly, coldly, but Cal's jaw flexed like he was biting down on something with his back teeth.

"Then what about Mikki, huh?"

"A nymph who is freed of her cultural incarceration by said Mr. White," Ink interrupted, scratching at his chin. "He sounds of a downright saint. First, attempting to remove the cancerous alpha."

"Or attempting to take over the pack and use them to his advantage," I interrupted.

"Then releasing a nymph with his own coin, for what purpose?"

"I..." I didn't know. Maybe Mikki would have interrupted whatever plans he had when she was trapped with the river nymphs. Or... "He could have been the one to tip off the hunters! Free a nymph, then tell them where to find her."

"To what end?" Ink pressed. "I see no great advantage he gains."

"What if he's a hunter?" I threw out.

It was Cal who snorted. "Then Lucien would have ripped out his throat."

"But the kelpie said..." I began, trying to lay out the evidence that amounted to nothing more than a gut feeling. Every time I heard that name, Mr. White, my teeth clenched and my hands ached. I couldn't say why, I couldn't even give a reason for how, but I knew deep in my soul he was bad news.

Shame the two men in my life couldn't believe me.

"The kelpie who spoke while you were drowning. A time when mortals are rather known for panicking," Ink answered without a care. He inspected his fingers, elongating the claws, then shrinking them.

Why didn't they trust me? The least they could do was help me, either by disproving this theory or discovering that Mr. White was up to no good.

Condescending arms wrapped around my shoulders, yanking me up to stare into Cal's concerned face. "Layla, please," he whispered, tugging me tighter to his body. I didn't hug him back, so he increased his embrace. A low rumble of annoyance rolled through his throat, but Cal said softly, "You've got to let this go. There's no vast conspiracy, no big bad guy. It's just a lot of coincidences, okay."

They had a thousand good reasons I was wasting my time, and I didn't have a single answer for any of them. But it didn't stop me from growing more incensed with every patronizing second. Cal kept trying to get me to open up, but I hardened my body to stone and stepped out of his arms.

"Fine. If you aren't going to help, then I'll do it my damn self. Like always."

The boys shared a glance like they were about to pull out the straitjacket. Cal ran his fingers through his hair and sighed. "I need to get back to studying, so should you."

I shook my head, anger percolating in my veins. Each little bubble was building to a volcanic explosion I might not be able to control.

Wafting his offering hand away, Cal turned to march back to the table, leaving me in the stacks. Before walking off, he said to Ink, "Come on."

"Whatever for?" Ink asked.

"Layla's liable to bite your head off," Cal said at me while talking to the demon. Ink shrugged as if that was the least of his concerns.

What was he doing? Ink could come and go as he pleased, and... Dana was watching, and Cal must have overheard her threat with his damn wolf ears. Great.

"I have some of those honey snacks in my bag," Cal said, instantly snagging Ink's attention.

Running ahead of the feet-dragging werewolf, Ink asked, "Do you have that sour sugar sauce as well?"

Cal paused to stare at me, his eyes pleading for me to follow, but I folded my arms tighter and turned away. With an exasperation, he trailed after the giddy demon. I was pissed as hell at him for refusing to listen to me. I was also grateful that he helped to keep Ink under control. That combo of emotions managed to make me boil even hotter.

If he's so damn thoughtful and considerate, why won't he fucking listen to me? Under my breath, I snarled, "I'll do it my damn self." Like I had any idea where to begin. A Google search ended in a couple hundred thousand hits, not to mention a laundry chain in Nevada, and a scummy-looking dentist who probably groped his patients. Would a secretive, rich, shit-stirrer who knew about magical creatures even be on Facebook?

I wrenched my neck and a pain spidered from the long-faded healing spell. Was that normal? God, I could really use a chatroom of other witches. Absently, I flared my fingers, watching tiny fires rise off every nail like I was a dead man's candle.

A shadow passed along the other end of the stacks. I shook my hand, praying no one saw the unexplainable puff of smoke. This deep in, I expected it to be a librarian checking on the crazy woman shrieking at two men. If so, this was the punkest librarian I'd ever seen. The man's slender frame was hidden below an acid-washed denim jacket covered in safety pins. An embroidered patch filled the back, but it looked about to fall off and I couldn't make it out.

The stranger had a single shock of neon-blue hair among his midnight-black locks. They were slicked up and back, not quite long enough to give him the mohawk he seemed to be going for. He hovered beside the book cases, staring down the spines, until his head snapped to the side.

Ooh damn, he was pretty, like a young Jet Li gone neon punk. The whites of his eyes blazed, twisting the deep mahogany brown of his irises to an impenetrable black. Rather than scare me, it ignited a curiosity. Were there little hints of gold hiding inside those browns, or was it an endless void perfect for anyone to fall into and never emerge?

I realized I was staring. Turning, I glared at the ground even with the back of my neck burning red. I tried to absently cover it with my hand, but the longer the stranger stood there silently inspecting the books, the further the blush crawled. I was going to look like a sun-dried tomato if he didn't move on.

Should I back away? Return to the others…while praying Ink didn't make some smart remark about the electric punk I discovered among the stacks? Of course he would. Probably in his smug and antiquated voice. "My bond has desires to caress her breasts betwixt the neck of an electric lute."

A loud whoomph broke me from thinking of Ink and I spun around to find a book laying on the ground and the heels of the stranger's boots turning a corner. "Hey," I began and rushed to the book he must have dropped.

The Conquest of Chicago: How White Owned the Mob.

White as in…the White I was looking for? The cover was a black and white photo of men in fedoras outside speakeasies, so probably not the exact man. But it could be an ancestor. I flipped through the pages, catching a few sentences on the ivory paper. "His alias was always the same, though no records exist prior to reveal his true name... In under a year, Mr. White claimed half the city...ruthless, tireless, endless."

With the book tight to my chest, my heart pounded at the possibility I'd turned a corner in this mystery. Maybe that was a librarian who overheard me, or a devoted patron. Either way, I had my first real break in the case. "Thank you," I called to the air where he'd been and dashed back to dig into this mysterious Mr. White.

Chapter Five

"Speaking on anonymity, one of Mr. White's lieutenants revealed to me the construct of what the man called 'his ants'."

The book shook in my hands, jumbling the tiny sentences my brain took minutes to piece together. Anger bubbled in my stomach, but a warm kiss was pressed to the top of my head and Cal whispered, "Sorry. Had an itch."

He shifted his back up and down against the corner of the couch. An old movie scene involving a pottery wheel played on his TV while March rain tumbled through Cal's weedy front garden. We'd left Ink back at my place, where the demon was getting up to the devil knew what. There'd been plans to study, but if I looked at drug labels one more time my brain would implode.

I leaned back against the itching man, his chest a comfortable place to rest and read. Cal had kept one hand across the arm of the couch and the other on his leg. Just as I got settled back into the wild west of gangster Chicago, my pillow swept a curious palm up my thigh.

"I always wanted to try that," he whispered, his touch now at my stomach.

My gaze darted up for a second to the screen and I said, distracted, "What? Make a vase? I think there's a pay-as-you-go studio downtown by the college."

"No." Cal laughed like I'd made a joke. "That."

The couple, one of whom was either dead or invisible, I couldn't remember which, were curled around each other much as we were...and making one hell of a mess with the clay. I was lost with not only the plot but why Cal cared, until the two leads began to kiss. Okay no, that was tongue fucking and they were all in. A flush tumbled down to my belly, lighting up right below Cal's palm. I squirmed and felt the stiff prod from behind the top of my butt. He was really enjoying it.

"I might..." I said, drawn into the unburdened sexuality of the scene, "have a spell that could turn you invisible."

His low laugh blew aside my hair and he caressed both hands up to just under my breasts. "That's not the part I care about." Drawing back my hair with his chin, Cal said, "I want to touch you." Slowly, he darted his fingers one by one up between my cleavage. "To feel all of you, to ravish you in love, no matter the obstacle trying to keep us apart."

"I think I saw bungee cords in your junk drawer," I said, tempted to get them.

Wanting to kiss him hard, then find anything to tie his hands to the couch, I turned in his lap. A flicker of lust danced in Cal's eyes. He raised his palm flat and drew it just a millimeter above my cheek. The warmth of his palm reached through the space between us and I shivered.

A smile flitted about his lips, Cal darting his tongue between them as if he ached to use it. Still, he toyed with me, keeping his fingers from my ample sweater or my naked legs. Was he serious about not touching me at all? My knee began to shake with impatience, and I leaped forward, pressing my breasts to his palms and my lips over his.

Shock reverberated across Cal's face even as his caress burned with need and tugged at my sweater. "I thought…" he whispered even while unhooking my bra.

Drawing my teeth up his square jaw, I breathed, "I don't like waiting."

Was I still mad at him and Ink for treating me like some foolish damsel with fluff for brains? Fuck, yes. Was I also horny as hell after an entire afternoon resting in my beefcake werewolf's arms with his gargantuan cock riding against my ass? I intended to answer that question while the ghost couple reached their own scripted climax.

Grabbing Cal's shirt, I yanked him off the couch for the floor. He wrapped his hands around my naked back, trying to lift my sweater with just his forearms. As I started to fall to the floor for better reach and flexibility, a loud jangle erupted from beside the couch. The moment wasn't ruined, keep going and…

Another two more text message announcements beeped from Cal's phone and he grimaced. "I should probably…"

"Yeah, yeah." Accepting my fate, I released him to check his phone, and slouched on the other side of the couch.

Cal bent over his phone, partially obscuring the erection in his... Damn it, Dana was right. I could either burn all his gray sweatpants, or make popcorn and enjoy the show. For now, I fell deeper into the old fainting couch, my ass flattened by the Victorian lack of cushions.

"Ah, Scott reminded me to pick up a couple bug bombs tomorrow." Cal hunched over, hooked both elbows to his thighs, and began to text using only his thumbs.

I watched the rather adorable and antiquated move while brushing back his fallen hair. "Not sure why you'd need a bug bomb for tomorrow. Unless you hope to pass via chemical warfare."

"Oh, no. They're worried about a silverfish infestation in the..." Cal's train of thought derailed off a cliff as he stared at me.

"The what?" I prompted, my skin itching. I've always had an impressive bullshit meter and thought it came from my mom. She could sniff out a nonpaying client in two seconds.

Biting his lip, ruffling his hair, Cal gave every sign he didn't want to tell me, which just threw fuel on my anger. "Did I not tell you about the cabin?"

"Pretty sure I'd remember a cabin. Tend to have bears or serial killers lurking in them. Sometimes rich people who may be secret serial killers."

He laughed and rubbed along his chin. "No serial killers, and it's not rich, or really fancy. For the past couple years, Scott and Jared and I all go to his uncle's cabin in the woods for spring break."

Oh. "And you didn't tell me because...?"

"I thought I did. I swear! You were with me when I bought those new rain boots." Cal gestured to the pile of stuff he had picked up while I was working at Bellpeppers. It'd all been left beside his front door instead of put away.

"Boots can be used outside of a cabin," I said, but my gut churned. There'd also been a net, and some pink plastic worms. Most people didn't use those when going to get coffee or catching a rainy matinee.

"Moon take me," Cal cursed to himself. "I'm so sorry about that, Layla. I swear, I thought I'd... You probably had plans."

Nothing concrete. We had a merciful week off from school so spending it wrapped up with my boyfriend would have been nice. There was also witch training which I'd been putting off because of midterms. Or the two of us trying out that whole chaining him up idea he'd floated earlier could be a nice way to pass the time.

Cal shook his head and texted rapidly. "I'll tell Scott I can't go."

"Don't." I reached over to catch his hand before he did something stupid. Wrapping my fingers between his, I said, "You should be able to go out with the boys, work off all that manly testosterone when you want."

"Are you sure?" he asked even while placing his phone on the table, the exit text left unfinished.

Don't fuck this up, Layla.

I nodded, my heart heavy with the admonishment from Dana and a long past of overreacting for no good reason. Swallowing down any vitriol, I let a smile slip free and glanced at his pile of gear, when an idea struck. "What if I go with?"

"Uh..."

"Scott and Jared, they like me, right?"

"Sure, I mean, yeah, they do. It's just, I don't know if you'd like being in the cabin. It's..." Cal stared everywhere but at me.

"It's what?" I tried to get him to finish. My mind churned with what three men would get up to alone in the woods. Was it a porn hut? Did they all bring in a girl for an orgy?

"There's a lot of..." Cal began, his hand flying freely. I latched onto it and wrung around his fingers, wondering what he was hiding.

A flash kicked into the back of my head and whiteness zapped over my vision. As it flooded away, I stared down at my hands—masculine, cracked-knuckled, thick-fingered hands. Flannel hugged around wrists which were far too square and wide to be mine.

"Morning, sunshine!" a voice shouted and flung...tapioca at my head. I absently wiped at it and stared up at Scott and Jared. They were barely dressed in only boxers and Jared held a bowl of tapioca pudding.

"Very funny," someone said. It wasn't me—I didn't find any of it funny. But the voice came from inside of me and it sounded just like...

"...the bathroom isn't really a bathroom, more a hole we dig and fill up after leaving."

Cal's voice rang through my ears and I blinked rapidly. We were sitting on his couch in his living room, the movie's credits playing and a screen asking what we wanted to watch next. What the shit just happened?

"Layla?"

"I...saw Jared and Scott," I said, my voice rising to a panicked squeal.

Cal twisted his head to stare out of the front window. "On the lawn?"

"No, in..." The floors had been wood, walls too. "That cabin you stay at?" I asked, closing my eyes to try to remember. "Is there a deer head over the door that you put...panties on?" I glared at Cal, but his eyes went white.

"How do you know that?" He gasped, before adding, "The panties are Jared's doing, I swear."

I couldn't find it in myself to be worried about random lady's underwear. Instead, I stared at my hands and my stomach flipped. "I...I think I became you for a second. Jared, he, he threw tapioca pudding at my — your head."

"He found an old can in the fishing shack stash and thought it hilarious," Cal grumbled before jerking his head to me. He gripped onto my hands. "You can see my...my memories?" Then he dropped my fingers like they were boiling hot. "How? When did...? Has this happened before?"

"I don't know. And no, this is the first time. I just...I wanted to know about the cabin, then I touched your hand, and boom, tapioca to the face."

Cal looked fully spooked and he wasn't the only one. What witch power was this? I reached for my spell book left by my feet and thumbed through a few pages. What would I even ask it? Can witches steal people's memories for a little bit? Manically, I flipped through the pages trying to find anything to explain what had happened.

"You had no idea," Cal said calmly, his hands falling until he gripped to his knees. Still, he wrung his pants back and forth while watching me carefully.

"Does it look like I do? Shit, am I gonna have to wear gloves all the time or risk seeing people take a dump?" There was definite panic rising in my voice. I tried biting on my tongue to calm down, but the tremble in my hands wouldn't stop.

Warm fingers skirted down my clothed forearm. My rabid hunting for answers paused and Cal gently caressed over my sleeve and held my hands. I froze, fearing another strange flash while he stared at me.

"Anything?"

Slowly, I shook my head.

A sigh of relief slipped from Cal and he pulled me back into his lap. He grazed his lips against my forehead. "Another question to put to your magic trainer."

I frowned, wondering if Ink would have any explanation for what happened. "He certainly didn't warn me about this," I fumed.

"Layla," Cal said, resting his cheek against my forehead. "Can you promise me if that happens again, no matter what you see, you'll tell me?"

Why? The question lingered on my tongue, but as I turned to stare up at him, I knew. He'd spent his childhood under the endless watch of an abusive cult and chafed at the idea of anyone even innocently spying on his whereabouts. It was a massive sore spot I knew I couldn't overcome.

"Of course," I said.

In response, he enveloped me in his arms and pulled the both of us back onto the couch. All the rampant sexual tension became a soggy tissue after that. Stupid magic. For every good spell, I had two damn curses put on my head.

Closing my eyes, I tried to pretend I wasn't a lonely witch struggling to understand anything of this damn birthright. Nope, just an average college student curled up on a rainy Thursday afternoon in her boyfriend's embrace. Everything was normal.

"Do you mind staying here tonight?" Cal asked. "I have to transform and I get a lot of looks climbing up your apartment's staircase as a wolf."

Completely normal with a boyfriend who turned into a wolf whenever he wanted. And there was that sex demon watching game shows on my laptop. Nothing about my life would ever be normal again.

"No problem," I said, snuggling into the warm abyss of pretend.

Chapter Six

My laptop beeped in agony and I blindly reached into my purse for the charging cable. Grizzly's, my go-to caffeine provider, was damn near deserted. On the Friday afternoon before spring break, anyone with a life was already on the road or waiting to catch a plane. Then there was me struggling to find the outlet hiding behind the table's leg.

Finally. The prongs went in and I moved to sit up, only to slam my back against the table's underside. It sent my purse tumbling off the edge...where the spell book slipped free. I reached for it, only for another pair of hands to get there first.

An insane anger rose inside of me, the kind a mother bear would unleash on anyone who'd dare approach her cubs. In a spitting rage, I leaped to my feet, ready to rip the book free, and came face to face with Frank. "This yours?" the owner asked before snorting mucus up his nose and coughing.

I suddenly didn't want to take back my book. "Yeah…" I whispered, reaching a single finger out to rub the spine. I'd swear the book cooed at me and, even if my baby was covered in another man's germs, I had to rescue it.

While I hugged my spell book tight, Frank stared at me. Grizzly's wasn't the hippest coffee shop in the city. Its distressed décor was less a design choice and more a lack of finishing the ceiling. Frank looked like the kind of man who'd drink black coffee he burned on a fire between cinderblocks. His face puffed out at the cheeks and forehead, shadowing away his sunken eyes, which couldn't stop staring at my spell book.

"That what they're using to teach you nurses now?" Frank asked.

I hoisted up my bag and stuffed the book deep inside. "Yep. Lots of books for college, you know." My spell book tumbled against the thinner biography of Mr. White. I'd read through it twice and learned practically nothing helpful. It seemed like this man who, for a brief time, had taken over all of Chicago, came from nowhere and went right back there.

"Right, right," Frank said. "Well, if you need anything…"

"I'll holler," I responded, already falling back to the chair I'd been squatting in for an hour. I'd finished with classes for the week, but we had another midterm happening right after break. Getting in a cram session while everyone else was out partying was Fariah's idea. Be nice to know where the hell they were.

I fumbled past the errant spell book that never liked to stay in place and grabbed the bag of rice. Inside was my poor phone, locked in its desiccant tomb as it had been for the past three days. Would it rise from its watery grave? I popped open the plastic bag and reached inside.

"Layla!"

I yanked my hand out so fast rice pinged across the table like a tiny wedding broke out for my coffee mug. "Cal? What are you...?"

Instead of his usual hoodie and jeans attire, my werewolf boyfriend was decked out in full camouflage. He even had on a ball cap with that woodland floor pattern. Sweeping an arm around my waist, he said, "We're about to head out to the cabin."

"Oh." They were leaving that soon? "Did you come to say goodbye?"

"Well..." He swayed on his feet, pulling me flush to his body until we both did a half dance together. "Your phone isn't doing so hot and I wanted to do this."

Sweeping both palms over my cheeks, Cal focused his crystal eyes at me. A flutter tumbled in my belly and I launched up on my toes to kiss him. The gentle peck of a girlfriend saying adieu to her beau burned away. Instead, I felt like a woman fearing she was about to see her man for the last time before he shipped off to sea.

I needed him to remember this kiss, for it to keep him warm while counting down every night we were apart.

"Are you trying to get me to stay?" Cal whispered.

All I could do was shrug. "Far be it for me in my red satin bra with those lacy bits..."

Cal's groan reverberated through every fiber of my being.

"...to dare compete with two other smelly men in the woods."

He stared hard at me and bit his lip. As his gaze drifted down, no doubt picturing the bra I sure as shit wasn't wearing, Cal's human tooth shifted to a full-on fang. We were getting close to another full moon. Would he make it back in time?

I hadn't thought to ask.

"Are you—?"

"Hey, Rollin. You done sucking face so we can head out?" Jared shouted, sticking only the top half of his body through the door and letting all the heat out.

"Give me a sec," he said, waving to his friends.

Jared shook his head as if there was nothing more unmanly than kissing a girlfriend. "Have fun with your long days standing in freezing water and nights...I assume smacking each other's balls until you're all sterile."

I expected a laugh, but Cal held my hands tight, his face twisted up in concern. "You're not going to be going after any"—his voice dropped to a whisper—"monsters while I'm gone?"

I hadn't planned on it, but if one were to pop up...

"Just wait, okay? Until I'm back. I don't like the idea of you risking your life like that."

"I can handle myself," I said, but it was sweet that he cared enough to track me down and ask me to not potentially die from magical creature of the week.

Cal didn't answer, just kept rubbing his thumbs over the backs of my hands.

"There's always Ink," I said, wondering why he was so concerned all of a sudden.

Cal sighed. "True. Can't ever forget or get away from the...guy. Do you promise?"

"What if there's—?"

"Humor me, okay? When those fucking hunters had you, I..."

I reached out to cup his cheek. Cal's gaze dropped to the floor. I'd been the one tossed into an unmarked van, no doubt destined for weird experiments at the whims of well-armed assholes. But I'd known my boys would come for me. It was Cal who'd wake up sweating and constricting around me until I swore I was safe in his arms.

"I promise, no monster hunting while you're away," I said and placed three fingers up in the air. "Scout's honor."

"For fuck's sake, Rollin. Stuff your sausage back in your pants and let's go!"

"Sorry," he said first to Jared, then me. "I have to...you know. I love you," he added, stumbling through the door with his canvas bag flopping from one shoulder to the other.

"I love you too," I said to myself as Cal was already climbing into the truck with the other two guys. Wrapping my arms around myself, I watched it pull out of the parking lot and onto the road eventually leading them to the woods.

Focus, Layla. I worked the night shift tonight and only had these few hours to study. Falling to the chair, I pulled out my text book. For a moment, my fingers grazed against the spine of my spell book and I sighed. Later.

"Frank? Can I get another cup?"

* * * *

Where the hell are they?

I tapped my pen against the table while staring at the clock. Fariah and Dana should have gotten here a half-hour ago. Dana being late was normal. Sometimes we'd tell her to come an hour early just to get her on time, but Fariah? Did something happen?

They didn't know what lurked in the lakes, what crawled through the sewers and owned the shadows. They were what I once was, happily ignorant and defenseless.

My ears started to ring in a stress-induced panic as I excavated my phone from the bag of rice. Moment of truth. If it wasn't fully dry by now, it would never be. I pressed on the button and prayed.

The screen flashed white and the loading animation appeared. So far, so good. While I waited for my phone to reboot, I stuffed away my work. I'd taken the practice test twice, my fritzing brain misreading a few of the questions so I failed spectacularly. *Can't do that on the real one, Layla.* Dyslexia, fun when studying, twice over on standardized tests. The only guidance counselor in high school stared at me like I was invisible after that score. No one wanted to waste resources on the kid with no parents to shout at them.

I had wadded up my laptop cord and slipped it into the side pocket, when the book on White fell to the front. There had to be more about him. Maybe someone at the library could help me find another book about this guy. The whole ancestor angle was turning into smoke in the wind.

A bead of guilt burned on the back of my neck. Cal only told me to not chase monsters. This guy was hardly a monster. Far as he and Ink thought, White wasn't even a nuisance. I'd just be wasting my free time checking up on it.

My phone finished loading, and a string of texts waited for me from Dana.

Forget Grizz's. F got tickets to a movie. Get to the Sunport cinema double time. There's full frontal in this one.

I glanced at the timestamp, then double-checked the little clock in the upper left corner. She sent that nearly forty-five minutes ago. By the time I got there, any potential peen would be long gone.

Hooking my bag on my arm, I rose to my feet. No doubt a full-frontal show waited for me back home. Ink didn't seem to be on friendly terms with pants, and I'd never seen him in underwear. Odd he hadn't popped in to check on me, or pulled me into an abandoned section of a used bookstore to rifle through my periodicals.

I shook my head. Trying to understand an incubus was like wondering what sequoias dreamed of. If I wasn't due to work for another three hours, and my friends were busy with a movie, then I had time to stop by the library. It shouldn't take more than a minute to ask a simple question.

On a late Friday afternoon, the public library was deader than an atheist church. I didn't expect to run into many people. But as I walked under the looming Roman arch of the doorway, dashed along the chipped floor marked by a zodiac symbol and stopped before the main desk, I didn't find a single soul.

Pushing the call button, I danced up and down on my toes and scanned along the back wall. A series of photographs commemorating the library's history hung there, some dating back to its Victorian beginnings. Curious, I was drawn to a picture of a man in a white suit and hobbled higher onto my tiptoes to get a better look.

A flash of denim flitted across the edge of my vision. I cranked my head around, both certain I saw the figure and doubting it was anything more than dust. My stomach twisted at the thought and goosebumps rose at a person vanishing through the stacks.

Wait! The jacket reappeared, moving down the aisle with that same back patch threatening to fall off. It was the man that helped me before. Shaking off the unearthly quiver, I dashed for the vanishing librarian.

"Excuse me," I called, trying to run without making a sound and shout in a whisper. It must not have worked as the man didn't even turn. "Hello? You helped me before and…"

Okay, he had to hear me. I was so close I could make out the folded-over patch on his jacket was a tiger with a guitar in its massive paw. But the man kept drifting deeper into the stacks, not even glancing back.

"Look—" Reaching a hand out, I cupped his shoulder.

Or I tried to.

Cold stabbed up my arm like a bush of thorns and my fingers slipped right through the man's flesh. A blast without sound burst from the stranger. It blanketed away the lights, casting the library into shadows only punctured by the sun peeking through barred-off windows. I ripped my hand out of the nothing of his chest.

Slowly, the floating figure turned, his eyes narrowing in on me holding my hand like I'd burned it. "What…?" I stuttered, the whole of my body shaking. "Oh, shit!"

Ducking into a half crouch, I scrabbled to escape. A lone, wailing voice scratched through the ether to my ears. "Wait…" he called, like I had any intention of standing around and letting whatever that thing was rip me to pieces.

That's what happened with every damn creature — strange encounter, minor greeting attempt, then claw extension and liver consumption. Not today. I struggled to keep my balance, slapping my hands into rows of books. The covers smacked to the floor, providing debris to slow the monster down.

Or it would if the thing wasn't non-corporeal.

Instead, it was my shoes that caught on the slippery books. I clung to the shelves, pulling my body along like I was pretend skating with my mom. Except this time an evil creature was actually chasing after me.

"Stop!" the monster called, quick on my heels.

Confuse it. I twisted down a row of books. A hint of sunlight shined down from the windows. Maybe the light would scare it away. Twisting around, I met the creature eye to eye.

Fuck, those are killer cheekbones. He was a beautiful man in profile, but straight on my heart skipped a beat tracing down the wide plummet of a bone structure as delicate as a stiletto dagger. The hot creature stopped, maybe realizing I was in the protection of the sun.

Slowly, I moved to ease my purse off my shoulder and reach for my spell book when the creature took a step forward. Shit! I dashed back, my gaze never wavering off of him. The mass of books in my bag smashed together, pinching my hand. Where was the damn spell book?

Ah!

Metal ridges smacked into my back and I realized I had walked right into the radiator. The awkward angle bit into my knees, causing them to buckle. I strained to keep my toes on the ground even as my ass tumbled to the hot metal.

Book, if you have some psychic link with me, I need you to find a passage to banish bodiless…okay. No. He has a body. A lithe, tortured punk kind of body. Stop staring at his body.

"Can you see me?" he asked. The voice of fingernails scratching from inside a coffin shifted. His gravel mellowed to a softer timbre until smooth as glass.

"Damn right I can!" I shouted and raised my spell book at him. It'd sent scroungers screaming, smashed in the heads of werewolves. No chance whatever this creature was could stand against it. "Now…begone!"

He darted his dark eyes to my tome of witchcraft, the red leather warmer than the radiator under my ass. Reaching out with his hand, he moved his arm through the sunbeams. I stared harder and watched a sheen of blue barely glimmer below the surface of his olive skin. Folding his fingers back until only a single digit remained, he tapped the tip against my book.

A surge of energy radiated across my splayed palms and up through the monster's arm. As it circled his body, the jacket darkened and a red stain splattered right above his heart.

With wide eyes, he gasped, "What are you?"

Chapter Seven

Light burst above, the fluorescents going nuclear and blinding me. I blinked furiously, certain that whatever I'd seen would vanish. But no, he still stood there, waiting for me to answer him. *What am I? What is he?*

Trying to stand, I said in my most imposing voice, "I'm a..."

"What are you doing?"

This new voice came from behind the strange man. Slowly, I leaned to the side and spotted the librarian staring at me like I'd lost my mind. "Me?" I squeaked.

"I heard shouting. There are books scattered everywhere. Why are you sitting on the radiator?" the woman scolded, causing me to leap to my feet.

I overshot and nearly fell straight into the strange man's arms. He lifted them as if to catch me, but I dodged away in time and stared at the librarian. Still, my gaze kept darting back to the man she was completely ignoring.

"It…it was dark?"

She crossed her arms in a 'you're a grown adult, stop being scared of the dark' way. "Please refrain from touching the radiator. It can burn you." The woman spoke like I had the IQ of a bran muffin.

Arguing with her could only spell trouble, so I numbly nodded. Loading her arms up with the books I'd tossed to provide coverage, the librarian stared at me. "Please keep your voice down or you'll be asked to leave."

"What about…?" I grew incensed being the only person she blamed. The librarian dead-eye stared at me and I jerked both thumbs in the stranger's direction.

A light laugh rumbled from him and I glowered. Did the weirdo have an in with the staff?

Wait. This time I watched the woman's eyes. She stared not at the man's face but over his shoulder, then right back at me. There was being polite, but he had a face worth gawking at. The woman didn't even give a cursory glance to his shrouded eyes or deadly cheekbones.

I folded my hands behind my back and tried to stand up straight. It was a default move from my time in foster care. "I'll keep quiet," I whispered. The woman gave me another curt nod, then swung on her crisp shoes and stomped away leaving me alone — at least as far as she knew.

"She couldn't see you." It was an accusation and not a question.

Another sustained laugh rose from the man. "Of course not."

"Why?"

He quirked his head to the side, causing that blue swish of hair to fall over his eyes. I wanted to push it away, annoyed at how it blocked his face. "The reason is quite simple. I'm dead."

"You're doing an awful lot of talking for a dead man," slipped past my lips before my brain could even catch up. Dead? Like a zombie, dead? Or was he insane and just thought he was dead. Could be some creature that lied, who was also invisible to everyone but me. Ink would know.

"Oh, I would love nothing more than to pour sonnets into your delectable ears," he said. "All these years, no one could hear me. No one could even see me. And now you, a flower blooming among the cracks of concrete, appears to speak to me. How?"

Just how long had he been dead? Even Ink didn't talk like an eighteenth-century poet late with the rent and he was over two thousand years old. The dead man's gaze burned into mine and his flower line lit a blush across my cheeks. "It's…see, I'm a witch."

Instinctively, I gritted my teeth. Every other time I had to reveal the truth, I'd either be dismissed, shouted at, or openly attacked. But the man parted his hands wide and shouted, "That's wonderful!"

"And my name's Layla?" I added, waiting for the boom. There was always a boom.

"Oh, forgive me. It's been so long since I've had to introduce myself. Introduce myself? It's been years since I've had the pleasure to speak with anyone. I'm Daniel. Daniel Lu."

He held his hand out and I reached to shake it. When my palm skirted through the air where his hand should be, a cold tingle raced across my skin, but nothing else. Daniel frowned and let his drop. I felt I should do the same, but for a moment, I let my fingers drift through the empty space where the strange energy lingered.

"My bond, you have need of me?"

Sashaying around the corner, Ink appeared. Right. I'd mentally called for him. Still wasn't used to that. Out of habit, I reached for him. Ink caught my hand, then brushed his nails up my arm while curling his body around my hip. Just before he could run his lips over my ear, he turned his head. "You've discovered a ghost? Delightful."

"How do you...?" I craned my head from Ink back to Daniel. He looked as solid as my incubus.

"Give me credit, my eternal bliss." Ink was laying it on thick. With the whole of his palm, he swatted through Daniel's chest. To my eyes, Ink's hand sunk into the man up to his wrist, but Ink only chuckled. "The energy of a soul tingles across the whole of his form. An interesting diversion for you, I'm certain. Shall we remove these infernal knickers and pleasure each other?"

I moved to push Ink away, when he playfully extended his claws and poked the tip of one against my chin. His smile wound into a deadly trap and I leaned forward to fall for it.

"Malebranche!" Daniel shouted. "Remove that woman from your foul deeds and return to the pits of hell!"

Both Ink and I stared at Daniel, his hand outstretched as if he was trying to exorcise the demon sneaking his hand down the back of my pants. "What?" I asked.

Ink chuckled in his baritone brimstone. With an arm wrapped around me, he didn't just lean beside Daniel, he drew the whole of his clawed hand up through the man. "I met Dante. Rather twitchy sort who liked to keep lists of his enemies around."

"This...this is a..."

"He's an incubus," I said, "not a demon." Daniel stared wildly at Ink and pointed to the claws. "Will you put those away?" I tried to swat Ink's two-inch talons, but he shook them back to normal fingernails.

"Why are we entertaining this remnant of soul droppings?"

"Says the creature born of darkness and hate," Daniel argued back.

"Darkness, yes. Hate...? Well, that depends on their kink."

Could I talk to just one man and not have it turn into a pissing match with my incubus? "Will you stop being so obstinate?" I begged my damn demon.

Ink shrugged and I didn't know if it was his way of saying he didn't care about stopping or that fighting with Daniel was nothing to him. It could be both. "My question remains valid. To what purpose have you called me to your side? I assumed you discovered another creature preying upon fragile mortals."

"I...I didn't know what Daniel was at first," I admitted, wincing. Ink was supposed to help train me in this witchcraft thing, but when I'd ask him a question, he'd act shocked I didn't already know everything.

"And now you do. A delightful opportunity to discover new wonders...well, minor annoyances of the world. Shall we be off?" Ink extended his elbow to me.

"Wait!" Daniel called. He took a step closer and Ink bared his teeth. The ghost wobbled to my side instead and stared only at me. "Please, don't go. Not yet. I haven't spoken aloud to anyone in...I don't even know." His voice cracked, the sound of tears gushing through, though none moved down his cheek. "You're the first friendly face to look upon me, to smile at me, to give me hope since I died."

The outpouring of emotion caused me to curl my toes and bite my lip.

Ink exasperated while rolling his eyes. "I see my time is already wasted. I will return to the drawing room to partake of more delightful court battles. If you have need of me again" — he glared at Daniel hovering just behind me — "it'd best be for a real threat."

Before I could answer, Ink vanished.

"The demon — !" Daniel shouted.

"He does that, a lot." Not sure what it said about my life that I didn't even blink at his vanishing. *You're literally talking to a ghost, Layla. Normal went out the window on Halloween.*

What did I say to the dead man? Asking him how he died felt as gauche as asking someone how they wound up in prison. He stared at me with his eternal brown eyes, his perfectly beautiful face, and his succulent full lips quirked in anticipation. All sentience fled my mind. If it weren't for my brainstem keeping me upright, I'd have fallen like a sack of cement.

"Wha…?" drooled from my lips and Daniel rescued me.

"Tell me all about you, please. Layla?" He repeated my name like a connoisseur testing a fifty-year-old whiskey. The last 'a' popped off his tongue and a blue halo rose around his eyes. "What a beautiful name, though it is but a tenth of a tenth as lovely as its owner."

"You…" My cheeks wouldn't stop burning. I absently covered my mouth, then the blush with my hand while trying to think. "You're good at that."

Too good?

The thought rattled in the back of my head, trying to warn me, but the rest of my libido trumpeted over the sound. Why'd Cal have to leave town now?

"Am I lying?" Daniel asked, his chin turned so a blue haze trailed from the corners of his eyes.

Of course not, my libido wanted to say.

Yes, my humility tried to throw in.

The loud shushing of a pissed-off librarian answered for me. Daniel's body, skin and all, faded to a dull gray. He shook his head and pointed in a direction. "We should speak elsewhere."

"It'd be nice to not have the entire town think I'm insane," I muttered to myself.

"Can all witches see ghosts?" Daniel asked. He traveled ahead, my eyes drawn to the flapping of his fallen jacket's patch. Though, on occasion they drifted south. Nice to know tight pants were in fashion whenever he died.

"I don't know," I said, then walked past an aisle just as an older gentleman turned at the strange woman talking to herself. I raised a hand up and jerked a finger to my ear like there was something in it. He frowned but didn't chase after me with a pitchfork.

"I haven't been a witch for long," I admitted, barely giving voice to the words. "It's been nothing but nearly dying, followed by long stretches of waiting for the next time something tries and kill me."

"Sounds terrifying."

I'd been having twisted dreams lately where I'd wake up to people laughing at me while I waggled useless fingers. They'd tell me I'd slipped into a delusional belief I was a witch in love with a werewolf and fucking a demon. Magic wasn't real.

Those stung deeper than any other nightmare.

Daniel paused and turned around to face me. I stared up and realized he'd pulled me back to an old room stuffed with newspapers hanging on wooden rods. A single table filled the darkened space, the rest of the area taken up with shelves of old news. "This is my room, at least I treat it as such. I come here often when the library is full and distracting. So many people, so many voices, life brimming and none of it directed at me. It's downright maddening at times."

"I don't know how you're still..."

"Sane?" He drifted for a chair left out and settled in it. To do so, he had to phase his legs through the table, but Daniel didn't even bat an eye. "The one good thing about being forced to haunt a library—I never run out of reading material."

"There's something I wanted to talk to you about." I fished around my purse and moved to sit across from him.

"Hemingway is highly overrated," Daniel said with a dismissive wave.

"Huh?" I asked, only to watch a sly smile rise on his face. A laugh rolled off my tongue and I laid out the book on White. "You were the one to drop this book at my feet?"

"Ah, yes. I overheard your discussion with the"— shadows passed over his face and Daniel's voice chilled—"blond man and thought it might prove useful."

"So you're like a helpful library spirit, floating around finding books for people?" That sounded adorable.

Daniel tipped his head to his shoulder. "Depends on the person. Though I regret not leaving *Lady Chatterley's Lover* at your feet."

Mental note, look up the Cliffs Notes for that book. And don't let Ink find out about it.

Coughing to try to cover up the fact I didn't have an afterlife to spend in a library, I twisted the book around to face him. "Can you help me find more about Mr. White?"

"Hm?" He studied the book's title page and flipped to a random chapter in the middle. *Are books the only thing he can touch?*

"The man I'm chasing, he's...well he's like me."

"A witch?"

"Okay, not exactly like me. But he knows about werewolves, and nymphs and other magical creatures."

That caught Daniel by surprise. "Nymphs are real?"

"Don't get too excited. Their reputations are greatly exaggerated. Look, I have to find him. He's still around, maybe he doesn't age. Or ages slowly. Or it's another man entirely using the same name. All I know is that he's...he's bad news."

Wow, Layla. That's sure to sell him on this. That guy, the one from a book about the thirties? Yeah, I just know he's still alive and a jerk. No wonder Cal and Ink kept brushing me off.

Daniel reached for my hands folded together in pleading. Only a slight chill wafted against them as his eyes burned in mine. "I'll gladly help."

"You will?"

"Of course. What fool would turn you down?"

I could think of a couple.

"But I need you to do something for me. Please, Layla, you might be the only one who can help."

It only seemed fair. Not knowing what the ghost could ask for—might be virgin blood, or the fang of a vampire—I said, "Yes. What is it?"

"I need you to find who killed me."

Chapter Eight

With a flick, I split open the tape on the massive box of paper straws. I filled my arms and moved to place the straws on their 'summer fun time' shelf. A shadow hid away the industrial fluorescent lights above me, but I didn't even pause. Flamingo straws on the left, red, white and blue on the right.

"I don't understand why you're bothering."

An announcement blared over the loudspeakers, the pre-recording telling everyone the store would be closing soon, so please get the hell out. Okay, it used corporate-speak niceties, which was probably why it didn't stop a single customer from browsing.

"Because," I said and moved to stand up. To my surprise, he dropped a hand and helped me. The scent of charcoal wafted in the air and Ink slipped his guiding hand around my waist.

"Many unholy things have been done in this world for little reason."

"Are you saying Daniel's unholy?"

"A ghost? A mere reverberation of a soul left to rot in this realm?" Ink laughed hard and shook his head. "No, I meant I'd like to slip from this place and do unholy things to you. Or you to me. That is the perk with the unholy, it's rather flexible in its malfeasance."

"I'm working." I slid from Ink's sticky grip. *Don't think about what he meant, or what counts as unholy to a sex demon.* Repeating that while keeping my periphery off of the man designed for fucking, I yanked open the next box. Floppy sunhats, those belonged on shelf A-3.

"This is what confounds me. Your life is already entwined with the power of the realms, this study of healing elixirs, and whatever compels you to place tchotchkes upon shelves in dreadful warehouses."

"The need to not starve compels me. Which reminds me, did you eat my damn yogurt?"

Ink shrugged as if it was no bother, ignoring the fact that he ate three pints in a day. Good thing incubi didn't seem to shit or he'd be in big trouble. "Given your hectic schedule, what has compelled you to assist the ghost?"

"Daniel..." I shifted on my haunches, wanting to tell him that I'd finally found someone who would help me. But no doubt Ink would laugh at that as much as he did my agreeing to solve Daniel's murder. "He asked."

"We are a charity now? Any who ask receive recompense and salvation from the witch of the Bellpepper Warehouse?"

Why the hell did he care? Most times, unless he wanted something, Ink said nothing about my coming and going. On occasion, he'd ask if I'd learned a new spell, but then get distracted by another modern trapping. "Are you jealous?"

The demon scoffed so strongly I knew I had hit pay dirt. "Hardly. Mere curiosity and perhaps a touch of concern."

"Daniel can't even touch me," I said, brushing him off.

"Which you'd do well to remember before your long looks grow uncomfortable between your thighs."

Fuck. He'd been...he was always reading my desires. How did I keep forgetting?

"I am surprised at the clarity the specter has maintained. A ghost's lot is to grow rabidly insane without the tether of a physical form, then fade into non-existence."

"That's horrible."

The demon who apparently didn't die shrugged. Life and death were meaningless to him, as he liked to remind me every now and again. "There are worse ways to live, better ways to die," he said.

I shook my head, too exhausted too early into my shift to keep up. Taking a step for the next box, my knee twisted sharply. The moment I felt myself falling, Ink wrapped his arms around me. I tried to steady myself to stand back up, when white swept across my vision.

A scream echoed from the blank field. As I opened my eyes, I was met with a man's body contorted like a dying spider. He lay on his back, arms and legs extended in the air. Both wrists and ankles were tied to a pole, then those poles roped to the ceiling. Red welts covered his body, which was splattered with blood.

My gaze fell further down and I started to find a whip in my hand.

The trussed-up man tipped his head down, revealing a face plumped from excess. He made me think of the corrupt banker trying to ruin the down-on-his-luck hero. "Well," he said, rattling the chains tied to his arms, "shall you finish the job?"

Fuck! Pain snapped at the back of my neck and I flung my head forward. It felt like someone punched me, but I blinked and stared up at Ink's slightly concerned eyes.

"Damn it, it happened again," I cursed. I'd hoped the one time with Cal was a fluke, but no luck. That one hurt even more, leaving my skin itching as if someone else had worn it. Pinching into my temples, I asked, "What the hell were you even doing?"

"Hm? Oh, yes, I was remembering my time with a bishop. His visage shared much in common with your shift manager. It's left me wondering how much that man would enjoy the rush of leeches upon his scrotum."

"Ink…" I moved to chastise him, but it wasn't his fault I randomly slunk into his memories. "How the hell do I control whatever this is?" I asked instead.

"I have no idea."

"You're supposed to be my teacher. That's the deal, you help me with witchcraft and I…feed you."

The incubus sighed. "While I would love nothing more than to answer your inquiry, I'm afraid my knowledge of whatever plagues you is beyond me."

"What exactly are you good for then?"

"Shall I make an annotated list? Your dog taught me how to create a spreading sheet."

For fuck's sake. I did not need this…whatever the hell it was. I didn't need to have a demon prodding into my business while at work either. And how was I going to solve a decades'-old murder?

Ink began to slip his arms around my shoulders, but I ducked out of the way. Last thing I needed was to wind up in a threesome with King Louis and Marie Antoinette. He didn't pout, and folded his hands against his stomach. "If this ails you so, then perhaps you should find other witches to inquire."

"How do I do that?"

My teacher could only shrug leaving me to wonder why I kept him around. "If you will allow me," he said, dangling his fingers above my skin without touching.

Pain at my cutting him off bubbled through me and I nodded. Still, I winced, waiting for my vision to be kicked to Ancient Greece. Delicate fingers danced up my shoulders and around the nape of neck. "I promise to focus only on you when we are embracing, my bond."

A nice idea, but it'd take only a second for his mind to wander. I should argue with him, but his massage increased, kneading away the stress-boulders I carried. "What you require is an eight-hour stay in bed with my body for the mattress."

I knew he didn't mean we'd be sleeping. Though, with Ink's talents, eight hours might feel like ten minutes. No. I shook my head to clear it, and heard the clip of shoes. We weren't alone and sure as hell shouldn't be talking about witch and demon stuff.

"What I need is for you to go home."

"Yes, the rooms in this place are far too cold and ungiving to properly enjoy each other's skin." Instead of puppy eyes, Ink cranked up his incubus flames at me. Orange and red flickered in his irises, and a sheen rose across his lips. He even managed to undo the first two buttons on his shirt without moving. I didn't have time to play, even if he was temptation incarnate.

"Look, I'll meet you back home when my shift is done."

"Excuse me?" Oh, god. My manager with the face of a masochistic bishop waltzed up. "Sir, the store is closing soon. Please make your purchases and exit."

Ink sized the man up while I scurried back to stocking the shelves. Stepping closer, Ink took in a deep whiff and said, "Not the leeches, no. A woman emptying your coffers and refusing you release."

"What?"

"I will begone," Ink declared with a dramatic flair of his hand. He walked around the corner and at least had enough sense to wait to vanish until he was out of sight.

"Leeland." My manager thought we all worked harder if he only used our last names. "You're behind schedule. Where are the tumblers?"

I finally glanced up at him, and Ink was right. He looked exactly like the trussed-up bishop. "Don't know, sir," I muttered and turned away.

"Well, you should—"

"Help!" Screeching around the corner, a disheveled elderly man ran right into the manager. "You gotta help me!" he shouted. His hair was wild and knotted, his clothing ripped at the knees and sleeves. A trickle of blood fell from his nose and he wiped it with the back of his hand.

"Help you how, sir?" the manager asked, struggling to cling to the wild man.

"It's coming! It's gonna kill me!" he screamed and whipped his head around. In doing so, he revealed a port-wine birthmark across his neck.

"Sir? Sir!" my manager shouted.

"Fuck, it's here!" The erratic man gaped in horror at…nothing. Absolutely nothing turned the corner, nothing lurched closer to him. But his face gnarled into a rictus and he twisted out of the manager's hold to resume running.

"Every fucking full moon," my manager groaned and called in. "Security. We've got another one." Just before he gave chase to the poor guy, he said to me, "You're staying until you finish the whole seasonal restock, Leeland."

I'd be clocking out at my usual time, but be stuck shelving hours after because there was nothing I could do and overtime didn't exist in retail. Pinching my fingers tight to keep from cursing at my manager, I turned to stare at the rows of boxes filling the floor.

All alone, it was going to take me until five, maybe six in the morning to get this stocked, cleaned up, and boxes squashed down. Or that was how long it would have taken the old Layla. I reached into my pocket to unearth a small piece of chalk. It'd been broken to a nub thanks to the books in my bag, but the bit was enough.

Dropping to my feet, I drew a wobbly circle around the whole of the boxes on the linoleum and whispered the simple spell, "Obey my command and fill the stand." Instead of floating up from the box, maybe getting into wacky hijinks and attacking customers, all of the stock appeared right where it belonged.

Thanks to whatever witch had owned a fruit stand and hated stocking shelves as much as me, I got to go on break. Maybe there was still time to explore Ink's skin after all.

Chapter Nine

The first day of a much-needed break and where was I? Rolling my tongue around a curly straw in a daiquiri while the surf licked at my toes? Racing down a mountain on skis for the last powder of the season? Hiding under the blankets with two men, one of whom was designed for my pleasure?

Of course not. Bright and early on Saturday morning, I returned to the public library. I took a deeper draught of my coffee, wishing I'd bought a gallon tub. A bundle of maple seeds twirled from above, their green wings scattering across the bucking horse standing vigil. First day of trying to solve a murder.

I could do this...probably.

Squaring my shoulders, I marched through the doors, slipped past the turnstile and took in a deep breath. Muddled paper, crayons, carpet glue, and the bouquet of colognes from men who thought showering optional rose from the shelves before me.

Where was my ghost?

Not *my* ghost. I didn't have a ghost. He was just…my partner. Ink's needling rose from the back of my brain and I tried to shake it away. Another kind of shaking rumbled from my hoodie pocket. I stuffed my hand in and felt my phone vibrating.

Aw, it was a text from Cal.

Morning, beautiful.

That was sweet of him. We'd only been able to exchange a handful last night before my shift and my phone freaked out. Seemed the water damage wasn't fully out of its system. The edges of the screen were still wishy-washy and out of focus. But I could make out his next text…which was a picture of a pair of antlers?

See, no panties.

I flexed my fingers and typed back.

That's nice, but I don't need to know Jared's underwear preference.

Cal responded with a gif of a dog smiling.

A thought struck me and I stared around the empty library. Even still, I hunched the phone close to my chest to type.

How'd last night go? I added a full moon emoji to make my point.

Cal had full control over his shifting, but things could get wild whenever the moon was full. I drew my fingers over my neck remembering the last one in February. That was a good Valentine's Day.

He responded with a curt 'fine' and I winced, wondering if I had stepped into something I shouldn't. He also wasn't exactly happy about being a werewolf. Not in a 'woe is me to have been cursed' way — more it reminded him of his abusive father...among other issues.

Missed you though

Oh yeah? How much?

My phone blew up with a photo of Cal's proof practically popping through the thin cotton of his boxer briefs. The gray fabric hugged it so tightly I could make out the vein I loved to trail with my tongue. *Shit.* My cheeks lit up hot and I slammed my phone to my chest.

Checking again to find no one but a solitary man hen-pecking at the keyboards, I dashed deeper into the stacks. I kept risking another peek, then smothering the screen in my hoodie. What the hell was wrong with me? This was hardly my first dick pic. Though it was the first one I wanted to have framed on my wall, maybe as a diptych with the photo minus his underwear.

Holding the phone at an awkward angle, I tried to type '*naughty*' without looking.

After pressing send, I took stock of my surroundings. I had nearly made it to the periodicals. My phone vibrated like mad and I found a series of eggplant emojis and smirking devils filling the screen. What in the...?

Autocorrect had turned my 'naughty' into 'mighty.'

I mean, it wasn't wrong.

Do you miss me?

The abrupt swerve from sexting to a plaintive request threw my heart into a loop. I felt another 'aw' rising in my throat but kept it at bay.

More than you know. The bed's cold without you.

What about the demon?

I typed 'Ink's not you' then deleted it. My cheeks reaching magma status, I fired off fast.

Ink can't bend me over the bed while holding my legs up, and fuck me until it aches like you.

"Good morning!"
Oh, shit! I moved to slide my phone into my pocket while looking up into the smiling face of my friendly ghost. I say moved because I forgot to slip it in and my phone careened to the ground. The twitchy screen went full glitch, my text app opening and closing like it was possessed.

Cal was typing something on his end, but I knew my phone was going to fail soon. I quickly sent him an update.

Got to go. Library. Studying. Work.

That had to be a good enough excuse. He was on practically the same schedule to hell as me. I moved to turn it off in the hope that'd cast a miracle and heal my phone, when Cal responded fast.

Say hi to Dana and Fariah.

I...

I will. Bye.

Before he could send any more texts or pics to distract me, I buried my phone in my bag and stared up at Daniel. "Morning!" My voice practically bounced off every window in the library. Damn it. "Sorry, been a long night." Ink had made certain of that.

"I'm elated you came back." Daniel drifted back from the table, giving me room to place down my bag. The spell book haphazardly fell out as was its wont.

"We had a deal," I said, hoping he wasn't about to renege on it.

"No, I know. I only... For the first time since I woke up in this prison unable to speak or touch, hope has bloomed. I suppose I entertained the thought you'd never return, or you'd been a delusion from madness just out of habit."

"I promise." I reached for him and was about to try to take his hand in comfort, when I remembered. Dropping my palm to the table, I said, "I'm real. See?" I knocked shave and a haircut on the table as if that'd been my plan the whole time.

"Two bits, which should be more than enough to pay the ferryman," he said to himself. "Do you ever wonder if Charon makes change?"

"He's probably got a money belt on his bony hips." We both laughed together and a flush warmed in my stomach that usually came from my werewolf instead. "Your death," I said, trying to drag us back on track.

God, Layla, you can't just ask someone about their death.

"Sorry, that was crass of me. I mean…the day that you, uh—"

"Died. I am dead. You can say it. If I hadn't accepted that fact, I…I don't know." The blue sheen of before was replaced by a bright yellow light sparkling at the edge of his eyes. I couldn't stop staring at the stars dancing off him. "I don't recall much of my death, only the date."

"That's a start," I said and turned to the mass of preserved newspapers. How old was the punk movement?

I fished out a small notebook and one of my handy markers. "Have you met any other ghosts?"

"Afraid not."

"No one at all?"

Daniel tipped his head back and recited, "'The loneliest moment in someone's life is when they are watching their whole world fall apart, and all they can do is stare blankly.'"

"That's *The Great Gatsby*," I said, surprised I recognized it. "We had to read it in school," I quickly explained, hoping that told him he wasn't going to find a deep well of knowledge inside of me. This also wasn't getting us any closer to an answer.

Armed for the fight ahead, I stepped to the first row of books crammed in with the archived newspapers. "Okay. What's the date of your death?"

"The twenty-fifth of June."

My mind shattered like a bird slamming through a window. I swallowed hard, trying to keep breath flowing through my body even as my throat swelled up. Daniel seemed to sense the change. "Layla? Is something wrong?"

"June twenty-fifth…" I licked my lips trying to keep the tremor out of my voice. "…is the day my mom died."

"I had no idea you were…suffering so."

"It's okay, it's fine." I was used to everyone apologizing if they harangued me about calling on Mother's Day The dead didn't make a habit of answering phone calls. "It's, it was a long time ago."

Please don't ask me to talk about it.

"If you don't mind, how long ago?"

Swiping at my nose in the chance of cry-snot appearing, I said, "I was nine, so…um." If reading was hard, numbers were damn near impossible with my dyslexia. They danced in my rotten brain like fridge magnets tumbling to the floor.

"If it's any consolation, I died in 1994. Though the coincidence is startling."

"Yeah." I nodded to him, trying to not shiver where I stood. I happened to walk into a library where a ghost happened to die the same date as my mother? Though, people had to die, and there were only three hundred and sixty-five chances so… I could ask Ink about the odds later. "June twenty-fifth, 1994," I repeated and scanned the shelves.

"Layla, if the pain is too much…?"

"No. No, I can. We had a deal," I said, locking back up that Pandora's box of teenage angst, rebellion, and self-hate. "I'm gonna see it through."

The massive book weighed down my arms and I waddled for the table to drop it in place. It'd have been poetic for a crack of thunder to strike in that moment, maybe the lights to flicker off. Instead, I heard a car alarm go off and a flock of crows screech at the interruption.

Paging through the book to June, I found the twenty-fifth. No mention of anything exciting on that page. If he'd died that day, it probably wasn't in print until the next. While I hunched over, squinting to read the tiny newsprint, I felt Daniel just beyond my shoulder.

I kept catching my breath in anticipation of his hand touching my shoulder or the small of my back. But then I'd shake my head at the stupid thought. He couldn't touch anything, which was why he needed me.

I frowned, staring at the front-page puff piece about a new racetrack. A man in a suit so white it'd faded into the newsprint stared out. His head was bald save a strip of dark hair circling the bottom, the eyes shriveled and sunken below a heavy browbone. Every time I flipped back and forth my eyes kept leaping to him and I had no idea why. He looked like any typical stuffed-up politician or businessman that'd be in the news for either selling a company or embezzling from one.

"Where did you die?" I asked.

"Here. It's why I'm doomed forever to haunt this place."

A murder in the library? Hm... I pinched my lips so tight they began to sting. "Are you sure?" I glanced over my shoulder to watch Daniel's face fall.

"What do you mean am I sure?"

"Well, you don't seem to remember much. Not who killed you or why?" He'd been rather tight-lipped about any biographical information too.

The ghost my demon warned me could be going mad shook his head and wrung his empty hands in the air. I focused on his hands, my hackles rising even though I knew they couldn't do anything. Daniel stomped around in a circle, every step lifting him an inch off the floor.

"I have been trapped in this purgatory, this unending limbo for...how long?"

"Thirty years, give or take," I said.

That caught Daniel by surprise, his eyes opening wide. "Thirty..." He stared at his hands beginning to shake. "I'd assumed it a decade, maybe two at most. The days they all...there is no end to them. One becomes twelve, becomes a hundred, becomes a thousand. What am I?"

He stared at me, his face stricken in torment from the dump of years. My voice caught at the beautiful features twisted into the terror of a man on the breaking point. That wasn't helping.

"You're a man who's going to get retribution," I said and held my palm up flat.

Daniel's wild eyes softened, the pupils dilating to a warm recognition. He too extended his palm and placed it against mine. I could only see his skin gliding over mine, but the ghostly touch made me smile.

"I am Edmond Dantes emerging from the Château d'If."

"That's a good thing?"

I braced myself for the man to either give me a derisive snort or explain whatever literary reference had flown over my head. But Daniel only smiled sweetly. "A wonderful thing that would be impossible without you. I'm sorry I...struggle to remember my life before. It's as if I've lived these past thirty years unchanging, my memories left as dust on the shelf. While at the same time, I've accumulated little to share."

"How are you so certain you were killed here? Maybe this was a favorite place of yours?" What if someone died and wound up haunting a gas station bathroom?

Daniel drew a hand down his jacket and tugged the open side away. Over his beat-up The Clash shirt, a red stain darkened the fading gray cotton. "A bullet rests inside my heart. I know that as surely as I know my name, perhaps better. This place, it meant nothing to me before, beyond being the last floor I walked across. Why? What have you found?"

"That's just it. There is no way the news wouldn't be going ape-shit over someone getting gunned down in a public library. That's primo fear mongering. But I can't find anything. Not the day after, not a week. It's like it didn't happen at all."

"No." The ghost bent over, hunting through the pages he hadn't read. "That can't be. I died, bled out right there on the seal in the floor before the entrance. It happened, I swear." The madness crept back into his words, his face contorting at the reveal that it could all be in his head.

"I did find this." Turning the pages past the big news, the local minor news, and even the personal ads, I stopped at the police blotter.

"'Minor noise complaint on Victor Street. Police called to investigate, declined. Caller believed it to be fireworks.'" Daniel slumped back, his eyes wide as he digested the news. "That's it. My death amounts to a couple sentences, a nosy neighbor, and fireworks? What do I do now? I've found Abbé Faria's treasure and it is empty."

I couldn't take his dejected look and scanned down the old pages of the past. "Why were you here?"

"Pardon?"

"If this library was nothing, why were you here at night after hours?"

Daniel scratched along his forehead without leaving a single mar to his perfect skin. "I...I cannot recall. There was no reason for me to be here. I'm not even from this town."

"You're not?"

"No. I live in, was living in Rockford, Illinois. We were traveling for a reason that's on the tip of my tongue."

"We?"

His pacing stopped and he stared at me.

"You said we. Someone else was with you. Maybe someone who knows what happened that night. Your family?"

"No, my mother would have never approved of... Fingers Strasborg!"

I eyed him up. "Your mom doesn't approve of you fingering Strasborg?"

"What? No. Fingers Strasborg. Not his real name."

"I mean, I've heard of stupider names."

Daniel tapped his lips, his pinkies flailing out at the side. As he raised his head to the ceiling, he shouted, "Bryan, Bryan Strasborg. He was with me when we came to this town for...there was a reason. A make or break one."

"Okay, we have a plan. I'll try and find this guy and—"

Daniel scoffed. "How can you possibly find him in a country of three hundred million?"

I held up my phone and gave it a shake. "We have the internet now." I tried to put in a Google search, but my phone was not having it and glitched out. "When I

find him, you'll have to come with me." Assuming he
didn't live in Hawaii, though that would be nice. A long
week at the beach, some minor murder solving, then
back to savor a soak in the surf with a werewolf, a
demon, and a ghost.

"For what purpose?" Daniel asked, jarring me from
my dream drooling over Cal and Ink in tiny swim
trunks.

He probably didn't want to hear why I mentally put
Cal in the blue ones and Ink in the skimpiest red ones.
Shaking my head to focus, I said, "Because I can't very
well show up at a random guy's door and say, 'Hey, do
you remember why you went to this town on this date
thirty years ago?' He'll slam the door in my face."

"You require me to travel with you," Daniel said
slowly.

"Yeah. Is that going to be a problem?"

The ghost didn't breathe slowly, but gave a good
impression of it. "Follow me," he said and took off for
the front of the library. I stuffed my spell book back into
my bag and took off after Daniel.

He wasn't moving quickly, but didn't stop to dodge
out of the way of book trolleys, displays or people. I
called, "Watch out!" when to the rest of the library
absolutely no one was about to knock over a stand of
picture books. *Keep being the town weirdo, Layla.*

Turtling into the collar of my jacket, I raced after
Daniel who stopped beside the door. "If I try to leave
the library..." he said and took a step through the front
door.

He vanished in a flash but not like Ink. A gut-
wrenching sound my ears couldn't hear and a
pounding color my eyes couldn't see clanged through
me. Sickness seeped from my pores and I found Daniel

splayed out on the floor right before the front desk. Blood bubbled up from his heart and splattered across the linoleum. The librarian calmly typed away while a man bled to death at her feet.

I tried to turn away, to look anywhere but the dying man, but I couldn't. I pushed him to this horror, and I had to suffer for my ignorance. Daniel's feet stopped twitching against the ground and his dying body fell silent. Oh god, was he gone? Did I kill his ghost?

"Do you see?" the corpse asked me. It popped up without a care and rose to his feet. The gallons of blood vanished off of the scratched-up floor. "I am doomed to forever haunt this library."

"You can't leave at all?" I tried to swallow, struggling to keep my guilt in check.

The librarian stared at me and said, "I leave when the library's closed. We don't live here."

"I am afraid not." Daniel stepped closer, his brow heavy, when a sly look crossed his face. "Though, there is one other place I am capable of haunting. Yes, that could be the answer."

"What is?" I dropped my voice and turned so the librarian couldn't hear.

"I'll tell you where and meet you at the location tonight after the moon's risen."

"Okay," I said, my heart pounding at the thrill of the chase.

Daniel gave me the address, then asked, "Are you certain you wish to do this? It could be unpleasant."

I wanted to laugh. If he knew half of the things I'd done in the past six months alone. Going to a random address to probably pick up an old memento he could haunt was nothing. "This is important. I want to help."

"A wayward ghost could not ask for a braver champion. Or lovelier."

Damn, there went that blush again.

Daniel skirted a finger over my cheek without touching me. I leaned closer, lost in his lips parting. "And, Layla," he whispered.

"Yes?"

"Bring a shovel."

Chapter Ten

The GPS kept shouting that I was at my destination, but there was no destination to be had. The street Daniel had given me came to a dead-end in a dirt patch with a chain-link fence circling it. On instinct, I reached for my phone to call and check the directions...only to remember the dead didn't have cell service.

Sighing, I put my car in park and — keeping my foot on the brake — tried to peer over the fence. A ditch turned into a river, or maybe vice versa, the blackened water chugging along thanks to the recent rains. Droplets clung to the bare tree branches, waiting for their opportunity to plunge onto my head. All in all, unpleasant weather to go poking into someone's industrial dumping ground.

I made a promise. Even accepting my fate, I gritted my jaw and reached for my purse tucked in the backseat beside the shovel. Dana had asked a lot of questions about why someone living in an apartment would need a shovel, and I had no answers. I went with 'in case it snows again.' 'Because a ghost told me to' would have held up worse.

"Now you see the futility in conversing with specters."

I didn't come alone either. Ink made a habit of pretending he gave me a choice while stripping it away. He whipped his head to the side so fast it reminded me of a hawk chasing a mouse. In that scenario, I was the prey. "If what remains of his cognizance hasn't fully rotted to mush, this must be a ghoulish prank."

"Why would Daniel prank me?" I asked. Ink's reluctance solidified my resistance. I pulled the shovel out of the backseat and slipped from the car. Traffic brushed past from behind. Was anyone wondering about the woman in the purple jacket standing before a fence? Or were they all too busy in their own lives to give a shit?

To my surprise, Ink followed. I half expected him to sit in the car and make 'I told you so' faces while I wandered around. "Why would a poltergeist fling picture frames off the walls? The dead do not make sense because death is nonsensical."

"Daniel made perfect sense to me," I said. The hairs on the nape of my neck stood on end and I turned to find a pitying look on the incubus. "What?"

"You are aware ghosts are incapable of physical touch?"

What is he going on about? "Yes."

"And yet you intend to follow through on this inane quest of the dead?"

"Yes!" I repeated, having to shout over the rise in vehicles.

Ink sighed and folded his hands behind his back. "Very well. I shall prepare myself for the unquenchable lust about to radiate from your loins."

Ignore him. Whatever Daniel wanted had to be over the fence. I took one more glance to the left and right. "You never stop," I said and leaped onto the chain link. Ten feet tall, with a wire running the top — I needed a few footholds to get up it. Thankfully, it wasn't barbed or I'd be in bigger trouble. Bending the wire down, I lifted my leg over the top and leaped to the other side.

I cursed, my boots sinking an inch into the sucking mud. Sneering, I raised my foot up and glared at the muck oozing up to the laces.

Movement cut through the skeletal saplings clinging to the edge of the ditch. Had I been spotted? "Layla?" a voice called.

I tipped to the side to try to see, still keeping my boots where they landed as if that could save me from trespassing charges. An arm in a jean jacket waved furiously and I traced it up to Daniel's smiling face.

"You've been summoned by the dead," Ink said.

I spun my head around, having not heard the jangle of the fence from his climb. "How did you…?" I began, before remembering he was a demon and did whatever he wanted. "Come on."

Stomping over the ground oozing with freezing puddles, I kept my sight on Daniel. Incapable of containing his enthusiasm, he danced back and forth. The sheen of industrial lights from the warehouses leading to the fields beyond cast shadows across the trees, but none of them touched Daniel. He always appeared in the same flat fluorescent light whether in the library or under a cloudy sun.

"You made it. I almost thought…" he began, when his gaze found the demon trudging beside me. "And you brought it."

"Him, if you please. I only use it when with particularly depraved company."

The ghost looked frightened of my incubus while Ink grinned nefariously. I didn't want to deal with this. "Ink agreed to help and I'm not going to turn that down."

"Truly? That's a new twist," Ink responded with a laugh.

"Can we please get whatever this is done," I said, waving the shovel for emphasis, "so I can get out of here before anyone spots me?"

Daniel bent his head deep. "Of course. I am sorry that the day isn't more pleasant."

I mashed back the curls already clinging to my forehead from the damp mists. "I've been in worse. So, why am I here and why the shovel?"

"You must dig up my bones."

I misheard that. Snickering at the joke, I turned to Ink whose grin twisted to a macabre smirk aimed at me. "I'm sorry, did you say you want me to…?"

"Exhume my body. If you'd be so kind."

He had to be…nope, he wasn't kidding. And the demon was a hundred percent laughing at me. "I can't dig up a body. Are you freaking serious?"

"Of course. Why else would I ask you to bring a shovel?"

"I don't know, maybe I needed to trade it with a gnome to get a magical rock or some shit. Stop laughing, Ink."

"As you wish, my bond." He at least had enough decency to stop chuckling at my decent into madness.

Dig up a body, exhume bones and desiccated flesh buried in the dirt. Why?

It was Ink who draped his fingers across my shoulders and whispered in my ear. "The dead can only haunt that where they died and that where their bones rot."

"So...I just need some of the graveyard dirt?" I asked hopeful, and my incubus slowly shook his head.

"If you find this task too macabre, we could always return to the car. I believe that olisbos has arrived from the invisible merchant."

"The...?" My brain short-circuited with three thoughts at once. *What's an olisbos? Why are you using my credit card to buy shit online?* I went with the third one burning through me. "No. I can do this. I've dealt with werewolves, and kelpies, and imps. Digging up a body is nothing...almost nothing in comparison."

My incubus parted his hands and left me to take a step. I raised the blade of the shovel and rammed it through the soil. It sunk all the way in and I pulled mud away. "How deep down are...you?" I asked Daniel.

"After all this rain and the erosion of years, I'd guess...four or five feet."

Oh, fuck.

Ink giggled, dooming me to a long night of grave robbing. I stubbornly focused on a small hole, digging my way down and down to the depths of the underworld itself. Every time I raised a shovelful of dirt, half fell back in.

It wasn't long before Ink joined in with a shovel of his own. "Where did you get that?"

"A pile was left inside that building." He pointed to one of the locked and bolted storage units.

"That's stealing!" I hissed.

"I intend to return it when this is finished. What would I do with a shovel? Though, we should have a wonderful spot to hide another body when done."

A shiver snapped up my spine at the thought. At least with Ink's help, the work flew by—lucky demon with his demon strength. My hands ached and legs trembled with every shift of dirt, but I couldn't give up now. All the while, Daniel stood beside staring forlornly at the pit we opened up.

How would he handle facing his own dead body? I'd probably scream...a lot. Most of it would be indecent or incoherent.

"The weather at least remains fair to our endeavors," Ink responded.

"Don't."

"Do not what?"

"Even hint at the clichéd 'it could be worse.' Shit, did I just do it?"

The two men shrugged and I paused in my filthy hole to stare at Daniel. I'd sunk with the dug ground so my eyes were level with his waist, which I wasn't entirely complaining about, but it felt rude to talk to his dick. Craning my head back, I asked, "Did you only recently learn you were out here?"

"Oh, no. I've always known."

"That someone dumped your body behind a bunch of warehouses like the sewage in an RV?" The injustice sparked inside of me and I slammed the shovel deeper into the ground. Dirt shifted down the sides of the hole, staining my jeans as I tossed its brethren to the pile above. "And you never got anyone to find..."

Who would he have asked? No police could see him, no patrons of the library could listen. Even I was gritting my teeth trying to dig up his skeleton and we'd been flirting —

No. I wasn't flirting with him. And he was, ya know…lonely. It was just a —

My shovel smacked into the dirt and a crack rose through the air. It sounded like I'd broken a stalk of celery. With my bare hand, I pushed away the crumbly clay and revealed a smooth piece of white rock.

That's not rock.

I wrenched my hand away and leaped back against the hole. Ink peered from his side. "Congratulations, you've discovered a dead body. Is there a mortal dessert to celebrate that milestone? Mincemeat, perhaps?"

Daniel was laid to rest here. No, there was no resting for him. Someone dumped his body in a shallow ditch and let nature cover up the crime. They didn't care if he received any closure or proper rights. He was nothing more than an inconvenience to them — trash in the backseat.

"Ink?" I asked through a prick of tears. "Finish unearthing him."

"What do we say?" he responded in full ornery mode.

"Please."

He snickered. "I'd prefer, 'Once we're finished you can sup upon my feminine delights,' but please will work."

No other word passed between us as we got to work. The fading sun fell below the horizon, leaving the industrial lights to guide us. They couldn't reach inside the grave, so only the pinprick of rising stars and the waning moon shone off the scattered bones.

Daniel's body prodded through the black earth like roots churning out of the soil. It looked as if he'd been tossed onto his back, the neck twisted so his head crumpled against the chest. I could only glance at the skull before a deathly chill crawled through me. Instead, I focused on the one thing I could — his hand.

I'd taken classes on anatomy — bones, muscles, tendons, all the organs. Dissection had been clean, clear-cut and obvious — this is a spleen, that's a femur. None of them were half buried in mud, rotted away to a strip of red leather inside of denim chewed to strands by bacteria and insects. But the hand I could understand. It was his left, the fingers strained apart so every phalange was visible.

"Well." Ink tossed his stolen shovel aside, straddled the bones, and placed his elbows across the open grave like it was a hot tub. "What shall we do next? Grave digging is typically followed with robbery. Light desecration?"

"Not funny." I shuddered.

"You presume it to be a joke. I've met quite the characters while traipsing through graveyards at midnight. Met the vandals there to rob them as well."

Why was he enjoying this? I couldn't stop shaking, my tongue drying as I stared at the scattered bones then at Daniel. My brain kept piecing together where every one fit inside of the man standing above me. The whole thing was obscene.

"Do we...?" I turned to the ghost, expecting to find horror or worse on his face. But he only stared down at himself with light wonder. "Should I...dig them all free?"

"What for?" Ink interrupted. "If you really wish to let him haunt you—an idea terrible on every level, I want it to be known—all you need do is take a piece."

"That's it?" I sputtered, my chest expanding with a breath I didn't realize I'd been holding. "All I need is a piece of him…?"

Ink drew closer to me and placed his blisteringly hot lips to my ear. "The piece you ache for has tragically been eaten away. So I'd suggest a femur? Ooh, it could help prop up that wayward table of Turkish beverages. Or the skull…?" He bent over for it and I shook my head hard.

"No. Not that." Dropping to a knee, I carefully crawled through the mud to that hand. I dug my fingers into the cold ground around the single white bone until I held the distal phalanx in my palm and unearthed just the tip of his middle finger. Would it be enough?

I tried to lift it to the light in the hope that Daniel might say something, when Ink reached over. He offered a hand to help me stand. When I went to catch it, my palm curled around the bone and it snapped in half. "Shit." I stared at the two pieces now broken from my stupidity.

What if that…?

Daniel floated down into his own grave and stared at the small bone made two in my hand. I tried to apologize, but he smiled. "If this works, then I will be able to visit both bones wherever they rest."

I hadn't thought of that. "Will it? Work, I mean. Or do I need a bigger bone…"

"The werewolf's isn't enough to fill you? You'd put some Roman emperors to shame," Ink scoffed. He leapt out of the grave like a cat reaching the top of the fridge.

I faced a long, muddy scramble out and instead stood beside Daniel.

He remained contemplative, almost in a state of zen staring at what used to be him. I wanted to reach out and rub his back, so I gently cupped my hand around the bone instead. A tiny part of my brain screamed that I was holding a piece of a dead man, but it was drowned out by the rest of me telling it the dead man asked me to.

"I've spent hours standing above the shallow grave," he whispered.

A low whistle broke through the night and I glared at Ink humming a tune as he walked back to the shed where he stole the shovel. At least he was keeping busy.

"This must be...I can't even imagine," I said.

"The first day I knew it was down here...that I was down here, I screamed and screamed without end in the hope that someone would stop. Someone would find my body. All those years, it lay here, turning to ash and soil for the worms."

He had died fifteen years before my mom. She'd been in the ground half the time he was. Did she look the same? Had all of her blonde hair shriveled to dust? Were her fingernails chewed away by insects? Would anything of her honey-scented skin remain?

"We should cover them," Daniel said. "Before the sun rises."

"First coherent comment I've heard from the mad ghost." Ink nodded his head as if he approved the idea and kicked the top of the dirt pile.

"No."

Ink stopped. He always stopped when I told him to, but he stared at me like I was the mad ghost. "My bond, perhaps you are unaware the danger an exposed body, no matter how decomposed, can be. This entire village could succumb to plague, or begin asking impolite questions."

"Your demonic sex slave is correct," Daniel said. I heard Ink's shadow wings flap against the sky, no doubt to defend himself, but I kept staring at that hand.

That perfect hand rested in the mud waiting for someone to take it, to save him, to carry him to rest. "They need to be found," I said. "They deserve, you deserve to be buried. Properly. Your family, wouldn't they want closure?"

The mention of his family caused Daniel to stop. He stared down at his bones and the taciturn, disinterested look shifted to the pain I'd expected. "How will you explain finding this to the cops?"

"I don't have to," I said, and turned to stare at Ink.

He rolled his eyes. "Very well. But once this is finished, I shall lay siege to your box of iced creams."

Chapter Eleven

"...yes, I caught what appeared like Councilman Rogers climbing the fence beside the war house. Sorry, warehouse. Bad connection. Mm-hm. Yes. You have all you need from me. Thank you, greatly." Ink slammed down the last payphone in the whole of the state.

Only the shed maple seeds tumbled across the sidewalk. No one was awake or wandering the silent campus grounds to watch us call the tip-line for the wayward councilman. I clung more tightly to the bones in my palm and turned to Daniel who'd been gazing in awe since he walked through the fence and into my car. "Hopefully they'll investigate and find the...your body."

"Of course they will," Ink said with a flourish. "I was magnificent. Every question answered with pinpoint accuracy at a speed rarely seen outside of an Inquisition's dungeon."

"You were interrogated by the Spanish Inquisition? The one no one expects?"

"Well, they weren't Spanish at the time. Bavarian, if I remember correctly. Though their depravity and desires would put an incubus to shame…if I had any. Shall I whisper them in your ear?" Ink quickly swept a hand around my waist, pulling my back to his chest. He rested his chin on my shoulder and parted a finger down my cheek. "Your glorious skin is coated in the mud of a pauper's grave. That will simply not do."

He swept the grime off my cheeks until catching my chin. I curled my toes as Ink turned my chin to face him, when he surged forward to kiss me. The cold of the night fell off me from the heat of his lips. I dug a fist into his hair, holding him tighter. Ink's acerbic tongue danced against mine, playing a sweet tune down my spine.

A cough interrupted the hot kiss and Daniel stared impetuously at us. I tried to wiggle out of Ink's grip, but he turned to stone and said, "Your soul flotsam is demanding attention."

Placing both hands to Ink's chest, I attempted to push my way free. "Could you…?"

His glower darted to me and his hands parted like the Red Sea. I stumbled away and stared around the silent campus lit with circles of streetlights above. "We should get out of here before anyone recognizes us."

Ink stared longer at Daniel who glared right back. "That must be a constant issue with your demon and his incapacity to understand buttons."

I didn't even realize Ink's shirt was open. When did that happen? Ink rolled the tip of his tongue across his teeth. As it went, it split into a fork and both ends licked his lips. "I'm afraid my body is not for your consumption. Oh, I forget myself, you cannot touch another's dewy, heaving, taut, warm skin."

"I'm walking back to the car," I said and marched in the direction of the parking lot. If it came to blows…it didn't matter. Ink couldn't be hurt and Daniel couldn't hit anyone. Only their voices were weapons, the words dampened by distance as I slid into the driver's seat and carefully placed the bone fragments in the console above my phone. For a beat, I stared at the phalanges and thought of Cal. Should I call him?

I wasn't getting into any danger. Solving a ghost's murder was nowhere close to fighting off a werewolf cult. Movement blurred beside me. It gave me a jolt the same time my mind brushed it off as Ink. But then a softer voice spoke, "Your demon has decided to walk home."

I laughed. "I don't think Ink's walked more than a mile in his whole life."

Somehow, in the darkness of my car, Daniel's form looked more solid. The shadows caught around him, only highlighting his cheeks, his lithe fingers resting beside mine, and the tips of his black and blue hair. Could I touch him in the dark? While pulling the car out of park, I let my right hand waft to the side.

Nothing but the cold air of night caught it. Feeling stupid and realizing I had just put my hand through his arm, I muttered, "Sorry."

It didn't take long to get back to my apartment. This part of the city practically shut down when college wasn't in session. Daniel had been quiet, nodding along to the passing cars and trailing me up the stairs. It wasn't until I opened my door and welcomed him in that the sullen scales fell away. He dashed inside while I limped to the kitchen table and dropped my purse, freed my spell book, added my phone to the pile, and was about to abandon the pieces of bone.

"What is this?" Daniel cried and pointed to my counter.

"Coffee machine?" I said, staring in my own confusion at the average one-cup maker. But he went wide-eyed at the appliance.

All the pent-up emotions and physical labor struck at once. I sagged to the ground and moved to rub my shoulders. The sensation of grit digging across my skin set my teeth on edge. Grave dirt that'd been under my nails was now worked into my bra strap.

"I'm gonna get cleaned up," I said. "Make yourself at home."

Leaving one bone piece on the table, I carried the other into the bathroom. Daniel was still gasping in astonishment at frankly a rather cheap and boring apartment. He made it sound like it was some secret billionaire's high-tech mansion.

"What is this wide black rectangle?"

I scrunched up my nose in thought while tossing my muddied clothing to the ground. "Black rectangle? You mean the TV?"

The sound of an infomercial selling juice cleanses blared from the living room, no doubt on the channel Ink had last watched. Daniel exclaimed, "Holy hell, that thing is huge. It must have cost a fortune."

"Not really. Store discount helped." I placed the bone fragment on the porcelain sink in the basin of my swan-shaped ring holder. For a moment, I paused and brushed a finger over the single amethyst embedded in a gold ring then shook my head and got in the shower.

I stood under the warm spray wishing it could wash away the churning thoughts in my head. It'd been years since my mom haunted my mind. Okay, not exactly. I'd think about that ratty caftan she wore all the time, or her homemade spaetzle come every cold afternoon. It was her death that I'd tried to bury. The memory of her body lying in that shiny coffin while I stood beside it haunted me. Why did the box they were gonna put in the dirt have to be polished? Who was it going to impress? I wouldn't let myself think about that day — I couldn't or it all came crashing down.

People always said that their moms smelled like cinnamon, or sugar, nutmeg. Cute things that made them think of happy times baking together. My mother smelled of charred wiring, frankincense, and copper. I'd tried to tell a school councilor about a memory I had of her stomping into our rented flat outside of Paris, her hair charred at the ends and smoke rising off her shoulders. He accused me of inventing fantasies and told me to stop lying.

Daniel shouted louder from the living room as if I should be able to hear him.

"I'm sorry," I called back and switched off the shower. "Can you say that again?"

"When did televisions stop being square?"

"Holy shit!" I shouted and slapped my arms across my chest. Daniel stood half through the shower door, his eyes bright with curiosity. At my outburst from a man partially standing in my shower, he blinked rapidly and stared downward.

Crap. I bunched up onto one leg, trying to hide everything I could. "What the hell are you doing?"

"I was...sorry. There, um..." He didn't turn any brighter, but his mouth fell open and he finally turned his gaze away. "There weren't any naked people at the library. Not often, anyway."

"Well..." I said, about to direct him out of the door with my hand — the hand trying to cover both my breasts which seemed to want to flop free for his inspection. My annoyance grew to a sharp snarl and Daniel winced.

"Sorry," he kept repeating as he backed slowly to the door. Just before he was about to vanish out of it, he paused and asked, "Does your demon easily grow jealous?" It sounded like he was concerned, which only caused me to laugh. "Is he a danger?"

"To me? Never," I said with full confidence.

Daniel blinked a moment, before stating, "That heartens me."

A part of me wanted to ask why he was worried, but the ghost returned to my living room and I was free to resume showering. The strike of endorphins from being caught naked kept zapping through me, heating a fire at the base of my spine. And there was no other cause of it whatsoever.

Once I was certain all the mud went down the drain, I slipped on my robe and a pair of tiger-striped panties. No reason, they just happened to be the clean ones on top. Before joining Daniel, I dug through an old box the state had given me after ripping me from my mom's apartment. There had been three boxes in total. I sold everything in the first one, threw away everything in the second, and kept the third.

Ah, there. Knotted around a mass of necklace chains was the silver locket. A heart of chipped rubies circled the outside. I'd never seen my mother wear it, but whenever I'd sneak it out for dress-up, she'd always get really mad and order me to put it back. She wasn't here anymore to stop me. I slipped the bone fragment inside, then draped the locket around my neck. That tiny piece of Daniel brushed against the top of my breasts.

He sat on the couch with an arm straddling the back, but the sagging cushions showed no sign of strain. In the library, he'd struck me as an educated professor doling out literary references like candy on Halloween. At the gravesite, he was a man deep in a depressive spiral struggling to escape. But by the glow of a screen, his legs splayed out across the couch, his head lightly tipped back, I could only see a guy in his twenties without a care in the world.

A damn handsome one at that.

Daniel drew his gaze from the TV and those enticing brown eyes daringly swept across my body. Around my knees, he winced. "Sorry for popping in like that. I don't know what I was thinking."

"You're a man," I said. My words were cross but the tone wasn't. He looked about to start whipping himself for his slight and it was kinda cute.

He shrugged with a lopsided smile. "Can you blame me?"

"For being male?"

"For being dumbstruck at you glistening in the shower?"

Oh boy. I wanted to laugh, but that same dumbstruck smile clung to my cheeks instead. The blush crept across to join the grin and I found myself staring like a fool at the ghost in my apartment.

Daniel glanced to my couch like he was inviting me to sit beside him, but I remained in place. He dropped his crossed leg to the floor and leaned forward, hands on his knees as if in prayer. "I am sorry if I made you uncomfortable. That was not, will never be my intention."

"It's not that," I said, realizing that he hadn't. I hadn't expected him, but I wasn't entirely aghast at the ghostly presence either. "I have a…a boyfriend," I confessed.

He tipped his head as if that was no surprise. "The demon, I know."

"Ink? Ink's not my boyfriend."

"I am completely baffled. Does this boyfriend of yours know of the demon?"

"Of course. What do you take me for?" I slammed a palm to my hip and glared at him for the insinuation. It might be a weird arrangement, but it was an honest one.

Daniel waved both hands in the air in a mea culpa. "Nothing implied. I'm merely shocked that any man would be willing to share you with an incubus."

I padded across the living room and sat beside Daniel. The cushion crumpled from my addition, causing the weightless ghost to lean against my side. Daniel drew a hand up and down his leg that nearly grazed mine—or would have if he wasn't a ghost.

"This boyfriend of yours either possess an ego of steel or…"

"You don't want to finish that statement," I said quickly. He might be charming and adorable, but attacking Cal's character would get his bone tossed down the garbage disposal.

A snicker rolled from Daniel's lips and he shook his head. "Then I shall refrain from any assumptions beyond saying he is a lucky man who is hopefully wise enough to know his good fortune."

I didn't know what to say. Trying to prove my boyfriend loved me felt like a fool's errand. 'Oh see, here's this text he sent me about how cute I am and that he wants to fuck. Total dreamboat.' Cal wasn't a romantic poetry and flowers type, but I trusted him more than I'd ever trusted anyone else in my life.

The momentary silence stretched on, Daniel staring ahead at nothing while I tapped the tip of my finger against the other. If I did it three times fast, I could start a fire. An urge to show off rose inside and I whispered the incantation, then finished with three taps. A flame the size of my nail sputtered from the end of my finger.

"You truly are a witch," Daniel said softly to himself.

"And you're a ghost." I waved away the fire with a flick and stared at him. "Actually, there's something that's been bugging me. If you can't touch anyone or anything, how are you not...?"

"Falling through the floor? I wondered about that for a time myself. In my purgatory, I discovered I could never pull out a chair, but I could sit in it. As if my muscles remembered the movements and mimicked them, while the chair did none of the work. Though, if I think too hard about it." Daniel started to phase through the couch and I reached to catch him.

Stupid! My fingers punctured through his body and a static tingle danced between them. Laughing, Daniel rose back up on his own, but I didn't shift away. His face floated a touch from mine, a touch neither of us could know.

I leaned back to my side and laughed hard. "I better keep you distracted then before you wind up in the basement gym."

His gaze darted down the neckline of my robe. "I suspect you will."

"Is it...hard? Being, not being alive while having to be around the living? God, I sound like I'm in a zombie movie."

He chuckled and shook his head. I watched the blue strip of hair waft from one eye to the other, wishing I could touch it. "For a time, I bemoaned my state. Thought I went mad, then thought the mad didn't think themselves mad. After that, I entered my groundhog stage where I did whatever I'd always wanted to do."

"What, like streaking through the library?"

"Sadly, I cannot remove these clothes," he said and a pang struck me. Why did I care I couldn't…no one could see him naked?

Daniel massaged his chin. "There is this single hair right here." He pointed to the divot in his chin. No doubt a tongue or five had traversed that dimple. "I shaved everything else but this damn chin hair. And I never will. No bathing, no eating, no…nothing. It's existence with everything turned off, both challenge and reward."

I turned to him, my brain screaming to offer comfort, but touch wasn't an option. All I had were my words and I'd fuck that up in ten seconds or less. It was Daniel who took over. He twisted on the couch without shifting it, pivoting to stare right into my eyes.

"Thank you."

"I haven't done anything yet," I said. Tomorrow we'd find this old Fingers friend of his. For now, I'd just talked to a guy and dug a hole.

But Daniel shook his head like I'd told the world's biggest lie. "You've done everything. I was slipping, I could feel it, the days melting into an unending slush of life. People came, people went, the sun rose, the sun vanished. It was relentless banality with no ending in sight. And then there was you."

He held his hands palms up in his lap and I placed mine right above his. Closing my eyes, I tried to feel his ghostly skin wafting so lightly over mine. It'd be like a down feather or a snowflake falling from the sky. It should be, but there was nothing.

"Layla, your beauty is striking enough to stop hearts in the street, but it is nothing compared to your generosity. I'm grateful anyone could speak with me after thirty years of silence. That it was you makes me the luckiest bastard in the world."

It was cheesy, but he spoke with such conviction and clarity, I believed him. My heart fluttered into a full-on throb for the gorgeous man dripping sonnets from his tempting lips. "For being my first ghost, I couldn't have asked for better," I said.

"Oh?"

"It's a crime that you're trapped in those clothes." My loose tongue ran away with me.

He didn't blush, didn't glance away. No, Daniel smiled with impunity and leaned closer. "If you'd like, I could describe to you what I keep under them."

I couldn't help myself and damn near leered down his ethereal body. The jacket hid some of it, yeah, but the arms cut tight to his biceps. And between the open buttons, I could make out a hint of his chest muscles. Not wide and pillowed like Cal's, nor toned and strong like Ink's. Daniel was lithe, like a fantasy elf running through the trees with long hair streaming behind. God knows he had the cheekbones for it.

What else does he keep in those tight pants?

Daniel leaned closer and slipped his eyes closed. Mine did the same, my lips pursing for a kiss. Didn't matter that he couldn't touch anything, in that moment all my body wanted, all it desired, was for his mouth to press to mine.

A hand locked around my wet hair and pulled me back. Scorching lips hard as stone plummeted to mine. I gasped in shock before tasting the familiar scent of leather and brimstone. Ink leaned above me, darting his tongue deeper down my throat while he tugged me into his lap. He managed to slip his hand all the way to my belly to pull me the last inch onto his thighs. Taking my top lip into his teeth, Ink drew the points back and forth in a threat.

I squirmed, unable to rise, clinging to his shirt's shoulder with my fingernails. He bit down, hard. The squeal shifted to a moan and Ink caressed his palm under my robe. The sides fell away to reveal...

Shit! With one hand clamped to my robe to keep it in place, I sat up and tried to edge away from the incubus. Though, that left me nearly falling into Daniel's lap. He was glaring ahead at the TV, red sparks snapping from his eyes.

"What...?" I gasped, dabbing at my lip to see if there was any blood. I spun around to challenge Ink, who was somehow completely perched on the two-inch wide armrest.

He didn't have his usual smirk or the cavalier shrug. No, my demon was fuming. The lips that'd plied mine apart were knotted in a snarl. "I do not enjoy being toyed with."

"Since when?" I snorted, remembering the many times Ink loved nothing more than torturing me before vanishing off to wherever he went.

But he wasn't laughing. "I already told you," was all Ink said. He rose to his feet and stalked off for the bedroom.

So it was going to be like this? Great. "Sorry, Daniel, um..."

The ghost didn't look at me. "I shall return to the library and we can reconvene tomorrow for the next stage." That wasn't what I wanted. I tried to reach for him, but he faded away until only a vague haze of his body remained. I blinked, and it too vanished.

Whipping around, I glared at the open door to my bedroom. *Damn it, Ink.*

Chapter Twelve

"What the shit was that all about?" I stormed into my own bedroom with righteous anger on my side.

The demon I'd taken in like a lost kitten sighed dramatically, shook his wild hair and shot me a single look. It said that I was being ridiculous, should already know the problem, and that he was exhausted with the whole conversation. My back bristled in consternation at how he brushed me off without saying a word.

With his piece un-said, Ink turned to the bed where he'd left my old tablet. Oh, no. I caught his shoulder and dug in. "You are not shutting this down. What the fuck is your problem?"

His body transformed under me, my fingers gripping not to his crimson shirt, but the crackling skin of a demon. The deep tan twisted to the color and texture of black coals raked over an open pit, red veins of fire burst from below. Horns sprouted off his head and he spread his wings of dark shadow until they blanketed away my entire room.

"My problem…" — he took a step forward so his cloven hoof clopped on the floor — "is that I am a creature of lust. I am bound by a hunger you can never understand. I was created for one purpose, mortal, to hunt and feed."

Ink drew his tongue out, the forked tips producing barbs at the end, which he flicked at me. "I have bedded kings, emperors, generals and warlords. I have seen the rise and destruction of entire countries. Yet you, you tiny mortal, treat me like your lapdog."

The air stank of suffocating smoke. I tried to raise my head above it, but my eyes teared. When Ink's clawed hand wrapped around my arm, I jerked back in shock. I didn't see him move.

Chuckling darkly, Ink shifted his head. He smiled wide, revealing rows of pointy teeth. Small veins of lava burst through his charred black skin.

I stared at the creature in my bedroom, the monster from beyond understanding, and I met him in his double-pupil eyes. "So the fuck what?"

"Come again?"

"So you're expected to do a little bit of work. Wash a fucking dish. Clean up the living room. Welcome to existence. You think I want to do half the shit I have to? You think I love losing nights of sleep in order to cram cheap plastic Chinese toys onto shelves?"

"Your constant observance of the place says so."

"No." I jabbed into his chest, only surprised to find the lava fields weren't hot after I did it. "I do it because I don't have a fucking choice. If you want to act like a goddamn baby because I ask you to help out, then you can sit on this bed until I muster up the idea of wanting to fuck you again."

Smoke puffed from Ink's nose and he was the one to step back. He put on that goddamn costume to try to scare me, like I hadn't spent my night digging up the dead. My plate was too full to deal with whiny demon-pain. I wanted to grab his horns and shake him, but I settled on turning around to stalk out.

"What of our deal?" he asked.

The voice was softer and refined, so I risked a look back. All of that pompous twat shit was gone. Ink was the sharp-faced, handsome model I had come to expect.

"How has that changed?" I asked, waving my hands around like a mad cheerleader. He taught me witchcraft, not that he'd been much help with that lately. I'd feed him via sex…or that massive food bill he ran up every month.

Darkness rose in the whites of his eyes, but the irises remained amber and he didn't put the wings back on. "Your pet ghost."

"Are you jealous?"

Ink bridled. "I am infuriated, not jealous."

"You cannot be…" I wanted to laugh at the suave, cold demon going all horns and declarations of doom because of Daniel. "You don't give a shit about Cal."

"The werewolf is more than capable of fulfilling your desires, but that unwashed stain on the mortal realm…" He muttered under his breath in another language. "I taste every desire he inflicts upon you." Ink caught my robe's shoulder and began to drag his hold lower. "How your mind churns with thoughts of what he must taste like, how his skin feels against yours, what his touch would do across the slope of your hips."

"That…" I shifted in place as if that could wipe away the dirty thoughts I'd let roll around in my mind. "So?"

"Would you invite a starving man to a feast and only allow him to smell it? Every moment he shares the same room as you is torture."

He sure as shit didn't look tortured. With both hands locked to my arms, Ink tugged harder on my robe. It slipped farther apart until the collar grazed my nipples. Goosebumps rose across the whole of my décolletage that had nothing to do with the cold. His fiery gaze circled down my cleavage and he caught the robe's tie. Rather than pull it apart, Ink gave a single little flick of the bow. "Your toy is a nuisance. A fly buzzing forever in my ear."

"Funny, I could say the same about you most days."

Bundling the whole of my hair in his fist, Ink yanked my head back until my gritted teeth nearly grazed his chin. He held me in place, his hot breath billowing over my face while he glanced his hand, fingertip by fingertip, from the bottom of my throat down my chest, past my breasts, until reaching the lone tie keeping my robe on.

"What..." Ink asked, then he grazed the edge of his teeth over my cheek. At my ear, he whispered, "...will you do with me?"

My scalp tingled where he yanked it, the sensation aiming right for my inner core. Ink toyed with the robe's tie. He twirled the heavy end until it slapped against my leg, then did it again. Heat pooled between my thighs and up into my belly. I wanted to rip him to shreds for how he'd been acting, not just tonight but for months.

I grabbed his chin and pinned his smiling face. Tightening my fingers until my nails dug into his cheeks and up his jaw, I leveled his eyes right into mine.

"You're exhausting," I said and wrapped my hand around his cock.

Ink ripped off the belt around my waist. He spun it to wrap around his hand while plunging his lips to mine. I kissed back just as hard, the anger boiling inside. I'd either fuck him or kill him — both options were on the table.

While he ran his tongue across mine, I jerked him off hard without a hint of lube. Ink didn't stop me. No, he thrust his hips to help. Every rock sent his cock slapping against my belly. He didn't care how fast I tugged on his skin — he only cared about it making me squirm.

I hated how hot that was.

"You like how I exhaust you," Ink said. He snapped his hand and the terry-cloth belt of my robe knotted around my wrist. I glared at his half-attempt at bondage and yanked my hand. The tether slipped through his fingers.

"It's not gonna be that easy," I said, shaking the falling belt away from him. I turned away to step back and take the high ground, when Ink hooked his claws around the empty loops on my robe, and pulled me against him.

The breadth of his cock pressed my robe into my ass. His breath curled down my neck while he rubbed his chest against my back. I struggled to shake him off, but Ink already had the end of the belt. In a second, he knotted my other hand so my arms crossed over my chest, my palms flush to my biceps. I could do nothing but glare at empty space.

"What if I told you to stop?" I said, wanting to stew in my anger.

His touch caressed up my breasts, the thick robe unable to block the heat of his hands. Ink ground the bones of his hips against my ass and traced his palms along my sides and down my waist. "Do you want to?" His frisking stopped at the top of my thighs.

Yes. Tell him to fuck off. That you've had enough and need some air to think.

Ink's fingers kept slipping under my robe until they nearly drew against my naked skin. Not because he was trying, but I was breathing hard, pushing my body against him. Every touch felt like the first drop of rain against a still pond. I traced the ripples down to my toes, my tongue buzzing for more of him.

Snarling, I spun in his grip. His cock nestled against my lower belly and the reminder of that goddamn magical wand sent me reeling. I walked forward, Ink having to take a step back. With only my shoulders for leverage, I shoved against his chest and he fell onto the bed.

"I fucking hate you," I said and climbed on top of him.

Ink fluttered his fingers under my robe, first up the outside of my thighs, then down the inner skin. He didn't scramble back even as I kept walking on my knees over him. He was the one in total control, no matter what. Always keeping shit back, playing games for his own reasons.

Latching onto my hips, Ink sat up from under me until his lips pressed to mine. "I don't care," he said and pulled me onto his cock.

"God damn it!" I cried, the whole of him puncturing through me. This wasn't gentle, it wasn't sweet. There wouldn't be any cute playing. It was a hate fuck on both ends.

Ink slapped against my inner thigh with enough force I buckled, driving him even deeper. Holy shit! He pulsed inside of me, the crown of his cock thumping against the whole of my vagina. I braced for the jar of it hitting my cervix, but Ink dug his claws into my naked hips and hoisted me up.

I was practically off of him, only the tip left inside to sweep in a circle while Ink swung his hips. He laughed at me trapped just beyond his offerings and said, "So much unresolved tension rampaging through you with no release."

From the side of the bed, Ink fished out the form of my destruction. Thirty patterns, ten different speeds, and he knew the exact one to drive me mad. Only the buzzing of the magic rabbit cut through the room as he placed it between my legs.

"Oh," I began to moan, rocking for the toy's vibrating silicone. Ink swerved it up and down my clit, pushing the strongest part right against the nerve ending, then yanking it away. My moans turned into whimpers as he kept doing it, all while his cock filled just that first inch. I kept clenching down, trying to will it deeper inside, and Ink laughed.

Was he torturing me? Trying to prove a fucking point?

Every rise of my orgasm was cut short by Ink. The bastard was in my head, in my body, he knew exactly how to keep me on that edge for hours. Rage burned hotter and I struggled to fight against the bonds. The ties pulled against my skin, my muscles bulging around the belt.

Ink ramped up the next speed, the rabbit practically punching against my clit. I rocked on my thighs, needing a swift ending, knowing he wouldn't give it.

All because I had flirted with a ghost…and didn't tell Cal.

The tie around my arms opened. In shock, I tumbled down to the bed. Ink met me by thrusting his cock as deep as before. He knotted a hand at the nape of my neck, pressing my lips to his and he guided the rabbit for its final number. I rocked against him, tears rising in my eyes at the electricity pumping through me. Grinding harder, cursing and moaning in the same breath, I bent down and bit Ink on his pec.

A life-changing orgasm socked me in the back of the head. My vision went white and I felt myself tumbling to the side. Tender hands caught me out of nowhere, caressing my cheeks and brushing back my hair as he guided me to the safety of the bed. For a time, my body hung in an unreachable state. I felt myself floating above it, aware but not feeling Ink's legs between mine, or his hands caressing my breasts.

Then it all struck at once. The tingle transformed into a full-on clench of pleasure. I locked my thighs around his leg, having to press my throbbing clit against his skin. As the bolts zapped through me, I grazed my teeth over Ink's body, crying out and moaning at the same time. And the fucking bastard tenderly drew my hair back with each comb of his fingers.

The bone-quaking orgasm passed, but I couldn't stop clinging to him, the tears falling faster. "Why did you…? How — ?"

He lifted me off his chest and wiped away the proof I cried. "You mortals, always punishing yourselves for the minutest of reasons."

"I am not… I didn't want…" I said even as my body betrayed me. It'd wanted him so bad. It craved his touch, how easily it brought pleasure to the weary flesh. Even while Cal was away, it wanted Ink.

Did it want something else too? Something impossible?

I tried to sit up, but my muscles were jelly and I oozed back to the bed. Ink laughed at my struggles and he swept his hand down my waist. "Why do you fight what is immutable?"

I didn't need him. The incubus was a momentary thing. That was our deal. Once he taught me enough witchcraft, I'd release him so he could seduce thousands to his bed to give them the same bone-melting pleasure. As I stared down the cut of his body glistening with a hint of sweat, I'd never felt more selfish in my life.

"You may desire the ghost with your whole…" He drew his hand against my heart, then swept it down to stop right above my cunt. Ink smirked at my frown. "But there is no body to caress, no fingers to suck, no cock to take up the…"

"All right, I get *that*, but what's your point?"

"Return him to his grave. Let him fade away to the madness that rots all who failed to pass on. That is the right of things."

Even with my desire sated, Ink couldn't stop railing against Daniel. Why? Was there actually a thread of jealousy there? One that he'd never admit to in a million years.

I finally found the strength to sit up and cinched my robe together. "I made a promise and I'm not going back on it."

Ink frowned.

"Not until I find his murderer."

In an instant, the dour and sarcastic incubus transformed to a wide smile. "Why didn't you say you intended such? I'd rip out this criminal's heart myself."

"You would?"

"Of course. I mean, if your intentions were always to help the spirit finish his final business —"

"What does that mean? Finish his final...?"

Ink put on his 'I can't believe you're this stupid and haven't drowned in the shower' look. With a heavy sigh, he said, "The reason a specter haunts these lands is typically due to some unfinished business. I'd say that discovering a murderer and achieving justice would be Mr. Lu's."

"Well, I guess so. I mean, yeah, that sounds right." Daniel'd been fixated on it to the point it was all he asked about. Made sense to be his unfinished business. "Why are you so excited about this?"

The demon who hadn't cared beyond getting a few good swipes in was practically glowing. "Once we find this malfeasance from his past, your lingering ghost problem will pass on to wherever they go."

What? "You mean..." *Daniel will be gone, forever.*

"Wonderful, isn't it?" Ink declared. "I believe I will eat a marshmallow sandwich to celebrate."

We've just met and once I find his murderer he'll vanish? Did he know when he asked me? Or was he trying to play me the whole time?

Ink popped his head back in to ask, "Shall I lick whipped cream off your stomach?"

Leaping to my feet, I stared at my demon who never lied but happily used me. "Get the caramel too."

Chapter Thirteen

I have to talk to you.

Are you trying to kill him? I deleted the whole message, then tried again.

Found something. When you get a sec can we talk?

I'd tried contacting Cal when I woke in a mess of sheets and had to take another shower to get all the dried sugar off me. It'd been left unread the whole morning. "He's probably doing male bonding. Tossing food at each other, ass slaps, running through the woods while a chainsaw murderer hunts them. The usual."

All my babbling assurances had done was get Ink to look up from his morning tub of cereal and locked another link of guilt to my heavy chain. So Cal was my boyfriend, and he was cool with Ink hanging around fucking me whenever I wanted. That part we all understood. It was the whole what do I do if I find someone else to flirt with?

Was that cheating? What if I knew nothing could ever come of it? Nothing physical could happen and he wouldn't be around long. Did I have to ask every guy if they approved of me finding someone else cute like I was pleading with the council of boyfriends?

"Why isn't there a manual on how to date three men at once?" I groaned, tossing my head back when the air beside me thickened. A tickle of wind caressed the side of my face and I turned to the ghost slipping into my car.

Daniel looked how I had left him, exactly as he had for the past thirty years. For a moment, I glanced a finger against the locket around my neck, as if to remind myself he was real and I wasn't delusional. Though, digging up a body and wearing a piece of it probably wouldn't play well against the insanity defense.

"Morning," I greeted him.

"Is it?" He turned to gaze out at the parking lot, then to the library he'd left behind. "Wow," he whispered quietly. "It's so small. Are we ready to commence?"

"Operation find your murderer is underway," I said and pulled out according to the directions on my phone. Silence filled the car as I got onto the highway and drifted deeper into farm country. Pockets of snow lingered in the ditches on the side of the road, winter unwilling to give up the inevitable loss to summer.

"You've come alone?" Daniel was the first to speak.

"Yeah?" I asked, before realizing he was referring to Ink. "I hadn't planned on bringing him. Do you think I'll need backup?"

"No, no. Fingers could be a pain in the ass, but he's…" A frown knotted the entirety of Daniel's face. He shook his head as if he'd lost whatever memory bobbed to the surface. "He wouldn't hurt you. I don't think, at least."

A sensor on my car dinged, and I glared at the console to find a red seatbelt-not-in-use warning. Mine was locked in place. What was its…? I turned to look at Daniel and the sensor flickered. That tiny piece of technology could sense something in the front seat, but it wasn't certain what.

"It's the damn sensors going off again. Would you mind, um…?" I tried to make the strapping the seatbelt on movement, but I froze when I realized it looked more like 'jerking off a giant' instead.

Daniel raised up his hands like they were sterilized. "I would love to if I could."

"Right, shit, sorry. I'll just…" I started to lean to catch the belt behind him, but my eyesight dipped off the road and I snapped back up. "…ignore it. It's fine. Barely a bother and we're only on the road for a half-hour. Not like the cops are gonna stop me."

"Did you not want to draw closer to me?" Daniel asked.

"What?"

"Appeasing your car's Big Brother, you gave up rather quickly. Have you been ordered to stay away?"

I snorted at the thought of Ink having the inclination to tell me what to do. "No." *We had one hell of a fight, then one hell of a fuck, over you. But no declarations of who I can and cannot associate with.* "It's a…a me thing. My mom died in a car accident, so I'm the annoying friend always on about seatbelts and what not."

"I'm so sorry," the dead man said to me.

"Some asshole came out of nowhere and...hit her. Worst part is, they never found him, just some seafoam-green paint at the scene. Not that they tried. All I got was a letter my Aunt Didi read to me about how they were shunting the case off to the cold files due to lack of evidence. Like they spent two seconds looking for an SUV covered in—!" Why was I shouting at him?

"Did this aunt raise you after the horrible tragedy?"

I squirmed in the seat. "She wasn't really my aunt, just a friend of the family. We all traveled together—my mom, me and Aunt Didi. I'm not even sure what country I was born in. Mom told me she couldn't remember 'cause we were on a train."

That felt another Layla ago. The lack of roots never bothered me because we always found somewhere new to land and explore, until the day it ended.

"Didi was supposed to take me in, but not even a year after, she suffered a heart attack and I went into the system," I said.

"I wanted to see the world," Daniel whispered. "Aside from when I was ten and my parents dragged us back to Hong Kong for an extended family reunion, I only ever got as far as Texas. Now I'm cursed to never leave a Midwestern public library. Fate is a cruel creature."

"Understatement. Fate's kink is fucking people over right before their dreams start."

"After thirty years of a banal civil building, even these brown fields of dried grass wafting in the wind are a beautiful sight."

"I think some trees are up ahead," I said.

"Trees," he whispered as we blew past a small windbreak forest before quoting, "'The wonder is that we can see these trees and not wonder more.' The color green,

I forgot its vibrant potency. When trapped within the labyrinthian shadows of shelves and sickly light, green is a color suffering consumption. Pale as pestilence and disquieting to the constitution."

He pivoted to a poet's words on a dime, making me stare longer at the enigma. Despite being dressed like he'd been about to attend a punk concert in the nineties, had he been an English professor? Or perhaps he was a beloved national author that vanished one night never to be heard from again?

"Shame that you won't be around to see when the flowers bloom," I said softly.

"Hm?" Daniel abandoned the striking nature to stare at me.

I opened my mouth to explain, when a blare of sirens jarred me to my core. Were they aimed at me? I stared through the rearview mirror at the flashing red and blue lights sidling up behind the car. *Damn it, hands, stop shaking. Just pull over…wait, slow down but not too slowly or he might think you're running for it!*

I drifted over to the side of the highway and rammed on the brake. The cop car followed languidly behind, the siren off but the lights sweeping around. *Should I grab my identification? What if they think there's a gun in there? Don't move!* I sat up fast and the car rocked forward.

Shit, I forgot to put it in park. My heart rebounded in my chest. I wrapped my hand around the gear shift and pulled it down to fully park. A knock at the window sent me leaping out of my seat.

Be nice, be careful. Should I take my hand off the gear shift or would that read as a threat? But if I leave it there, then they might think I'll take off. Fuck.

Oh, no. No, no, no! Tiny fires spurted from my fingertips. I twisted my hand around, praying no one saw that as I turned to my closed window.

There wasn't a gun, so that was nice. The man standing outside had short-cropped hair buzzed at the sides. His eyes were hidden behind a pair of sunglasses. They rested astride a nose as flat as a two-by-four all the way up the long bridge. "Will you roll down the window, ma'am?" he asked.

My ears tingled at a hint of an accent, one I had no chance of placing. I glared at my hand, making certain the fire was out, and pushed on the window button.

When the glass between us fell, the man said, "Driver's license and registration."

"I'm going to have to reach into my glove box," I answered but didn't move a muscle until he nodded. Straining against the seatbelt trying to pin me in, I reached for the passenger side and stared at Daniel's lap. He inspected the officer at my window with a curious look. Maybe cops looked different back in his day.

After tugging out the small wallet from my purse, I opened the glove box. It swung wide, smacking into Daniel's knees. Without thought, I said, "Sorry."

"For what, ma'am?" the officer asked, and my face paled.

For thinking I hit the knees of the ghost in my car, but that's silly because you can't touch ghosts.

"For whatever I did to cause you to stop," I said. *Keep it together, Layla.* Steady fingers fished out my driver's license from behind the plastic window in my wallet. Slowly, I handed him that, then the registration and proof of insurance.

He took each piece of my life with a shrug and walked back to his car.

"Fuck, fuck, fuck," I kept mouthing under my breath, my eyes closed tight as I leaned back into the seat.

"Why would he stop us?" Daniel asked, the ghost twisting in the seat to stare at the cop no doubt running me through the system and hoping for a hit.

My being a brown shade without enough cream in it to pass came to mind. "Maybe I was speeding," I said. Not likely. I had a habit of going a couple under just to try to avoid shit like this.

"Layla, what's up with your book?" Daniel asked.

I followed his line of sight to my splayed-open purse where a red light pulsed from my spell book. It'd never done that before. "I don't know." I reached down to push it under the seat, hoping that'd hide the strange glow.

The cop ordered from beside me, "I'm going to need you to sit up real nice and slow, ma'am."

Shit. The beam of light was unmistakable. What was its fucking deal? *Don't make the cop wait.* Swallowing, I began to inch my back up like I was easing into a hot shower. As I went, I splayed my hands on the dashboard, proving there was nothing in them.

The edge of my eyes kept darting to the stupid book, its pulses increasing in speed. "Here," the officer said, handing back my IDs. As I took them, my fingers brushed his gloves and a wet chill clung to me. I looked closer to find a handful of water droplets running the length of his hand up to his wrist.

That was weird. Had it been raining here?

"Do not try anything funny," Daniel said, not to me but the cop.

I worried my ID back into my wallet, and was about to toss it into my purse, when I remembered my damn book was going haywire. Instead, I left it, my registration and insurance card in my lap while the officer stared. I bit my lip waiting for whatever the hell he wanted.

"Aren't you gonna ask why I pulled you over?" he asked like it was so funny.

"I assumed you'd tell me," I said, then blanched. *Was that talking back?*

"Please tell us why you're wasting our time," Daniel talked back. I tried to shut him out.

The man chortled and leaned closer. I stared at the reflection of my panicking face struggling to keep calm in his sunglasses. "Name's Conway. Officer Conway," he said and touched his badge.

"Clearly that was the information we've been pleading for this whole time, your farcical name," Daniel groaned.

I barely looked at it, my body screaming at me to get out of there as soon as possible. "As long as you're straight with me, you got nothing to fear, Ms. Leeland," he said, putting all the emphasis on my name he'd just entered into his database.

Right. Because anyone who says 'you have nothing to fear' has never harbored sinister motives. What could I do if this went bad fast? The Mace was probably lost in my purse. *In the time I'd try to get it, I'd be... Don't think about that.*

"What do you want to know?" I asked softly.

He pointed to my backseat and smiled wide. "Were you going to return your library book on time?"

What? I craned over my shoulder to find the book on Mr. White sitting where I must have tossed it without thinking. "Ye...yes. Of course. It's not due for another week."

Officer Conway smiled so bright the sun's rays glinted off both his teeth and sunglasses. It turned his face an impenetrable white, but I wouldn't look away. "Then..." He slapped the roof of the car, causing me to leap. Standing back, the cop said, "You have a good day." I looked up at him, my smile in place, when his eyes skipped straight past me to Daniel. "Now."

Not thinking, I reached into my purse, prepared to use my spell book to stop whatever was coming. But Officer Conway strolled back to his car and got inside. I kept glancing up in small bursts to my rearview to watch him calmly take a sip of coffee, press buttons and give no shits about the woman he had just terrified.

"That man!" Daniel fumed.

The cop car started up and rolled back onto the highway. As it did, dust from the tires kicked into my open window and scratched my eyes. Still I sat there, struggling to get my heart under control. I clung to my spell book like a safety blanket.

"What the hell was your deal?" I asked, not the ghost glaring in the vanishing cop's direction, but my book. Whatever set it off was gone, the pulsing red light fading to nothing. "Please don't tell me this is going to be a new thing with you." I moved to place the book on Daniel's lap, then remembered his being a ghost. Except, instead of sinking through him, it happily landed on his thighs, like a fat cat wanting to get warm.

Calm down, Layla. It was a weird traffic stop, nothing more. And you didn't get a ticket so that's nice. Still, I placed a hand to my heart and pulled in a deep breath. It was Daniel who kept up the evil eye despite the car and strange officer being long gone.

"Let's get out of here," I said, needing to put as much distance between this as possible. Checking three times, I pulled back onto the highway and resumed our quest to find Fingers Strasborg.

In a quiet voice, Daniel said, "I can't remember why Officer Creep seemed so familiar."

"Welcome to the future. They're all like that now."

Chapter Fourteen

A chain-link fence barely hid the dilapidated house. Muddy gray siding dangled off the side of the falling-apart house. I stopped across the street and rechecked my phone while Daniel stared at it.

"This is where your research discovered Fingers?" he asked incredulously.

"Bryan Strasborg, says right here."

"How did you find this place?"

"Google, Facebook then Zillow. I did it while I was microwaving old Chinese food. Found him before it finished re-heating the rice."

Daniel's stare of awe and confusion didn't lessen, so I said, "Would you believe magic?"

"More than the stream of made-up words you used."

A dog barked incessantly, but judging by the lack of vigor, it probably did that all the time. Bundling my purse to my side, I jogged across the street. The sidewalk was cracked, the first weeds of the season sprouting through unsealed seams. Daniel took his time joining me, still staring in disbelief from my locked car. When I found a mailbox with 'Strasborg' painted on the side, I pointed. This was it, the home of whatever this Fingers was to him. Ugh. I didn't know what to make of that nickname and doubted I wanted an answer.

I took the sagging porch steps slowly and pressed on the doorbell. Daniel floated just behind. "How exactly are you going to get him to talk?"

"I've got a plan," I said just as the door opened.

A pile of wavy, slicked-back hair graying at the temples prodded through the gap. Then a nose followed, and finally a face lined with age around the baggy eyes and the sides of his thin lips. His brow furrowed before he stared harder and his entire body language changed. The hunched shoulders dropped, elongating his neck. He tugged the door back to reveal his frame straining at a full height.

"Good morning," he said first.

"Are you…Bryan Strasborg?"

Daniel shook his head, the ghost practically leaping through me to glare at the man. "No way. This old fart? I've never seen him in my life."

"Yes," the supposed Fingers said. He pushed back his gray hair with his palm and damn near shot a set of finger guns at me. I'd never been happier for Ink to stay home. "And who might you be?"

"I'm Gina, a college student who's…"

"A co-ed?"

That term made my spine shiver, but I swallowed it down with a warm smile. Bryan read that exactly how I didn't want. He hooked a hand to his doorframe and hung off it to push his face even closer.

Tapping my notebook filled with drug side effects, I said, "And I was wondering if I could ask you a few questions regarding—"

"Is this about Tiger Whisper?" he talked over me. Daniel's face lit up, his mouth dropping open in recognition.

I leapt on the opportunity. "Yes, precisely." Whatever the hell Tiger Whisper was.

"Come in, come in." He waved me inside. "I've got a few hours till my…" Bryan glanced to his polo with a landscaping service emblem on the pocket. "I've got time."

The décor's vibe had that "once married but now a bachelor" feel. A nice-looking couch with a couple of small stains sat next to a blow-up chair sagging to the side. The coffee table was covered in dishes and looked like it was a slab of plywood under a stained bed sheet.

"Maybe he has an older brother," Daniel mused, staring closer at Bryan. "One with the same name."

I took a step for the living room, and Bryan failed to move back. A 'sorry' rose in my chest and I moved to dodge away, when I realized he did that on purpose.

"For fuck's sake, man," Daniel chided while pushing his hand through Bryan. "You could be her dad. Stop being creepy."

"What can you tell me about Tiger Whisper?" I asked Bryan, but stared over his shoulder at my invisible ghost.

"That name, how did I forget? It was…it was my idea. Or was it Michael's?"

Bryan snorted over Daniel's reclamation. "Not sure where to even start." He gestured to his living room and nearly smacked a hand into my boobs. I took the opportunity to leap for the couch and tuck my purse with the spell book in my lap.

Over that, I laid my school notebook and pretended to take notes. "How about with the name?" I said, clinging to the only thing I could tag for further research.

Bryan shuffled around the coffee table and I realized he was aiming to sit right beside me. At the last second, I placed my purse on the cushion and pretended to dig for something vital inside. He had enough decency to read that cue and fell into the deflating arm chair. Scratching at his neck, he said, "That was all my idea."

"No, it fucking wasn't," Daniel interrupted. He took to pacing around the room staring at the walls. One hanging picture was of Bryan and a mystery woman in their late-twenties smiling in a park. That one he kept focusing on while casting furtive glances at the older man with a balding patch.

"What's scarier than a tiger in the jungle?" Bryan asked. He spread his legs wide and slapped both hands to the bowed-knees. I had no idea, so I shrugged. "The sound of a tiger right at the back of your neck. Whispering. So, Tiger Whisper."

"That is not what it means!" Daniel shouted so loud I flinched, but Bryan showed no signs of hearing. Damn it, I was supposed to be pretending to interview him. I scribbled the pen over my paper while Daniel kept ranting. "The tiger is not an animal but a state of being, and that state of being is to roar so loud it becomes a whisper. Gah!"

"You...um...?" What the hell could I ask that wouldn't sound insane? In sweeping my gaze anywhere, I eyed up a plant drooping in the window, a stack of old magazines propping up a speaker, and a guitar tucked into the corner. "Do you — ?" It's a band. They were in a band together. *That's why he's called Fingers! Oh, that's a lot less disturbing than what I'd feared.*

"Do you still play?" I asked, jabbing at the guitar.

Bryan smirked and stepped to the instrument. "Do I still play?" he repeated, then strummed a few tinny chords. There was no amp in sight so it came out more like a kitten's mewl than a tiger's roar, but I nodded along and smiled. For a beat, he let loose with the solo from *Stairway to Heaven*, then stared at me. "Still got it."

Sure. I hunched over my notebook writing nonsense fervidly while staring up at Daniel. He'd frozen in place, his rant vanished as he gazed at the guitar with a couple of skull stickers and one of a nearly-naked woman on the case. About what I'd expect from a washed-up has-been.

"We were going places. Two tours back-to-back across five states," Bryan bragged. "Even recorded our first album."

"If you don't mind my asking, who else was in the band?"

"There was Mick on drums, Jed handling vocals." Bryan smiled wider. "'Course I was the biggest name on the posters."

Daniel snorted and cursed under his breath.

I tapped my pen against my notebook. "And that's it, just guitar, drums, singer? No one else?"

For the first time since I had barged in on his Sunday probable whack-session, Bryan darkened. He smacked his tongue against his lips so hard it sounded like a gunshot. "Yeah…" His body started to rock in the chair, the plastic screeching with every twist. "Yeah, there was."

"What happened?" I pressed, leaning for him.

Suddenly, Bryan shot to his feet. "I'll get the old album. We could listen to it." He scratched his chin and stared around like it was an egg hunt. "Sure I've got it somewhere. Give me a minute." He scrabbled for the stairs as fast as possible.

I watched him go, the hair on the back of my neck standing on end. "He knows something. What do you think?" When Daniel didn't answer I turned to find the ghost hovering just above where Bryan dropped the guitar.

He held his hand out for the neck and reached to press down on the strings. His fingers passed clean on through and Daniel winced. "We'd practice for hours in Jed's garage. No, his grandfather's. Almost no one came to hear us play, except for this fat raccoon that'd waddle by for food. We were gonna be huge. A modern Clash or Sex Pistols, all that teenage rage and angst for the alt-gen."

With a swipe of his hand, Daniel tried to pluck the strings. A small one barely vibrated but no sound escaped. "How did I forget?" he sputtered, grief rampaging over his face.

I stood up and walked to him. "What did you play?"

"Bass. I kept ditching orchestra practice to play with the band."

"I can't believe," I said, then stared again at the man in a punk uniform.

"What?"

"The way you talk, how smart you are, I just assumed that you'd been... I don't know, a professor."

Daniel snorted at that. "I got Cs and Ds. The only reason my mom even let me learn an instrument was because she thought I'd..." A shudder shivered through his whole body, his skin warping like an ocean wave. "My mom. My little brother. Cousin Hui. What do they...? Do they know I'm dead?"

"I don't..." I said, when Bryan returned with a cassette tape in hand.

Turning from the weeping ghost, I watched the man wave the tape. "Prepare to have your mind blown."

The music was typical fare for four teenagers standing in a garage screaming into microphones. I'd heard the same when I wanted to be anywhere but the foster homes. Though, the lack of tepid bars in the middle made it feel half finished. Where was that one white guy wearing fake dreads rapping about stacks of cash?

By the third song, which sounded exactly like the first two, I sat up to say, "Mr. Strasborg—"

"Wait, wait, here comes my solo," he said, then tipped back in the blow-up chair and pretended to play along.

"Mr. Strasborg," I tried again. "Bryan?" Still nothing but his head banging. Getting pissed, I shouted over the noise, "Can you tell me about Daniel Lu?"

Cassette tape scratch. He shoved down a finger so hard on the player, the tape didn't just stop but eject. "What about him?"

"The last member of your band, who vanished on J..." Telling him the exact date might spook him. "The summer of 1994."

"Yeah, I fucking know who he is. Why do you?" Bryan thundered and all my hair stood at attention. Why didn't I bring Ink with?

Because you've dealt with entitled assholes before, Layla. This one's no different from a drunk college kid at two a.m. trying to steal gum, or a middle-aged woman trying to use an expired coupon. Witch up.

"What do you know about the night he vanished?" I pressed, refusing to back down.

"That it was thirty fucking years ago, and I don't have to tell you shit. What even is this?" His eyes narrowed. "Are you with his mother? I told that she-beast everything back in ninety-four. I sure as shit ain't telling you now."

This was going swimmingly. I glanced to Daniel, who paced about the room, but that turned out to be the wrong decision. Bryan lashed out and grabbed my cheeks. "What the fuck are you looking at?" he snarled, his face right in mine.

I didn't have to get him to tell me. I could just see it. "June twenty-fifth, what do you remember?" I said in a cold voice and lashed my hand around his wrist.

Come on, white light, put me in that scraggly body. Hello? I blinked, finding only the fifty-something Bryan staring at me like I had a stroke. Why wasn't this working? Stupid, fickle witchcraft.

Bryan peeled my hand away before I could get the spell to work. "You need to leave," he said and I was lost. We got nothing beyond pissing him off.

I reached for my purse when Daniel said, "Ask him about Madison."

Madison? Who was she, a girl they fought over? So not the time for a twinge of jealousy. Before Bryan could haul me to my feet, I asked, "What about Madison?"

The huffing and puffing tone changed in an instant. Bryan slapped a hand to his forehead and collapsed to the chair. "That was... Look, I'm tired of this game. Every couple years his family sends someone asking about him, and I'd have to hold my tongue, but I can't. Not anymore."

This is it! I clicked my pen and placed it to the notebook, prepared to write down everything he said.

"Danny...was dealing."

What?

"What the shit?" Daniel shouted, stomping to stand right beside Bryan's face.

Tipping forward and placing his elbows to his knees, Bryan continued. "None of us knew. Every stop he'd use our van to deal crack and heroin."

"You fucking liar," Daniel kept screaming, his mouth right against Bryan's ear. I couldn't believe any of this. But Daniel didn't even remember he'd been in a band. Did he forget this too?

"Don't, don't get me wrong, he was a nice guy. Real nice. But he got mixed up with some shit people. Madison was where it all went down. They wanted money Danny didn't have. I guess they musta followed us here, cause we all woke up to find him missing and he was never seen again."

"You cannot believe this...*this*. Layla, he's lying," the ghost pleaded even though the explanation made sense. He'd been shot in a library then buried in the back of a warehouse. Sure sounded like something people who financed small time drug dealers would do.

"Look...I don't know what to tell his mom. I'd hoped she'd stopped looking. Praying at that shrine of hers."

"She built me a shrine?" Daniel's anger shattered to shock and sorrow at once.

"That's a very interesting story, Mr. Strasborg," I said, slowly closing my notebook.

He snorted. "It's the fucking truth, for once. All these years and they never found his body."

"What would you do if they did?" I asked.

Bryan snapped his wandering gaze straight to me and for a brief moment fear claimed his eyes. He shook his head and stared out of the window. "I dunno."

I reached fast for the table and grabbed a spoon left lying in a nearly empty bowl of cereal. Bryan turned back just as I slipped it into my purse. "Put flowers on his grave, I suppose. That's what people do."

"Yes." I nodded, clenching my bag shut and standing up fast. "That's what they do when mourning a lost loved one. I think I've wasted enough of your time." Backing up, I eased along the edge of the couch until I felt freedom and was about to turn.

"I don't think so," Bryan said and my heart dropped. Shoving my hand into my bag, I found my marker and plucked the cap off. If he came for me, fire spell first. It was the easiest to draw in a panic.

The older man didn't rush over but lumbered slowly, and I risked turning around. "Here," he said, bumping an old four-by-three-inch photo into my hand. "For the…whatever you're doing."

As I reached to take it, I tried to will that memory stealing spell of mine to happen, but Bryan snaked his fingers away before I could even touch him. "If you'll excuse me, I have to get ready for work."

With the old picture in my hands, I walked crisply to the door. It wasn't until it slammed behind me that I took a breath and stared at what he pushed into my hand. The image was faded, the edges grainy and yellow. Four men stood on a stage together, streaks of red and blue lights illuminating them as they posed next to silent instruments. The three were so young they almost looked like kids to me, friends who thought they'd never get old. At the end was the only one who didn't.

Daniel phased through the door still cursing under his breath. "I swear, everything he said was...it's bullshit."

"How can you be so sure?" I asked, the lingering question pressing on my brain. He didn't seem to be sure of anything in his past but this. Why?

"Because," Daniel fumed, looking about to stomp a foot. "I just am, okay."

Shaking my head, I dashed down the rickety stoop for the street. "We need to get out of here."

"But we didn't get anything," the ghost shouted.

Reaching into my bag, I carefully picked up the spoon by the handle. "You'd be surprised."

Chapter Fifteen

"That fucking liar. I swear, I had nothing to do with...with all that shit he was saying. Making up. Acting like we had to drag it out of him for my mom's sake. My goddamn mother."

Daniel's rant kept on while I held the spoon above two sheets of paper. For all I knew this had no chance of working. I ran my finger along the spell and waited.

"Layla." The raving ghost dropped to the bench seat across from me. Winds rattled the paper on the table outside a bakery and I slapped a hand to it. Last thing I needed was to lose that. If I lost the spoon, I really didn't want to have to steal another from a guy named Fingers.

Daniel eased closer and moved to take my hand. He passed his palm right over the back and I flattened mine harder to the table. "You have to believe me."

"Why? Why do I have to believe you?" I asked, exhausted with the damn refrain I'd heard the entire drive out of Fingers' rundown township back to something passing for civilization. Daniel couldn't shut up about how his old friend was lying, and I'd just had to sit there taking it.

"Because…" he began, but I finally shouted over him.

"You couldn't even remember the man before yesterday. You didn't know you were in a band until he told you. Maybe if I dug up your crackpipe it'd all come flooding back."

A snarl lifted up Daniel's lip, but he had no response.

Where the hell was he? I glared at nothing above the ghost's shoulder and a strangely warm wind from the south crested against my neck. "Look, truth is, I don't care."

"How…why not?"

I shrugged, unable to explain. There was the time gap—thirty years of punishment seemed like enough. There was the fact he was dead and couldn't serve his sentence even if he wanted to. I was tired of being judge and jury.

"What is pissing me off is how you keep insisting it's not possible. How are you so certain?"

"I'm…" His face shifted, his eyes darting away on their own, his lips pursing to keep the secret away. "I don't know."

"See, there you fucking go lying again. That's what I'm sick of." Liar face, every damn time. Sometimes it was about shit that barely mattered, staying an hour late to futz around in the back. Sometimes it was about the worse betrayal imaginable. Either way, they all made the same stupid face while trying to convince me I was the hysterical one. They all had something to hide, and when they did it to protect me, it managed to make me three times as mad.

"Fine, you're right. I'm uncertain if I've committed the atrocities he's accused me of."

Funny how his vocabulary shifted to Ivy League when he wasn't ranting about his innocence, or how it code-switched to a twenty-year-old kid around Fingers. Pinning down the spell book with my elbow, I leaned across the table. "Daniel, if you know something, even if you think I'll hate you for it, you've got to tell me. 'Cause right now we're working with…"

"A spoon," he said, his lips twisted in confusion, his eyes asking what the point of it was.

I opened my mouth, finally ready to tell him, when the air shifted and an incubus popped in beside me. "What did I tell you about the geese?" Ink hissed. His hair was festooned with a full crown of white and black feathers and he bore tiny pinch marks all up and down his arms.

With a smile, I leaned against him and plucked the longest feather from his fingers. "Last one, I promise."

"Ah yes, a witch's promise. About as steadfast as an ice cube above a volcano," he full-on grumbled, crossing his arms. I'd never seen anything, from a werewolf pack leader to murderous imp horde get under Ink's skin the way a goose did. It was damn near adorable to watch him pout.

I shifted closer even while whispering the incantation and hovering the feather above the paper. As I inched up into his lap, I leaned back to give him a kiss. Just when my lips were about to touch his, Ink grabbed my hair and pinned me in place. "Never again. Next map, you cook your own goose." He answered for me with a scorching kiss. I was certain he'd forgiven me, when fingers pinched against my sides.

Fuck, I tried to leap away, but he kept at it, honking in my ear as he went. "Fine, fine, no more geese. I'll get one myself."

"That shall be entertaining to watch. Especially when they are nesting."

Holding the spoon above the floating feather, the tip nearly touching the paper, I recited the last of the incantation and collapsed my hands together. The spoon flattened between my palms like a cheap magic act. But as I opened them, sprinkling the spell's last ingredient over the paper, the feather began to write.

"Yes," I shouted excitedly. "I was afraid it wouldn't work."

"Are we planning a heist to remove the rest of that cutlery's brethren?" Ink asked. He draped a hand over my shoulder and leaned closer.

It was Daniel who stared at the feather magically scribbling out a map across the notebook sheets in utter confusion. "What is this thing doing?"

"Tracking the DNA of whoever I told it to. And I hope there was more of Bryan's saliva on it than whatever bacteria ran rampant in his house," I said, then glared at my hands that just touched what he'd had in his mouth. Where was that hand sanitizer?

"What is this good for?" Daniel asked.

"I'm gonna watch him. See if he goes anywhere or does anything suspicious. More suspicious than throwing us out of his house for asking about you."

"So you do believe me?"

I looked up at his hopeful face, but it was Ink who interceded. "Young whisper on the wind, you are too inexperienced to understand the machinations of the female mind."

Bunching my fist to my hip, I glared at the incubus sweeping around Daniel like a wise old mentor about to teach him the ways of the Force. "For you see," Ink said, "when you've effectively perjured yourself before her and she knows of your misdeeds, there is only one eventuality."

"What's that?" Daniel asked.

"Eternal damnation, typically in the form of purgatory upon the settee. If you weren't already deceased, I'd suggest investing in a better pillow."

Fucking hell, Ink. The demon was all smiles while the ghost stared at him like his head had fallen off. I wanted to tell him off, but...he wasn't exactly wrong either. Daniel was hiding something, I felt it in my bones. Was it about his past, the reason he died, or that once this was finished, he'd vanish and he didn't have the balls to tell me himself?

"Look, I've got a shit ton of research to do on these guys." *Shake it off, Layla. You're not doing this to get Daniel to like you. You're only in this mess for one reason.* "Shouldn't you be heading back to the library?" I asked Daniel, then cast my eyes toward Ink.

Daniel followed suit, and Ink perked up right away. "Should I place my fingers in my ears and hum a chant loudly? All the ones I know are about the sexual predilections of monks with too much time on their hands."

"Our deal..." I prompted and jabbed at the paper. *Find me information on Mr. White because any time I tried I smacked into a cement wall.*

A loud sigh escaped from Daniel and I'd swear I almost felt it brush back my hair. "Yes, of course, the deal. I will be returning to the library post-haste and shall find you once I've unearthed something."

I nodded sharply, and Daniel faded from view. Still, even as he went, I traced my finger over the locket holding his bone. I was exhausted and needed time to myself, but I didn't want to entirely lose him. Not yet.

"Now that the peeping Tom has been handled, what shall we do to pass the time?" Ink asked, practically oozing around me. His hot breath brushed over my ear, but I slipped away.

Picking up the map, I said, "I need you to take this home. Put it on the kitchen table where it's safe."

"Shall I also fetch mistress a cup of tea? Lay upon the floor to cushion her beleaguered heels? Pick every seed from her strawberries with my teeth?" He asked all of that even while accepting the map and holding it flat for the eternally drawing feather.

"Whatever gets you off," I said, waving a hand at him and shoving my spell book back in the purse.

"In that case, we will require ten feet of steel wire, a plank from a haunted pirate ship, an excommunicated bishop, and three pomegranates."

"Three pomegranates?"

Ink shrugged. "In case the first two go missing." He stared at the bakery and the line of cars backing up in the drive-thru. "You intend to gorge yourself upon a buffet of fried dough, do you not?"

A flush rose over my cheeks. Slowly, I nodded my head and looked away.

His deep laugh rumbled and I looked up into the flaming embers in Ink's eyes. He cupped my chin and pulled me so close our lips nearly touched. "Then avail yourself freely, my bond." Ink kissed me with a surprising sweetness and stepped back. "And bring me a cruller," he added before vanishing to nothing.

Touching my lips to seal in his kiss, I stared a moment where my not-errand boy had been. He was due two crullers and an eclair after dealing with a goose. Feeling lighthearted despite the mess before me, I moved for the shop, when a familiar truck caught my eye.

It pulled into a parking spot across the street, revealing a decal for the university on the dented bumper. I was imagining things. Long day, all my emotions wound up after having to deal with Ink, then Daniel, then Ink again. *There's no way that's...*

Scott leaped out of the front seat and struck the cement. The Scott who was supposed to be off in some backwoods cabin doing male bonding with my boyfriend. Before I could think, I took off across the road, waiting for Cal to leap out too. Maybe they were dropping things off and he was going to surprise me about coming home early.

Or they could have to restock. That was a thing woodsmen did, right? Restocked when they ran out of beer and jerky.

Rather than head inside, Scott began to round to the back of the truck, which was when I shouted for him. "Hey, Scott!"

He stopped making his long circle to the passenger side and turned to me. "Layla? Hi. Fancy meeting you here."

"Yeah, I was..." I stopped a few feet away and peered through the back window. There was no head with short blond hair, not even a hint of a gray dog hiding. Where was Cal? "I was getting donuts," I said. "What are you...doing here?"

Something's wrong. A whole hell of a lot of something is wrong. My fingers itched and my leg started to shake, but Scott just kept smiling like he was enjoying the lazy Sunday. "Ah, picking up stuff from the drug store. You know."

No, I didn't have a fucking clue. He stared at me like I should nod understandingly, but I just kept staring. The sound of a door opening punctured between us and my heart lifted in hope. Cal was in the passenger seat, of course.

I tried to peer around Scott, but it was taking Cal a long time to move. When a voice shouted, "For fuck's sake, where's the damn crutch?" I was eighty percent certain that wasn't my boyfriend.

Scott rummaged around in the bed of his truck while I dashed to the side. Clinging to the roof in basketball shorts with the bottom half of his right leg in a cast stood Jared. He tried to sidle closer, but screamed when he put the injured foot down.

"Will you stop?" Scott said and he shoved a crutch right under Jared's armpit, then handed him the second.

"I've fucking got this, you pain in my..." Jared muttered under his breath, when he caught me staring at him. I went numb, unable to piece together why they were here and Cal wasn't. "If it ain't the ball and chain."

Scott rolled his eyes at the toothless attack. "Ignore him. Someone's been cranky since he ran out of pain pills."

"Like that's my fault," Jared snarled back.

"When...when did you guys get back into town?" I asked, trying to not freak out in front of them. The urge to grab Scott by the collar and scream "Where's my boyfriend?" surged through me.

"Saturday, when this idiot put his leg through the floor," Scott said, jabbing at Jared.

"Like I meant to do it, jackass."

"I didn't ruin the vacation one day in," he kept bickering with his friend in that concerned masculine way. Then he stared at me, his eyes calculating. "Didn't Cal tell you…?"

"Yep." I flat out lied because what was the alternative? Tell them that I was dating someone who couldn't let me know his friend broke his foot? "Yeah, I just…lost track of the days. Studying haze, you know."

Both of the fellow students groaned and shook their heads.

"Do you have any idea, um…?" *I can't ask them where he is, they think I already know. Why didn't Cal tell me? Oh shit, my phone.* I yanked it out and stared at the glitching screen. Scrolling up through Cal's texts, I watched the last one I sent about needing to talk dance up and down. Did it go through? Had he tried to send more but my phone didn't load them?

"What?" Jared asked.

"Hm?" *Cal was lost in the forest. The werewolf pack found him. He was lying somewhere bleeding to death.* "I don't remember," I said. "Sorry, I've…I've gotta go."

Placing the phone to my ear, I twisted my fingers around the string of my hoodie while the line rang. *Come on, Cal. Pick up. Tell me you're okay.*

"She may be hot but that one is fucking damaged," Jared said.

Instead of Scott's reply, all I could hear was the eternal ringing of a phone no one would answer.

Chapter Sixteen

Where are you?

The text taunted me with every panicked step up and down the sidewalk. I was vaguely aware I dashed my way to the crumbling section that felt like Main Street long swallowed up by urban sprawl. Cars parked not only herringbone beside the sidewalk but in the middle of the street. It created a vehicular manslaughter labyrinth I navigated like a blind frog because I couldn't stop staring at my texts.

Where was Cal?

The werewolf council had found him. Was there a werewolf council? Had to be. They probably all got together during solstices, stripped naked, and howled at the moon.

Or there were those hunters that had caught us in Oklahoma. They'd seemed to only want a nymph and a witch for their collection, but Cal said they'd hunt werewolves for sport. What if they found him out in the woods? What if he was somewhere bleeding and nearly unconscious, freezing naked while running through streams to avoid their traps?

Answer the goddamn phone!

I'm a witch. I stopped dead in my tracks and hauled out my spell book. The leather binding popped open to a random page about disemboweling. Was my own book fucking with me too? Closing my eyes, I asked it, "How do I get someone to answer me?"

I knew how to track a person and even eavesdrop on them, but I'd need Cal's DNA. Unless some dried sperm in a Kleenex counted, it wasn't happening. The pages stopped on a spell that'd encourage a subject to do whatever I wanted. That could work. If I cast a spell to make him call me, and he wasn't able, then that'd mean he was in trouble.

Scanning through the jumble of words written at an angle, I checked the ingredients. No DNA needed.

So far so good, no toad's eyes or dragon warts, but I'd need…a hangnail from a hung man. Where the fuck do I even – ?

A horn blared, causing me to leap back. My leg slammed into the bumper of a truck, slicing the skin. Clutching my spell book to my chest, I stared up at the eyes of a man glaring death at me. I didn't even realize I'd stopped in the middle of the street.

His warning stare of bodily harm didn't leave me until his truck had passed by. Even then, I was certain he kept watching me from his rearview mirror. *Take a deep breath, stop panicking. Focus. Cal could be fine and you're freaking out for no good reason.*

What if he wasn't?

I'd slit the hamstrings of whoever hurt him and leave them in the forest. If the bugs and blood loss didn't finish them off, the miles it'd take to limp to civilization would.

Another car blew past, a white flag rattling on the driver's side window, then two more rolled after. I risked looking down the road and spotted an entire caravan of cars bearing white flags. Who had died? It was probably very bad luck to cross a funeral procession, so I turned back to the sidewalk and read through the spell.

Everything else was easy enough to obtain but that damn hangnail. Where would I even find a hanged man, much less one with a manicure issue?

The jangle of a bell drew me to look up. Sunlight glinted through a multi-colored window cling, casting a rainbow over the pages of my book. Written across that door was a welcome for all to enter 'The White Witch's Emporium.'

No. It couldn't be that simple. Witches… Witches were real, and maybe I had found another hiding in the city.

It wouldn't hurt to look. I checked my glitchy phone once more — still nothing — glanced at the impenetrable funeral caravan, and caught the door before it closed.

Old wooden stairs beside a bowing wall met me at the entrance. Clinging to the banister, I worked my way up the steps and my heart sunk. Silk scarves with white price tags dangled from the ceiling. The scent of cinnamon and myrrh incense filled the hazy air. Tables lined all along the wide room crammed with baskets and handmade signs declaring what waited inside. The windows were nearly blocked by handmade earrings and necklaces. It was exactly what I feared, mystical bullshit peddled to gullible people.

Shaking my head, my hair already feeling heavy from beads of incense, I turned to slip back to the real world. A woman appeared from behind the counter as if she'd been waiting for a dramatic moment. She looked to be in her late thirties to early forties with the kind of face that'd hock smoothies on Instagram. But instead of yoga pants and power ponytails, her hair was curled in falling ringlets studded with gold beads. Massive gold hoop earrings strained off her poor, tiny earlobes. A pirate chest's worth of gold coins hung from her necklace.

"May I help you?" the woman asked and she threw back the divider.

Of course she was in a peasant blouse and giant skirt. I wouldn't be surprised if she was barefoot too. "No. I'm...I'm just leaving."

"Really? It's not every day a witch I've never seen before enters my store."

I froze in my tracks and turned to the woman practically screaming cosplay magick with a hard k. A painful smile tugged on my lips. "I'm not a witch."

"No? Your aura tells a different story entirely."

"My..." I tried to stare at myself by rolling my eyes back. "I don't have an aura."

The woman chuckled like silver bells. "Perhaps you are not capable of seeing it, but it is unmistakable. Also, you're carrying a spell book."

Fuck. I glared at the red leather peeking out from under my arm. But, there was no lettering on the top other than my name. No proof of it being a spell book to any except those who knew what a witch was.

"You're a witch too?" I gasped. "I mean a real one, not...ya know."

She smiled tight smearing plum lipstick over her bright white teeth. "Indeed, I am Sybil, aura witch and reader of fortunes." With her arms raised high, Sybil jerked the heels of her palms up and small golden butterflies burst free. As they flew, they vanished into puffs of vanilla-scented smoke.

Having proven herself, she slipped back to her counter and the cash register. When I touched the butterfly, transforming it into smoke, a strange sensation rolled over my finger. It felt like…calm but only at the tip. That single finger fell into a happy stupor while the rest of me looked at her.

"You're the white witch of…goodness?"

Sybil chuckled. "That's just for the mortals. They like to be comforted with the lie that if they're dabbling in the dark arts, it's all in the name of goodness. Now come, tell me who you are and why I've never seen you before. Did you move here recently?"

"Uh." I scratched the back of my head and stood before her. "No. I'm Layla. Got this"—I shook my book for emphasis—"last October."

"And where is your coven?"

Was I supposed to have one? "Don't…um, yeah, never been in one."

"No coven? How?" Sybil gasped like I told her I kept a pile of skulls in my car. This started to feel very wolf pack with insiders, outsiders, and decent people caught in the middle. Was that what happened to Cal? My clawing increased tenfold from worry.

To my surprise, it was Sybil who waved a hand. "Forget I asked." More of her butterfly glitter rained down and my fingers stopped. A fuzzy sense of calm swept through me, but it felt fake, like a blanket made out of polyester instead of wool. "Every witch has her own tale to tell. Please, what has you in a state of near terror?"

Well, my werewolf boyfriend's gone missing and I don't know if I have to burn down the forest to find him yet or not. Also, I have a ghost in my apartment and an incubus probably sitting naked on my couch.

I opened my book and laid it flat on the counter, which was when I remembered that only my eyes could read it. Sybil gave a wry smile as if she found my bumbling adorable. *Great, I'm the freshman witch.* "Do you have any hanged man hangnails?" I asked.

"Ah." She beamed bright at that and slipped behind an old blanket strung off the ceiling. "I believe you mean hung hangnails," Sybil's voice called along with the sound of plastic containers opening. "Popular ingredient for many spells."

"Pretty sure it's hanged," I said. Or did my dyslexic brain get hung and hanged mixed up again? "How do you get them? It can't be easy to find."

Sybil appeared with an old margarine tub. Inside of it were tiny dime bags each holding a single clipped nail. She wore a knowing smile while passing me a bag. "We have our ways. Not that you can trust the man to be truthful."

About his being dead? I stared at the tiny scrap of chitin cut off a man's finger, then looked up at Sybil smirking almost exactly like Ink. *Oh, shit. It's not a hanged man, it's a...* In a fluster, I nearly tossed the tiny bag aside. But my overwhelming panic to find Cal kept it pinned between my fingers.

"What...what does this cost?"

"I couldn't take a thing from a fledgling witch. On the house."

"First one's free kind of thing?" I asked, grateful but cautious.

Sybil chuckled. "I wouldn't recommend snorting it, unless you like fingernail cuts in your nostrils. Layla, if you ever need the comforting embrace of a coven, I'd be more than happy to welcome you into mine."

"Does joining come with ten percent off the toenails of a guy with a porn star dick?"

As she laughed, she shook her arm. The mass of bangles all tinkled together and shifted in color. A rainbow of light cascaded from her bracelets and arced across the whole of her tiny shop.

"It's dangerous for a witch to be on her own. Your book can guide you, but there are other magics in this world, innate ones."

My utter failure with Strasborg roared in the back of my head. Did she see that in my aura too? I needed to get in contact with Cal, but for all I knew, Sybil and her little shop could vanish once I turned a corner. "There is something, a…a spell I have. It's not in my book, and it started at random."

For no good reason, I tugged back my sleeve to expose my hand. Sybil noticed the stick-pin tattoo on my wrist warding off scroungers and smiled. "I see you've dealt with those pests already." She tugged back her hair to reveal the same on her neck.

So other witches drew the symbols as well. The way Ink kept going on about how I had to learn to recite them made me feel like a failure. Maybe this coven idea wasn't such a bad one.

"Please, child, tell me of this spell that troubles you?"

"When I touch someone, sometimes I can read their memories. It's like I'm in their body reliving it."

Sybil's warm smile faded so fast, I didn't realize she'd been using it. A cold, calculating stare watched me and I floundered. "I can't control it. When I don't want it to happen, I'll steal someone's memories for a few seconds, maybe a minute. When I do try, it's nothing. Just me randomly touching a person. How do I harness that?"

I really didn't want to have another accidental peek into Ink's debauched past.

"Hm," she mused, tapping a finger to her lips. "I've never heard of this spell, natural born or incantation based. But I've found that when you most want control is when it bucks you hardest. As strange as it sounds, try asking for permission. The 'magic word' can be just that if your magic is misbehaving."

A simple please to whatever the hell gave me powers was all it took? Maybe there was more of the hippy stereotype to witches than I'd thought. Tugging my book back and holding it under my arm, I said, "Thanks, I'll...I'll try it."

"Always pleased to assist. But I'd suggest you consult your mother. No doubt she's had the same problem."

There were days when people'd ask about my mom and I wouldn't even flinch. There were others when I'd be near tears, apologizing for making them feel bad with the truth. I found myself tipping farther to the latter, June twenty-fifth forever hovering in the back of my mind.

"I can't," I said, drawing Sybil's curiosity. "My mom's dead."

"I don't mean your adoptive mother." The knowledgeable witch laughed. "Your birth one."

"Like I said, she's dead." I gritted my teeth, the hair on the back of my neck rising.

Sybil shook her head and dismissed my life with a wave of her hand. "That's impossible, not if you have magic."

Not this again. First I got it from Ink, now a random woman who cuts toenails off guys with big dicks? "My mother is dead. She died in a car accident when I was nine."

"I don't know what you think happened when you were a child, but your mother, your real mother, cannot be dead. If she were, you never would have inherited her magic."

I full-on revolted at what she said — downplaying my pain, all but calling me a liar to my face. Slamming a hand to the counter, I moved to shout at her that I was there at the funeral. I had to stand by my mother's corpse in her coffin for hours greeting people I'd never even met because there was no other family.

Sybil beat me to it. "Did no one tell you? When a witch comes of age, all of her mother's power and knowledge passes directly to her. But if the mother dies before her daughter reaches the age of twenty-five, that line is cut forever."

"You're lying. You're…fucking lying. That ain't…it doesn't do that. It works some other way."

"Dear, it's been that way since the great awakening. There is no other path," she said, parting her hands. I spotted the damn mood-altering butterflies rising but I wasn't having it.

Swiping with my palm, I cast a halo of fire igniting every little bastard. Smoke and flames erupted off their tiny, light bodies, the magic butterflies now in a panic and flying for her stock. Sybil had no choice but to retract them, and I was already dashing for the door.

"You're wrong!" I screamed at the stairs. "My mother is dead!" Before she could spin more lies, I shoved open the door. "She's dead, damnit."

A soft drizzle picked up accompanying the last of the funeral procession. It must have been miles long. Whoever was in that casket was beloved by thousands. Only twenty people had come to the services for my mom. They'd sat at the back, black veils over their faces, whispering together. My first time in that church was because my mother died from a hit and run. She went into the ground while sun shone around us.

"Cal," a tiny part of my brain whispered to keep me out of a grief spiral.

The damn spell! I fished out the hangnail and opened my book, only for my pocket to buzz.

Hey babe. Just checking in. You good?

He texted me. Thank fucking god! Wait. Just checking in? Where was the *I'm being chased by a pack of werewolves, but I've got them on the run. Send backup?* Even an "I discovered a secret cave and went exploring." I'd accept, "Fell. Hit my head. Thai for dinner?" What was this?

The urge to ask him "Where are you?" in full caps swept over me, but I tossed it aside.

How're the guys?

The three dancing dots telling me he was typing took off, then just as quickly, stopped. A painfully long moment played out before Cal resumed typing and sent me a single word.

Usual.

What was he hiding? I wanted to order him to tell me, but he sent another text.

Heading back home later. See you soon.
Love you and your naughty ass.

Oh yeah, Cal, I'll see you soon. But you getting to ever see my naughty ass again hinges on you coming clean.

Chapter Seventeen

I barely got a foot in the door before Ink called from my kitchen, "This human is particularly dull."

"So?" I struggled to slide my shoes off. One caught on my ankle and rather than bend down to finish it off, I kicked. Hard. The shoe whizzed through the air, right over my pass-through on a collision course with an incubus' nose.

At the last second, he shot his hand up and caught my sneaker, his fingers clamping almost fully around the laces. Unperturbed, Ink turned the shoe around in his hand to stare at it. "Have you suffered an abysmal diurnal?"

"I don't want to talk about it," I huffed and slammed onto the couch. The TV was running because it was always running. Rather than suffer the marathon of *As Seen on TV* ads Ink adored, I pushed the button. He was lucky cable came with the apartment or I'd have cut the cord long ago.

A shadow passed in front of me, one I didn't care to take the time to look at, and the couch buckled. Sometimes Ink moved like he weighed as much as a prima ballerina, other times it was like a ten-ton moose. The mythical ruminant reached for my hand but I jerked the remote away.

For a beat, it stopped on the news talking about that missing councilman who'd been found floating backside up in the river. They showed footage of the funeral, which made my blood boil more.

"I would ask if you intend to speak of your toils, but…" Ink began.

"No." I shook my head fast and fished out my phone. It'd been behaving better, though there was nothing from Cal. Not that I wanted to text him. Instead, I scrolled through my mass of music to find an old, scratchy MP3.

Just as the single woman's acoustic voice warbled in the air, I said, "What does she know?"

"The tiny fairy you have trapped inside your mobile device?" Ink asked, pointing at my phone.

I stared at him in confusion. "That's my mom. My dead mom. No matter what you, or some *witch* says. She's dead. Okay? Dead!"

"Yes, yes, your materfamilias is worm chow. Understood." Ink raised his hands like a beleaguered housewife trying to calm her husband in a sitcom.

I leaned back, letting my mother's not good, but soothing voice call from beyond the grave. When shit in my life hit its breaking point, I'd crawl into a dark room and play it on loop. Some days, it felt like the only thing I had left of her.

"Do you know what that is?" Ink asked.

I shook my head. "We visited a lot of countries when I was a kid. I'm guessing my mom picked up an old nursery song from one of them." She sang it every night while tucking me into bed. I'd wait up, no matter how late her work kept her, just for that song.

Then it was gone in an instant. Taken from me by a fucking monster who didn't see a jail cell for a minute. He was probably still out there, pleased as shit about getting away with murdering some girl's mother.

Ink had his head cocked at an unnerving angle, his eyes staring hard through nothing. "That's a protection spell," he announced like solving a crossword.

"What?"

"Yes, more intricate than I've heard, but a general 'please keep this ground safe' so on and so forth request to the other realms."

"How do you...? My mom's not—" I nearly said my mom wasn't a witch, but she'd have to be. "How do you know so much about witchcraft?"

"You'd be surprised what people will tell you when at their most vulnerable."

That wasn't an answer. Mentally, I put a pin in that, growing more aware of every time that Ink didn't directly answer my question. He said he couldn't lie, but he was really good at dodging. What was he hiding?

"Layla, I've found..." The air barely had time to shift before the ghost strode through my apartment. Daniel's hurried speech slammed into a wall at the sight of Ink sitting beside me. "Or should I wait for you to find me at the library?"

Ghost and incubus glared at each other like it was high noon. Too bad I wasn't in the mood to be the comely saloon girl coming between them. "Can you go check on the map? If Bryan goes wandering off…"

"Your magic will follow him, as it has for the past ten hours."

"It was a long day at work," I muttered, wishing I could fall into bed and wake up with everything solved. Not just Daniel, but Ink, Mr. White, my mother and whatever the fuck Cal was up to. He was lucky I had to work because after his text that answered nothing, I was tempted to drive out to the woods to find him myself.

Rather than stomp off to his errand duty, Ink reached over and dug his fingers into my shoulders. The tension in my body melted despite the heaps in my head. He kneaded a deep knot and I released a moan of gratitude.

Ink glanced his cheek against mine from behind and whispered, "That sound gives me life." His gaze swung up to Daniel and I wanted to push his face back, but Ink slipped away. Rather than walk around the ghost, he walked straight through him and gave a wave upon sitting at the kitchen table.

For a time, Daniel glared in his direction but said nothing. "You can sit down, if you want," I said and patted the couch.

"Are you certain that's what you want?"

After a long day of men's half-truths, I wasn't in the mood to pussyfoot any longer. "I'm sorry for snapping earlier. I guess I'm just…coming to terms with what happens when we find your killer."

"Why?" Daniel asked, taking the seat beside me. "What will happen?"

"You'll be…ascended. Or whatever. Move on to the afterlife. I thought you'd know that, being dead and all."

"This didn't exactly come with a handbook," he said, his eyes dead ahead and shoulders in a slump. "I didn't even think I could move on. If there was a place to move on to."

"Your philosophers do enjoy spilling oceans of ink debating that topic, or talking someone's ear off while their ass hardens to stone," my incubus shouted from the kitchen.

I ignored Ink's need for attention and dropped my voice. "If you didn't know that it'd free you, then why'd you ask me?"

"Even as my past slipped from my mind, the one truth storming through my mind was my murder. Someone shot me in cold blood and I want the bastard. I want him to suffer, if not consequences, then literal pain for what he did." Daniel's voice turned sharp as broken glass and he clenched his hands against his knees. "It's all that's driven me for thirty years. I learned the library, discerned how to shift books to read them, just to try to find him."

His head swiveled as if he realized I was sitting there beside him. Blue light danced in his irises, small swirls twisting off like tears. "Perhaps that sounds cruel of me, but…"

"I'd do the same to my mother's killer," I said without a second's pause. What if I did find him? The cops might have not given a shit, but now I had magic at my disposal and a ghost. At least for a little bit.

"If I'd known that finding him would…" He didn't finish the thought, his gaze sweeping over me.

Layla, you have enough problems in your life. Keeping a vengeful ghost out of selfishness won't help anyone.

"What did you find?" I asked, trying to change the discussion.

Daniel tipped his head to the side to match the shift. "I dug into this Mr. White and you're right. Whoever that man is, whatever he is, it's…all I can think is unnatural."

That got me on edge. "What do you mean?" I asked and prepared for him to dump a mass of books out on the coffee table. *He's a ghost and doesn't come with a storage system. Duh.*

"It wasn't easy, there are an unending number of Mr. Whites throughout history, but I re-read the book I gave you and noticed a pattern with another newspaper story from the seventies. Horses."

A spoon fell to the floor in my kitchen but ignored it. "Horses? What, he owned them? Raced them?"

"Nothing so concrete, but wherever there is mention of a Mr. White, say, purchasing a night club, the establishment is named White Stallion. Or if he donates a particularly controversial piece of art, it's of a horse."

"Great, first water horses, now a man that's really into horses."

"From that I began to find stories, some actual articles, others little more than tall tales over hundreds of years old. They all mention a man with the family name of White, a horse and…"

"And what?" I asked, goosebumps rising from the tone in his voice.

Daniel patted his fingers together, met me right in the eye and said, "An end."

"An end? An end to what?"

"To whatever he was involved in. The man seems to be a force of destruction, an unending, unstoppable force."

I tapped my foot in thought and stood up. "That would explain the werewolf pack, if he was sowing discord. Or even the nymphs. What if he really was the one to tip off the hunters?"

The ghost stared at me in confusion and I realized I didn't tell him about my previous encounters. Never mind. Dashing to my kitchen, I asked Ink, "Do you know of a creature or monster that's long-lived, thrives on conflict and has a horse theme?"

It took a moment for the demon to think, only his profile facing me. "No, I've never heard of such a creature," Ink said softly, then he turned to me and smiled. It wasn't his typical smarmy smirk, nor his jovial grin. This was the smile of a man who just watched a friend go off to war. "Perhaps your book would have more information."

Why didn't I think to check it before? Probably for the same reason I didn't do a Google search for man named White. I pulled my spell book out without even having to look in my purse. Sometimes it felt like the pages would leap into my hand if I held it out. Was that a witch thing too?

My mind flitted back to Sybil in her little shop. What could she teach me that a demon hiding a mass of secrets wouldn't? I shook the thought away and collapsed onto the couch with my book in my lap.

"Do you have anything about horses and a man causing distress?" I asked.

The pages flipped on their own and Daniel reacted. "Is that…is that a new piece of technology?"

"Pretty sure it's all witchcraft. Right, demon?"

"Not a demon!"

After a time, the book landed on a page about centaurs marked as mythological. Though there was also mention of a man who once tried sewing half a human to horses to reanimate them. Blanching, I shook my head and asked, "White. Horse. Death?"

The book slammed through the first half with a loud thud, then kept paging back to the end as if sifting through time. I felt Daniel staring at it over my shoulder. He was probably wondering how I could read anything in the sea of blank pages.

"Damn it," I cursed, my eyes watering at the cramped, teeny text scribbled across the page. Didn't help it was also in a cursive. "'Beware, whosoever en...enters?'"

"'Whosever encounters the villains of blood, hunger, failure, and death. They will mark upon their souls the rite of...'"

I stared slack-jawed at Daniel, his beautiful eyes watering from the strain before he darted them to me. His face crinkled in confusion. "What?"

"You can read that?" I practically shouted at him.

"Should I...not be able to?" he asked slowly.

"I was told that only my eyes could read my spell book." Whipping my head, I glared at Ink to explain.

With a sigh, he said, "I believe the correct phrasing is that no other living eye may read that of a witch's spell tome. They must have never concerned themselves with the impressions of a whisper on the wind. Congratulations, you've discovered a loophole."

Daniel inched away as if he'd trespassed in my diary, but I started flipping my pages back to one I had marked with an old pharmacy receipt. Holding my book before him, I asked, "Can you read this?"

"I'm not certain if it's…" He started glancing at Ink already hiding back in the kitchen. "Here, let me look. Is this in German?"

"I don't know. I've been trying to figure out how to say it for…"

"Five months, two weeks, four days," Ink said.

"You might as well give it a go."

"We sawine vegarin nav lace min," Daniel read slowly while I wrote the words down in my notebook.

Raising my head, I repeated exactly what Daniel read. From my palm rose a ball of pure light. "Yes!" Giggling, I bounced the small ball to my other hand. The light never dimmed, a soothing cool washing up my arms. With every wave of light, the ball shrunk until it was the size of a marble.

"What exactly did I read?"

"Exactly?" Ink interrupted. "'Please put the blood back in my body.' Though your accent is atrocious."

"It's a healing spell." I'd been trying to read those complicated, always dancing letters but could never get them to work. "Maybe I won't have to rely on Sharpies, not if Daniel can tell me what to say."

"Is that wise? You are entrusting your entire line's secrets to a piece of soul flotsam."

I glared at the demon who seemed less inclined to teach me anything. "You're the one who kept telling me I had to stop relying on wards." Ink responded by throwing up his hands.

"This is amazing, I can't believe…." My euphoria shattered as I turned to Daniel. To my eyes, he was solid, whole, a living, breathing person. To my mind, he was a ghost, as ephemeral as Sybil's butterflies. To my heart— "I've been fighting with my brain. The words don't like to stay put, or I'll read them and my tongue does whatever it wants. No one else could help me until you."

Daniel cast his gaze over my spell book. He managed to close the cover, then caressed his hand through mine. I wanted so badly to feel it, even for a second. "I'm happy I can at least do that for you," he whispered. "I'd wish for nothing more than to help you."

Until we found his murderer, until he got his peace and was released from this world. Every second we'd spend together I'd get more attached until that last string had to be cut. There had to be another answer. I could study the book harder. Maybe try reading it aloud?

Leaning so close, I would feel his breath tickle my cheek if he was alive, Daniel whispered, "You don't have to—"

"I'd love to," I interrupted.

If there was one thing I learned from attending my mom's funeral, then my aunt's, life didn't do fair. I might get five days with Daniel or five hours. But I should enjoy the shit out of whatever we did have left.

A smile rose on his lips I could never touch. At the thought, I absently brushed my fingers against mine and grinned harder. Daniel pulled open my spell book and asked, "Where do you want to start?"

"Am I allowed to speak during the unresolved sexual study session?" Ink pipped up from the kitchen.

I tossed my head up in exhaustion and caught Daniel's glowering eye. He lightly rolled them at the reminder we had the strangest chaperone. "Only for good reason," I said and pulled back the pages to find an earth-twisting spell I'd wanted to try out.

"Would your target abandoning his villa for an empty stretch of river count?"

Chapter Eighteen

"Where do I turn?"

A blur of dark streets with solitary street lamps buzzed past my car's window. I tried to keep my focus on both the road ahead and the navigator stretched across the backseat.

"Left...two blocks back," Ink declared.

"Why didn't you say something before?" I snarled while struggling to find a place to turn around.

"Because your map is updating as this dullard of a man stumbles around. If I'd known he'd intended to turn left up a series of...oh, that's grass. Here I'd assumed he took to frolicking through a field of seagulls."

My tracking map was fantastic at keeping tabs on someone who didn't want to be followed, and absolutely useless at giving directions. I had to leave Ink with both the magical map and a paper map of the whole city. Teaching him how to use the apps on my phone just ended in him playing more Sheep Wars.

The whole of the car bounced up as I hit the curb trying to pull off a U-turn. When the back wheel smacked down onto the pavement, I rammed on the accelerator. Ink crowed from behind, "This reminds me of my viking days."

"You were a Viking?"

"No, I went viking a handful of times. The Norse barbarians smelled far better than the locals. Ah, you will be happy to know your prey appears to have stopped. In a spot where there is no topography. Do you have an opening to hell around here?"

"Those are real?" I shouted, turning down a maintenance road.

Ink answered me with a slow chuckle and a shiver zipped up my spine. I turned to catch Daniel stewing in the front seat beside me. He'd been gung-ho about following his old friend, but the closer we got, the more he shut down.

"I looked into your old band," I said, my gaze darting to the fading streetlights in the rearview. Wherever we were heading, the city didn't see a need to illuminate it. "Tiger Whisper had a couple of hits."

"Really?" Daniel gasped, turning to me. "I'd assumed, with where Bryan wound up, it went nowhere."

"Funny thing, the Tiger Whisper that got big with *Make a Wish* didn't have a Fingers Strasborg in it. Seems our friend out there slipped and broke his hand right before a gig with a music exec that changed their lives."

"Well, that's…something."

"The other members seem to be living in California. For my bank account's sake, I hope we don't have to track them down."

The road came to a dead-end with a locked metal gate. I glanced behind to Ink, but the demon was already crawling out of the backseat. "He's in there."

With a shrug, I put the car in park, turned it off, and followed. Dead grass barely disguised the water cresting above the ground. Every step was another slosh as I approached the metal gate and the chain-link fence around it. "I do believe we go over," Ink said. Holding the map flat in his hands, he stepped back, flexed his legs, then launched straight up into the air.

I girded myself for the demon to crash and impale himself on the fence, but he landed safe on the other side with a bright smile on. Daniel shook his head, muttered, "Overinflated ego," and floated right through the gate.

That left me. I patted the bag with my spell book against my thigh, squared my shoulders, and tried to squeeze through the bars of the gate. Oh shit, that was a tight fit. Ouch. Not like I needed a spleen — it was just good for the immune system and other things I should be studying instead.

Holding my breath and trying to think myself thin as a piece of paper, I slid one leg to the other side. My foot splashed into a puddle up to the ankle. I thought about trying to wiggle so I could at least keep one shoe dry, but it didn't work. Fully soaked from the ankles down and suspecting there'd be more, I stood before the two supernatural beings who didn't even try to help.

"Shall we?" Ink asked, a skip in his step. That petulant mood of before was long gone, probably because he knew this would get rid of Daniel.

My stomach churned and I risked a glance over at the ghost. Without much outside light beyond the stars,

Daniel faded into the shadows. I squinted, trying to keep him in focus, but the longer I stared, the faster the darkness overtook him.

"Layla," he said, the ghost nothing more than a whisper in the night. "I need to tell you. I should have told you before."

"What?" My teeth began to chatter. I didn't want to know what he had to say and I had to know.

"That accusation Bryan made about me. I don't know if it's true, but there's something in my mind about Madison and...a bag of pills. I can't say whose drugs they were, if they were even drugs. It could have been an unmarked bag of aspirin. Maybe."

"Daniel," I said, pausing in the trail. Ink kept on ahead. "Look. I'm...I'm here to help you, not forgive you."

"I know, but if this works, if I am free to move on, doing it knowing I caused you pain would wound me for the rest of my afterlife. I am sorry for the lies and for not trusting you."

A gasp of shock burst from my lungs. I didn't realize how badly I needed to hear that from someone until it was said aloud. Turning on my soggy heels, I caught only a hint of his blue strip of hair and those deep eyes. I raised my hand and placed it to where his cheek was. Only the cold of the darkening night pricked against my palm, but I imagined it was warm skin. "I forgive you."

For a moment, the lingering light caught his teeth as Daniel smiled and I found myself leaning closer to his lips. *I know there's nothing for me to touch, but I don't care. Just let me kiss him this one damn time.*

"We have a problem."

Ink's deadpan voice shook me to my senses. I found him standing with one foot in the grass and the other...on fire! Smoke billowed from the sole of his shoe, invisible flames turning his slacks and socks to ash as it climbed up his leg. Before reaching the knee, Ink yanked his foot back and the smoke vanished. His pants reappeared undamaged and he crossed his arms.

"Some pompous twat consecrated the ground."

I ran up right next to him, about to place my toe into the grass to test it, when the stench of burned skin burst in my nose. "Consecrated ground, out here? Isn't that something they do in churches?"

Ink cackled at that idea. "I've never known a church to not debauch itself within, at most, five years of creation. Usually a priest becomes carnal with two nuns on the pile of foundation bricks."

"Then how...how did it—?" My curiosity got the better of me and I tapped a single tip of my toe to the purified land. Nothing happened. Growing bolder, I placed the whole of the ball of my foot down, then the rest of it. Still nothing. Confused, I looked at Ink.

"You're a witch, not a demon," he said, already reading my question.

"I thought you weren't a demon either."

"I'm not, I'm... Consecrated ground will keep all manner of netherworld creatures and those associated with it from walking its trails. Typically by burning our bodies to cinders. The celestials are never creative in their punishments. Burn this, dismember that. Whatever happened to the days of turning people to salt?"

Whipping my head around, I tried to find an answer to something I couldn't even see. "Is this why Bryan came here? Does he...did he consecrate it?"

Ink rolled his eyes. "There is no chance of a human —
even one deep into religion's claws — consecrating
ground. No doubt an angel took a little walk about here
and..." He ended by waving a hand out as if I should
see the obvious.

All I saw was an unending field of dead grass. If it
wasn't for the black patch where the sole of his shoe
had melted I'd have no idea what was considered safe
and what holy. "Wait, did you say angel?"

"Celestials, always prodding their noses where it's
not wanted and causing trouble for centuries beyond."

Daniel took an elongated step to my side...and
didn't vanish, or melt, or have his eyeballs explode. So
that was good. I nodded and he said, "Bryan is still
ahead. We need to get to him."

"No, you are not. Well, you can go on and watch him
silently like a perverted piece of Scotch tape," Ink said
with a wave of his hand. "But you" — he jabbed a finger
at me — "are not leaving without me."

"I'm sorry, what? Last I checked you thought I could
'handle it on my own.'"

"Yes, as long as I can reach you, you're fine to futz it
all up in your own way."

Oh, that was not what I wanted to hear. "Futz?" I
stormed in front of him. "I've futzed it up?"

"Would you prefer bumbled? Good natured, of
course, the ends work to our means, but..."

"Daniel!" I shouted, spinning on a dime and
marching away from Ink. "We're going to find Bryan."

"My bond, that isn't wise. Hello. My bond? Layla!"

Ink's panicked flailing faded in the distance as I
walked away from him. What was he so concerned
with? It was just a human. Besides, I had Daniel with
me. Okay, so he couldn't touch anything, but this was

nothing more than reconnaissance. We wouldn't even talk to Bryan. Though, if I could touch him, I might get my damn spell to work and solve all of this mess.

We climbed up a hill together, leaving Ink nothing more than a cursing crimson dot in the distance. I did glance back once, surprised he wasn't shooting flames into the sky. Maybe this wasn't the best idea after all…

"Layla, I see him!" Daniel called from atop the steep incline. Digging my toes in, I scrabbled up beside him and stared down into a river.

That was the blank spot on Ink's map. All the trees had been cleared for the massive drainage pipes flushing water into the stream. Nearly unscalable cement walls lined the embankments surrounding the water itself. A single silhouette cut across the silver reflection, his body bent so the knees sat in the stream.

"What's he doing?" Daniel asked. He waited at the top staring at his friend silently resting in the runoff river. "Bryan!" he shouted once despite the man being incapable of hearing him. When I reached the top of the overhang, Daniel took off. He managed to walk down the forty-five-degree angle like a cartoon character. I, however, had no choice but to try to slide down it.

Lurching down on my haunches, I attempted to step down, inch by inch, my hand clinging to the concrete below. Daniel was already ahead of me and reaching for Bryan. He moved to shake the man awake, perhaps as he'd used to while alive, but his hand went right through the still shoulders.

"Fuck!" My toe folded and I fell onto my ass. Gravity yanked me straight down, my jeans burning from the speed at which I slid down the concrete slab that was a lot longer than I thought. Rather than fight it, I grabbed my bag, hoisted my spell book above my head, and plunged into the icy cold waters.

Luckily, they only splashed up to my knees. Unluckily, the fall was cushioned by more concrete. A string of curses rattled in my jarred teeth and I stumbled to my feet. The cold breeze struck through my jeans, stinging my ass. In pain and limping, I eased my way to Daniel's side. He'd drifted around to face Bryan but Daniel's entire body was eclipsed by shadows. I touched Bryan's shoulder and mentally asked *Please show me his memory of June twenty-fifth.*

Nothing. I dug my fingers in tighter and asked again, this time adding a pretty-please for good effort. Still nothing. I knew that witch was full of shit. Maybe she wasn't a real witch anyway and her butterfly effect was just a projection or glitter bombs.

"Layla," Daniel whispered from the darkness.

I jerked Bryan's shoulder one last time and let go. His body came with revealing scarlet glittering across his throat.

"Fuck!" I shouted, Bryan's corpse plunging onto his back. Freezing water burst into the air, splattering his pallid face and washing away the blood that'd gushed from his neck. No, it wasn't washing it, the blood was already in the water.

"He's dead. Why is he dead? He's not supposed to be dead!" Daniel shouted, sounding about to lose his mind.

The moonlight glinted white on Bryan's chest. Could be the murder weapon, or a clue. Rolling down my sleeve to cover my hand, I picked away the side of his open jacket and realized his jacket wasn't left open, it was cut apart. That wasn't a knife in his chest. All the ribs were stripped of their muscle and the sternum broken in half so it was exposed to the air.

"We need to get back to Ink," I said, splashing in the water to get away from the body missing its heart. "Daniel." I looked at him, but he stared down at his friend in twisted grief.

"Fingers, what did you do? What were you doing to cause this? How...? I don't understand. Why would you do this?"

"That's why we need to find Ink. He'll know. Come on." I kept waving him on, wishing he'd stop staring in horror. That never helped. The longer he stared, the deeper the memory would etch until that's all he'd remember of his friend. I tried to reach for him and my hand flew through his. Damn it!

Daniel was inconsolable, unreachable, but whatever could crack a man's ribs open and take his heart wouldn't be more than a few minutes away. I had to get him out of here, I had to get out of here.

Layla, he's dead. And he can only go where you do.

Fucking duh. I smacked my head and turned on my heel, only to come face to face with a nine-millimeter pistol.

Chapter Nineteen

As stupid as it sounded, the very first thought in my head was, *That has to be a toy.*

Some idiot had brought a toy gun down to the river and wanted to scare us. An idiot dressed in all black, with what looked like a bulletproof vest underneath.

"What are you doing?" I spoke first without knowing why. To my surprise, the armed man reacted by raising his pencil-thin eyebrows in shock. His straight arm bowed, momentarily dipping the gun. Could I just yell at him to get out of here?

He rested his palm under the butt of the gun. Well, so much for shouting my way to safety. Now what?

"The boss didn't say anything about the mark having a girlfriend." The voice oozed like jelly dripping down the fridge door. I could taste the mold build-up from his breath and shivered. "Tell me, sweetheart..."

Sweetheart? Oh, fuck this guy.

He re-leveled the gun in case I forgot he could blow my head off with it. "How much did you see?"

So that was it, he'd been sent here to kill Bryan. Why? And by who? Was he involved in Daniel's death as well?

It wasn't easy to tell in the dark, but gray swept across the jelly-man's hair. And the longer he stared, the more wrinkles deepened across his cheeks. He could have been the one who killed Daniel.

Layla, he'll kill you too if you don't do something.

I could cast a shield, it'd protect me from bullets, but needed time to voice — ten seconds at most. There was a 'See Spiders' spell I'd been wanting to try on someone but hadn't had the opportunity. Though, now seemed like a bad time to start testing.

Opening my hands so my fingers splayed out, I started to whisper an incantation under my breath. "Dol ita…"

The gun slammed closer. "He didn't tell us about no witches either."

Fuck!

Us?

"Layla!" Daniel screamed.

Splashing burst from behind me and I tried to turn to stop another, shorter man dashing for me. He had his hands wide apart, his strangling gloves on in preparation for the next victim — me. Holding my palm to the man, I started to whisper the next part of the spell in the hopes of beating both.

Daniel rushed for the running man, but he couldn't do anything. I was on my own, and I only had one second to stop… A hand slammed into my shoulder. I moved to kick water into the eyes, but instead of pulling me toward him, I was tossed to the side. A crack of gunfire shattered the air and I'd swear I felt the bullet whizz right over my cheek as I tumbled into the freezing water.

In shock, I watched the short man plow right into the armed one, hurling the man onto his back so hard a loud thunk burst when his head hit the cement. The shorter man wrestled for the gun, plucking it from a man no doubt suffering serious brain damage. I pushed myself up onto my knees and spun around, ready to yank the gun back before he could shoot me.

Grabbing the stranger's wrist, I pulled myself to him and dug my nails in—when a twist of blue light streamed from his eyes. "Layla, stop," the short man said.

How did he know my name? I didn't let go but my ability to worry the gun away became impossible.

"It's me," he kept on. "Daniel."

"That's some fucking game you're playing," I said and pinched as hard as I could. "How do you know I'm working with a ghost? Shit, what are you?"

He didn't even yelp, just stood there staring intently. *Please don't be another demon. I have no idea how to stop them.* His hand didn't shift, the gun locked in tight, but the eyes pleaded with me to look at him. "I think I possessed him. I'm not sure."

"You can do that?" I gasped, still not believing a word. "Prove you're Daniel."

"You keep an abhorrent demon in your apartment who, if the laws of nature applied to him, should be in a diabetic coma due to his diet."

"Daniel?" I let go and stumbled back, my feet slipping on the slick bottom of the river. "How? But it doesn't…" All I could see was a stranger, younger than the one knocked out in the water. Gaunt cheeks, no chin to speak of, wide-watering eyes, and a nose that fattened at the tip. There was no sign of Daniel's handsomeness anywhere. Except...the eyes, a flat hazel gray, would shift and for a moment turn a dark brown.

"You can possess people?" I said, accepting the madness before me. "Then let me take the gun."

"I'm trying." His voice grunted, half his lips tugged up in a sneer. The other side hung slack as if the person was internally screaming. "The man in here is fighting back, hard."

Swinging my bag around, I found the Sharpie in two seconds and popped the cap off. It went floating off down the river, but I didn't have time to deal with that. After running a test scribble on the barrel of the gun, I drew a ward, touched the middle, and stepped back.

The entire barrel of the gun melted like chocolate in front of hair dryer. The metal droplets hissed upon striking the cold water. As the immense heat reached back along whoever's hands were holding it, they opened and the half-melted gun splattered into the river.

One problem solved. The second was answered by the man on the ground moaning to prove he wasn't dead. I stomped for him, extending my fingers like I was about to soothe a tiger.

"What are you doing?" Daniel used the other man's mouth to ask.

"Finding who killed you," I responded and shook the oldest of the two contract killers. Blood seeped from his head, his pupils dilated to the point he probably couldn't even see me. "June twenty-fifth," I said.

"Wha...?" he whined.

"You helped kill someone on June twenty-fifth, didn't you?"

He shook his head, no doubt about to insist I was full of shit despite the evidence missing a heart. Luckily, it didn't matter what he said. Closing my eyes, I whispered to myself, "Please, let me see into his memory." I grabbed his chin and the world went white.

Fingers covered in grease appeared before me. They reached for a rag hanging off a toolbox and the gaze focused on an exposed engine of a car or truck. A screech of tires leaping off pavement into dirt burst through the air. The body I borrowed picked up a caged light bulb hanging off the hood of the car and raised it into the dark night.

From the side dashed a thirty-something man whose entire face was white as a sheet. "You gotta help me, Mac. Fuck. Shit." The man couldn't stop trembling, his hands clenched like he was still turning an invisible steering wheel.

"Whoa, calm down," Mac spoke from me. So that was who had killed Bryan and tried to kill me. Helpful. "Tell me what happened."

"What happened?" the skinny stranger shrieked. "What fucking happened!" He didn't have that covered-in-tattoos and granite-jawline look of a contract killer I'd expected. He looked more like the weasel accountant the mob hired to cook their books. And he couldn't stop shaking.

Mac reached out to catch the man before he fell onto the manifold and I could feel his trembling. "Terry, man, I can't help you unless you tell me."

Yes. Tell him, Terry. Reveal it was you who killed Daniel Lu.

His teeth chattered so loud I winced at the sound, while Terry raised his head. Green eyes against sandy white hair stared up at Mac and I tried to memorize that face. Age it a couple of decades, of course, but he couldn't be that hard to find.

"Mac, I...I think I hit someone."

What?

"With my SUV..." A finger trembling like he watched his own death pointed to the Odyssey, a sea-foam-green Odyssey. As Mac looked, my heart stopped. The entire front of the vehicle was dented like it plowed into a person as fast as possible. Red stained every sharp metal spike. Blood. June twenty-fifth, the right date, the wrong year, the wrong death. That was my mother's blood.

"Terry, Ter, come on bro, focus. You didn't hit no one. It was a deer. All we gotta do is clean it up and repaint her," the bastard who helped protect my mother's killer said.

I ripped myself out of the memory. Mac tried to fight me, a hand raising to either punch or hold me. I didn't even blink at it. Ramming my knee forward, I smashed in his crotch, wishing it'd been the speed at which his friend killed my mom. Mac tipped backward into the water and I went with, punching, digging, pushing in his throat, then returning to punching. There was no method, only madness as I sunk fifteen years of grief into him.

"You fucking sonofabitch!" I screamed. He tried to wiggle away, but I hooked my thumbs into his eyes. Mac kicked wildly, landing hits against my legs and back, but I didn't feel it. Everything went numb as I raised his head up, then slammed it down against the cement. Then again. Every hit I saw that SUV, I saw the mangled bumper, I saw where my mom's body lay in a coffin.

"Layla," Daniel shouted.

He wanted me to stop. He thought he should be the one to do this. Or he didn't think I was a murderer. Either way, he was wrong. I had spells. I could make this so much worse for the bastard. Transform his liver into a brick, make his intestines weigh a thousand pounds and rip from his body. Burn only his skin off until the entirety of his musculature was exposed to the air.

"Layla!" Daniel screamed and I whipped my head around just as the ghost was purged from the body he possessed.

Daniel flew through the air, his feet stomping into the water even though nothing splashed up. The other man stumbled to a knee, one hand planting to the ground, when he looked up at me wailing on his companion and a glint appeared in his eyes. Without pause, he drew a knife from his pocket, and stood up.

A massive spotlight ripped through the darkness. My vision whitened. I held a hand up, my eyes tearing, when a familiar voice shouted from the darkness on the other side of the river. "I wouldn't do that if I were you."

Blinking madly, I risked a peek and a laugh slipped from me. Officer Conway stood next to the spotlight. He didn't have a gun out, but the killers instantly stopped fighting back.

"Step away from him," he ordered to me. I held my hands up, trying to prove I wasn't armed and slunk to the edge of the light's circle.

Like he owned the place, Conway slid down the embankment without any strain. As he approached the water, the river shifted. It looked less like he stomped the water up and more the water moved out of his way. That made no damn sense. I shook my head, wondering if sneaking into other people's memories could cause brain damage.

Conway stopped before Bryan's body and bent over to inspect it without touching him. I rubbed my shoulders, cold climbing up my skin. He didn't show any signs of disgust or even surprise, only an exhausted acceptance at the barbaric nature of man. Abandoning Bryan, he strode to the two, the nameless one helping Mac to his feet.

"What do you think you were doing?" the officer said to them. "A dead body polluting the water!"

The two killers hung their heads. This didn't feel like a cop catching a criminal, but a teacher scolding students. My skin prickled more and I started to ease back.

"We were just—" Mac began.

"You." Conway turned on him and Mac's whole face paled. He didn't look half as scared when I nearly beat him to death. "You did everything I told you not to."

What? Run!

I took a single step back, prepared to spin and sprint from them, when the water hardened around my ankle. It didn't feel like ice, but tiny hands clutching at my skin refusing to let me go. Conway didn't even glance back to me, all his focus on his underlings.

"We killed the guy you said to," the second man said, sticking up for Mac. "And got his heart right here." From behind his back, he swung around a cooler. The sound of it unzipping reverberated off the cement walls.

I folded my fist up and leaned down to try to punch my ankle free. Water splashed up onto me, but whatever held me wouldn't let go. Damn it! It only had the one ankle. If I could just get it out... What about lightning? That'd kill me too. Fire?

Conway plucked the muddled brown heart from the cooler. As he held it up, the last of the blood that'd pumped through Bryan's aortas dribbled down his wrist. With a laugh, Conway opened his mouth...then opened his other mouth. Five rows of teeth filled the second hidden mouth, all of them glistening against the light while he unhinged his jaw like a snake. Joyfully, Conway tossed the heart onto his blue tongue and swallowed it whole.

Bile rose in my gut and I turned away for fear of puking. I could hear the monster licking his fingers as he said, "Fear is a delicious flavor."

"So...we good?" the second man asked carefully.

"You did an acceptable job, but you." He whipped around to Mac and slammed his blood-licked fingers around the man's head. "You let a witch into your head."

"No, boss, I swear. I didn't mean to. I — AAAHHH!"

The sick crunch of splintering bones burst from Mac. Conway squeezed with his palms, his fingers elongating and blue scales warping over them. Mac's eyes bugged out and his back teeth shot from his wide-open mouth like popcorn. Every crack churned my stomach and I tried to look away. He'd protected my mother's killer, let him get away with his crime. But even he didn't deserve this slow torture.

Conway didn't turn away. He met the rupturing eyes of Mac, watched the jaw break and fall open with only tendons to keep it in place. Still, he kept squeezing even as Mac fell silent and his body slack. When a crack formed on the top of the skull and brain matter splattered out, Conway stopped. He took a step back, opened his hands, and let Mac tumble dead to the ground.

"As for the witch," Conway said. The monster spun in place—not with his legs. No, he moved without turning them, like the upper half of his body was on a ball bearing. I gripped tighter to my calf and pulled with everything in me. "You've been prodding into affairs long since dead." With that he glanced right to Daniel and smiled.

"Why did you kill Bryan?" Daniel shouted, striding forward and raising his chest.

Conway chuckled, but it sounded like the bubbles bursting from my mouth when I'd nearly drowned. "Because he was foolish, as all these clumsy mortals are. Do not tell me you are showing sympathy for him, not after all that he did to you, land cretin."

"Why did you kill Daniel?" I took over, hoping to buy myself more time. An idea struck and I bent closer to the water to whisper a spell against it.

"I didn't," Conway said. "Nor did I care to. Your little companion was simply too curious for his own welfare."

"You were the cop! The one who was..." Daniel's voice dropped to a growl, "the dirty cop who was dealing with Bryan."

He answered with a slow laugh. "To a mortal's eye, perhaps."

"Then what's the truth?"

"He made a wish and I granted it in exchange for a simple task, one which you decided to involve yourself in."

Come on, stupid fingers. They grew numb from how tight I held on to my ankle. No, wait. It was working.

Conway sauntered closer, blue scales shuddering over his flesh then fading back to skin. He stared Daniel directly in the eye and the ghost gasped, "What are you?"

"The last voice the witch will ever hear," the monster said. He raised his hand and I let my spell go. Ice flew across the top of the water, freezing everything in its wake. Folding my fist up, I rammed my knuckles and shattered my leg free.

"Very clever, witch," Conway said. I risked looking back and the man walked over the sheer ice layer. How? "But you're a mere annoyance to a being such as my..."

A hand lashed out and grabbed Conway's hair. As it tugged him back, the monster screeched, "What are you doing?" into his underling's face. But that wasn't who had control of the body.

"Providing a distraction," Daniel said and he slammed the knife into Conway's ribs.

I only heard the shriek of indignation, my back already turned as I ran as fast as possible. The water tried to grip my feet again, but I dragged the ice spell while thinking. A sickening sound of a heavy weight falling a hundred feet to the ground struck from behind. Still, I didn't look back, the hair on the nape of my neck rising.

Consecrated ground. *Whatever the hell Conway is, there's no way he can walk on it. I have to get out of here.*

Daniel floated past, looking the same as before, aside from worry etched across his face. "I did my best to slow him down," he said as if I didn't know.

"Did you get tossed out again?"

"Not exactly." Darkness crossed his face, his eyes sunken and lips tight. So that meant... Not the time to worry about the villain's henchman.

"We have to get out of here," I said, when a spike whizzed right past my shoulder. Fuck! I dashed to the right, trying to serpentine to throw off the crazy man hurling blades made of water at me.

"No kidding," Daniel said, before shouting, "Layla, the left!"

I dropped and spun in a circle, keeping the fingers inside the water from getting me while also avoiding the next attack. My breath ached in my lungs, but I had to get out of here. Popping up, I increased speed and ran straight at the cement wall. My momentum worked and I shot up it, freeing myself from the water.

Yes! This was…oh, shit. All the force I'd had died a quick death. I dropped to the cement to keep from sliding back, my hands flattened to the wall that strained above me. Helpless, I stared up at the climb a good five feet above my head. There was nothing to hold onto, no way to continue.

And the monster was coming.

His laugh echoed with the river, bubbles rising from the surface like a taunting hot tub. I stared at the consecrated ground and freedom beyond my reach. Spinning around, I planted my ass onto the concrete.

Yanking the marker from my pocket, I pressed it to the cement and drew fast while staring at Conway. He'd nearly abandoned his human disguise, his skin entirely blue with scales of varying sizes across his arms and face. The cop's shirt was ripped open from Daniel's attempted stabbing. No blood dripped from the hole, but gold scales shifted, changing to a royal blue with each breath. It'd be beautiful if he wasn't trying to kill me.

The face looked like a mad scientist tried to sew a shark's head onto a human's skull. The elongated nose came to a point and fanned out to fit his massive jaw. While the eyes were sunken in where a shark's would be, they weren't the lifeless eyes of a doll but glowed gold with radiating light.

He lifted his hand, the fingers all webbed, and swatted at the water. Thousands of ice shards shot off the river's surface. I slammed my palm on my drawing not knowing if I had finished, while watching the shards grow bigger and bigger.

"Ah!" I cried, a razor-sharp sting cutting through my hand. I tried to fold up into a ball, when my spell finally took. The whole of the cement shifted under me. I began to slide back to the water, but my wall rose three, then four feet tall. Every other shard smacked into the barricade and shattered to a harmless icicle.

"Layla!" Daniel stood watch beside me. Rather than stare at the monster, he gazed down in worry at my hand. "You're bleeding."

"Yeah," I grunted, unzipping my jacket and tugging on the bottom of my shirt. I wrapped as much as I could around my bloody hand and gritted my teeth. The wound was deep, but I could worry about that later when I was safe at home — with a cheesecake the size of my head.

I didn't risk staring out, but I clung to the wall and shouted, "We're at a stalemate, Conway."

The creature laughed, sounds of splashing bursting from the water. "It had to be a damn Leeland that got in my way."

"How do you know my name?" I shouted, just as my brain remembered that he'd pulled me over. Because he'd been stalking me. That meant he knew where I lived.

"A witch of your line happens to appear right when the... Do you take me for a fool?"

What the shit was he taking about? Didn't matter.

"How much do you know about water?" Conway, or whatever his real name was, chortled.

"It's down there and I'm up here," I said, not feeling a tenth as cocky as my words. I had to get out, I had to get up, then come back with a flamethrower or something. Hauling out my book, I begged for it to find a way to make me climb.

Conway's laugh became a chortle of wet and sticky laughter. "Do you know anything of hydrodynamics?"

"What's with the fucking questions?" I shouted back. The pages flitted past, but I couldn't read anything without light. "Daniel?" I asked, waving him closer. "Can you see this?"

"I think so."

He bent down, his head nearly in my lap, when Conway shouted in pure villain monologue, "Did you know that, with enough pressure, water can cut through anything?"

"Anything?" I gulped. A massive smash pounded against my wall and I leaped back. It let me see Conway floating above the river on a spiraling waterspout.

"Every carefully laid plan, measures taken and accounted for, and a witch should appear now!" Conway shouted, sending another two water fists slamming into my wall. Cracks spidered up the sides and I watched my last hope crumble.

"Tell me you have something," I whispered, tears rising in my eyes. I didn't ask to be a witch. I didn't ask to be anything but a nurse, and all these assholes kept making that meager dream impossible.

"Maybe. It's tricky, but I think I can read this incantation," Daniel said.

"You witches are maggots in an open wound," Conway taunted. "Festering and gorging on the flesh of your betters."

"Joke's on you, maggots help clean the wound!" I shouted back, like that'd help. A massive one-two smack pounded into the wall and the cracks rose even higher. I traced one almost at the edge. One more hit and... "Daniel!"

"Hang on, here, repeat after me. 'Dama ko-tay.'"

"Dama ko-tay," I said, then yelped at the loudest attack. *Good wall, sound wall, stay standing.*

"'Ee-long a-tum-o.'"

I repeated his words, nodding fast to get him to speed up already. Daniel bent closer, his lips opening. I followed suit, prepared to match him the second I heard the syllables. The cement world shattered beside my ear. "Fuck!" I shouted, erasing all that work, as a chunk of my barricade cracked and fell to the river below. Numb, I stared at the monster with both fists wound inside an unending column of water.

There was no escaping Conway. I could hide under the remaining barrier, but he'd just hit it again until I was exposed. Lifting both of his hands high into the air, the monster said, "So much for the spawn of Isobel."

That's my mother's name!

He launched both fists forward, a cacophony of water gushing out of the river. I ducked, wrapping my arms around my spell book and tried to draw that air ward on my palm. Pain seized up my sliced hand, but I couldn't stop, I couldn't give in. I owed it to...

Leaping from the darkness, a large body on all fours sailed through the air straight off the far embankment.

It landed on Conway's shoulders, claws shredding up the scales down to the gold below. Cal?

"I believe this is our exit."

I whipped my head up to find Ink holding a hand down to me. "If you would be so kind as to take it, I am on fire up here."

Shit! I leaped to catch his hand and dug my toes into the cement. Even as I scrabbled up, I kept looking at the werewolf in a deadly battle against whatever Conway was. Cal held his own, but the monster was quickly getting the upper hand.

When I reached the top, I dug my foot into the grass and stared up at Ink. His flesh was peeling off and blistering black. It'd reached his face — the magma veins exposed while his wings fluttered in agony.

"Ink," I gasped, struggling to breathe.

"Yes, it is I, saving you. Again. Please save your rapacious gratitude for when I am not smoking."

"No." I pulled in air and pointed at Conway. "The river's not consecrated."

A malevolent smile twisted about his flaming lips and the incubus strode down the cement like a god woken from its slumber. He ran through my barrier, shattering the cement into pieces. "You dare to hurt my bond," he shouted and kicked off into the air. His shadow wings extended wide, flapping once to give him altitude, until he stared directly into Conway's eye, and shoved his hand through the creature's chest.

In the beat of an eye, Conway vanished. All the water fell to the earth, along with Ink and Cal. I leaped to the edge, prepared to run to them, when Ink caught Cal in his arms and the two tumbled to the ground together. Water splashed down like a heavy rain on them. Ink landed on one knee and Cal twisted in his arms like a dog wanting to be let go. The demon did just that.

Trotting in a circle, the werewolf faded to reveal the naked form of my boyfriend. He shook his head, splattering water against Ink's cheek. The incubus merely swept it away.

"Are you okay?" I shouted, prepared to cover both in every healing spell I had.

"Yes," Cal said. "Are you?"

I stared at my ripped-up hand still dribbling blood and held it flush to my stomach. Pain sundered my face, but I knew they couldn't see it at this distance. Nodding, I gave an, "Uh-huh."

"Good, now maybe you can tell me why you nearly died when I begged you not to!" Cal screamed, stomping a foot on the ground. "If the damn demon hadn't come for me…"

That explained how he got here so fast.

"Um." I stood up to try to get my bearings. "Well, I was trying to help…" I turned to Daniel who'd floated up beside me.

Ink wrapped his arms around Cal's naked shoulders and leaned close to his ear. In a bellow loud enough for the whole city to hear, he said, "We have a ghost now."

Chapter Twenty

It was a silent ride back to the apartment with a naked werewolf in the front seat beside me and the demon in the back. They'd maintained their "we're very disappointed in you" stance the whole way, though Cal latched onto my hand and refused to let go. The tension erupted when I opened my front door and three men tried to be the first to enter. Exhausted, with my hand aching, I left them to figure it out.

The bathroom light was a cruel traitor and the mirror even worse. I looked like I'd been up all night in jail waiting for someone to wake up and bail me out. Biting my lip, I dumped alcohol onto my palm. The burn seared through me, but I stared at the little cuts across my cheek. When I blinked, I saw Conway ramping back his fist about to throw a punch.

Breath spattered from my lips and I clung to the sink. Not wanting the others to overhear, I cranked on the tap and watched the water twirl down the drain. It spun just like the spouts under the creature that had nearly killed me. Damn it! I didn't have time to freak out. Digging into my pocket, I fished out the Sharpie and placed it to my hand, only to find I'd ruined it during Conway's attacks.

Except, I didn't need the ward anymore. Holding my hand close, I whispered the words Daniel revealed to me. The ball of light formed on my aching palm. Instead of rising, it sunk under my skin. As it did, magical morphine flooded my system. Not only did it mend and soothe away the puncture that nearly reached bone, but all the little pains of the night too.

I felt almost right as rain as I walked out of the bathroom into an ambush.

"What in the hell were you thinking?" Cal shouted. He was still naked, but didn't seem to care while Ink lingered near the door. On occasion, the demon glanced down Cal's exposed backside and smirked but said nothing more. This was my wayward boyfriend's show.

"I..."

"You could have been hurt. You were hurt! You could have been killed. Fuck, I don't even want to think if Ink hadn't gotten me." He tried to rip his hair out while pacing frantically in a circle.

I didn't know what to say. Everything that happened wasn't supposed to. Bryan sure as shit wasn't supposed to die. There weren't going to be any goons with guns. And I still didn't know what the fuck Conway was. Oh, shit.

"Conway," I said, causing confusion in Cal and Ink. "That...water shark thing. He's, he's posing as a cop. He ran my info and knows where I live."

Cal's eyes widened as big as mine and he whipped around to Ink. For his part, the demon shrugged.

"While an attack at your abode seems unlikely, I shall remain vigilant."

"As vigilant as when you let her face off against that thing?" Cal bit back.

"You should know me well enough by now to expect that I put up a valiant effort to stop her, but that is impossible when she is of a mind."

Daniel butted into the ganging-up. "This isn't her fault." I didn't expect him to defend me, but he gave me a sweet smile before facing down Ink. To Cal he only gave a cursory flit of his eyes, probably because all of him was on display.

"No," Ink said. "You're correct. The ghost is mostly to blame for putting Layla in danger. I suggest an exorcism. I'll get the salt."

"What?" Cal watched Ink practically skip to the kitchen. "Why do we have a ghost?" He swiveled to me to plead and accuse, "Why didn't you tell me about him?"

"I tried!" I shrieked, tears tumbling down my cheeks. That froze every man in his tracks. Even Ink's gleeful dance to rid himself of Daniel soured. I slammed the heel of my hand to my eye to try to hide away the rising tears. It was exhaustion yes, fear to some extent, but most of my outburst was a grief I thought I'd put behind me. "I texted you two days ago about needing to talk, about something I found!"

Cal's staid shoulders finally crumbled. He wafted his foot around on the floor and wouldn't meet my eye. "I didn't think, the reception was awful, and I thought we could…"

"And you fucking know none of that was supposed to happen. You were there," I screamed at Ink who was doing his damndest to pretend he'd had no part of this.

Like he wasn't excited at the prospect of getting rid of Daniel before everything fell apart. The demon shrugged.

Another sob clawed its way up my throat. Rather than let it free, I shouted, "If you want me to feel like shit, you're both doing a great job."

"Babe." Cal softened immediately. He swept his hands over my shoulders and pulled me closer but I held firm. Instead, he bent his forehead to the top of my head and skimmed his lips against my skin. I didn't know what he said, my stomach churned so loud I could only hear the anger gurgles.

After a moment, Cal shook his head and stood up. "I should..." He stared down at his un-werewolf state and winced. "Get dressed. Do you have anything...?"

I jerked my head to the bedroom despite having no idea if he'd left any of his clothes behind. "Come on, I'll find you something. Where's your stuff?"

"Back where Ink found me," Cal said, jerking a thumb no doubt in the direction of the woods.

We shuffled into the bedroom that remained a colossal mess. Bending over, I began to dig into the haphazard clothing piles that needed to either go in the wash or closet.

"You scared the shit out of me," Cal said softly, his voice wobbling.

I was tired of being reminded how fragile they found me. But away from Ink, he let his terror show and I crumbled. "I didn't mean to. I thought..."

"What exactly were you doing?"

I told him everything. Who Daniel was, why he'd asked me to find his murderer, how it had led to an old bandmate who had turned out to make some deal with water Satan. It sounded like total nonsense, but when I finished, Cal wrapped his arms around me and pulled me against his chest.

I buried my cheek against his white chest hair and pulled in a racking sob. My mother's killer, the vague terror from my childhood was finally given form. My mouth opened, prepared to tell him, when I remembered Jared and Scott staring at me like I was an idiot. Slipping from Cal's hold, I resumed digging for clothing so he couldn't see my face.

"Where were you in the woods? At the cabin? Fishing?"

"I was running," he said, "on paws."

Could be the truth. He showed up in full werewolf, but I hated that I was questioning his every word. "I saw them," I blurted out, unable to take this dance of waiting for him to either reveal the truth or fuck up. Tossing down my pile of scrubs, I turned to Cal. "I saw Scott and Jared...and his broken leg."

Cal's mouth plummeted as if the lies became too heavy. I stared at him, waiting for an answer, an excuse, anything.

"They left on—"

"Saturday," he interrupted. "Jared was clowning around, jumped off a counter and slammed his leg through the floor."

"Why didn't you come back with them?"

He shrugged. "The cabin needed to be re-set. Fires put out, the floor fixed, the boat pulled off the lake. I stayed behind to do that while Scott took Jared to the ER."

All things he could have finished in a day. I wanted to throw that in his face, to cackle at the evidence I had stacked against him. No, I didn't. I wanted him to give me a good reason why he lied because I fucking loved him and didn't want to stop.

Those damn tears rose back up and, through them, I pleaded, "Why didn't you tell me?"

"Because…" His chest rose, Cal breathing like the air was on fire. Shaking his head, he whispered, "Because I'm a selfish jackass."

No shit.

"I'm not over it yet. Eli…" he began, when his voice clogged in grief. A part of me wanted to comfort him, but the angry part kept me pinned. "I love you, so much that this night damn near killed me."

I closed my eyes, my heart screaming as it read ahead. "But…?"

"I've never had to combine my life, my past as a werewolf, with"—He waved a hand at me—"my girlfriend, my job. It's always been one or the other. Jared, Scott, Dana, they can't know about Eli. What do I tell them? My brother was murdered by our father and then I killed him?"

"You can tell me. I'm here, I want to be here for you. With both the petty human stuff and the wolf shit too. Please, talk to me."

He pulled me close and promised, "I'll try to not be so moody."

"That's not what I said. Just, tell me what happened in the woods. You had a lot of time to yourself."

I expected him to snort, insist that it wasn't interesting, maybe even hope he'd tell me a small story. But his face hardened and he repeated, "In the woods? Nothing happened."

Yes, it did. Now tell me… I reached to hold his cheek to get Cal to look at me, when white swept over my vision.

Damn it. I didn't mean to slip into his memories. Smoke curled in front of my darkening vision. I watched them swirl farther apart than usual and my eyes narrowed down the long gray snout. I wasn't just Cal, but his wolf form.

I hadn't even thought what it'd feel like with all that power. Cal pulled in a sniff and my brain lit up with information I couldn't processes. A handful of the scents I recognized — wet forest, frosted moss, exhaust from cars — but the rest was a jumbled mess of things I'd never experienced before.

He swung his head to the side, a single eye landing on a massive chain-link fence. Was he smelling people? Groups clustered around, everyone dressed in camo gear. Oh god, did he stumble into hunters? I tried to get him to run, when a howl broke the air.

Cal whipped his head up into the dark night cut only via flood lamps attached to buildings high in the trees. I knew this place. It was the cult's compound out in the woods. What was he doing there?

Another howl shattered the air and a wolf the size of a grizzly bear leapt from the bridge. Its paws smashed into the leafy underbrush, claws gouging into the mud. The eyes of the giant wolf were a bloody orange and the fur a rusting red. As it tipped its head back, the jaws opened and every cult member howled too.

"...we didn't even bring enough food. I wound up scrounging on the third..." Cal's voice twanged through my ears and I stared up at him. For a beat, his blue eyes looked blood-stained. I shook off the lingering memories I'd stolen and swallowed. Concern rose and he asked, "Layla?"

He'd asked me to tell him. It *was* an accident. I didn't even say please. I should tell him. "There's something you should know," I said, running my teeth over my bottom lip. Cal's interest increased, his hold on me did too. "I...I think you were right. That cabin sounds awful."

Cal's smile tried to warm me but it couldn't reach past the anger pacing inside. He refused to tell me about the other werewolf hiding in the woods. What was it to him?

In the end, I was able to find a men's T-shirt that fit, but jeans were impossible. Though, I did get to know what a guy with Cal's blessed endowment looked like in yoga pants. He insisted it was fine, he only needed to borrow them for the night it'd take to drive back from the woods.

As we headed out to the others, I whispered in his ear, "Promise me you won't wear anything like that around other girls."

"What? Why?" He laughed even while swinging around that Mack truck vacuum-sealed against his thigh.

I stared at him with a 'You know why' look while returning to the bickering duo.

"You think you're so much better?"

"And what precisely could an impotent eidolon do to protect her? Other than place her in a more precarious situation than she managed to bungle herself into!"

Running into the living room, I feared I'd find Daniel and Ink about to come to blows, but the ghost couldn't touch anyone and the incubus didn't care. Ink was spooning globs of store-bought frosting out of the canister while taunting Daniel.

"It does not escape my notice how you left her despite being capable of stopping the creature," Daniel thundered.

Darkness eclipsed Ink's eyes. He slammed the frosting tub onto my kitchen's pass-through and loomed over the ghost. "You are balancing upon a precarious line, spirit. Watch your tongue or I will burn it and your lips to cinders."

"I'm not afraid of you."

"You say as if it's brave to be ignorant."

"For fuck's sake!" I leapt in between them. Neither man moved. Daniel glared at Ink and the incubus…puckered his lips against my palm. Without taking his eyes off the ghost, he grazed his teeth over the skin and rolled his tongue around my finger. When he reached the tip, I yanked my hand back.

"Can you please stop antagonizing him?"

Ink blinked contemplatively, them smirked. "No." He sauntered away, swaying his ass like a beacon, but I was strong enough to endure. "Your pet vapor is incorrect. I could not have stopped that creature if it wanted to kill you."

"Sure as hell was trying." I absently rubbed my palm, dipping from Ink's kiss to the healing wound.

"Hardly. You were in the way of its plans, thus it intended to dispose of you. Upon our interceding, which only worked due to catching the creature off guard, he decided it was in his best interest to forgo the fight, possibly for another day." He said every word like he was reading an article on an ancient battle for a report. As if I wasn't the one that nearly became paste, as if that wouldn't have doomed Ink to hell too.

I wanted to strangle him but I knew if I even got close enough to put my fingers around his neck, we'd wind up in bed. Reading my desires, Ink flicked the tip of his tongue off his teeth and grinned.

"What…?" Cal took a step forward, joining into the fray. "What was that thing? I couldn't see much."

We all looked at each other, waiting for someone to reveal the truth. "Oh, come on. You're a demon fresh out of hell. You've been a werewolf your whole life. And you've studied anything you can find in the library. No one? He could shapeshift or pretend to be human."

"That removes trolls and little else," Ink declared.

Daniel raised his head. "The creature, it said it granted Bryan his earthly desires."

"Is it like you?" I asked my incubus. "Not a sex thing, but, I don't know, a sin of Pride?"

"Pride wouldn't be caught dead in those shoes. But no, if it'd been a creature of sin I'd have known before we left the car."

"Sin radar?" Cal asked.

"Except, he didn't grant Bryan his desire." I snapped my finger, remembering. "Tiger Whisper didn't take off until he'd—"

"Broken his hand," Daniel added.

Ink nodded his head thoughtfully. "Sounds like a djinn. Given its predilection for water, the blue scales, the golden blood, I'd guess a Marid."

"What's a…?" I started to ask him what he had just told me. "A djinn? How dangerous?"

"Depends."

"On what?"

"On how deeply you angered it. Djinn are an entire species from the nether realm."

I asked, "He's from hell?"

The demon in my apartment laughed. "Don't be foolish. Nothing escapes hell."

"Except for you," Cal pointed out softly. He turned to me, the hair on the back of his neck rising. I reached over to soothe it down as much out of habit as needing to touch him.

"I am a living exception to every rule." Ink dragged a hand down his body as if that would prove his anarchist worth. "The nether realm is simply neither the mortal realm, nor the celestial. It is made up of many other realms. Some have claimed ten, others seven."

"So what's the real answer? Ten or seven?"

"There isn't one. Space and time mean little in the realms within realms. Nor does it matter. A djinn is not a mindless beast hunting in the forests." Ink jerked his head to Cal, and a soft growl started. "They are wise, malevolent to those who don't serve their purpose, and ruthless. If it is a djinn, as we feared, then you've just faced your first real trial, Witch Leeland."

That was what the Marid had called me, and he mentioned my mother. Did he have something to do with her death? "These djinn, Marids, would they go after witches?"

Ink shrugged. "Find a djinn and ask one. This is my first time meeting one, and trying to slice him open...which I lost a claw attempting." He twisted his hand around and extended four of the five off his hand. I caught his naked finger and whispered the healing spell.

As the sharp talon re-emerged from the base of Ink's cuticle, the demon leaned closer. "Shall you kiss it next?"

"I think your claw's all better."

"That's not what I was referring to."

Daniel scoffed from behind. "Never turns it off, does he?"

"You get used to it, like tinnitus," Cal responded before locking eyes with Daniel and both of them scowling.

I didn't have the energy to deal with three men having a cat fight. "I'm going to research how to stop this djinn."

"Does that seem wise?" Ink asked.

"He's killed people. A lot of people." Like my mother. Shaking the thought away, I said to Ink, "You should get Cal back to his stuff."

"I'm not leaving you behind." He dashed beside me, swooping one hand around the small of my back and resting his cheek against mine. I wanted to be mad at him, I was, but the assuring beat of his heart thumping against my back calmed me. Unexplained red wolf or not, I loved him.

"I'll be fine. I doubt Conway, the Marid, will attack tonight. It's your one opportunity to get your things and come back to me."

I'd girded myself for a long night of trying to read through my incomprehensible spell book. I didn't plan for worrying about Cal worrying about me.

"She makes a fair point," Ink said. "It's highly unlikely. Well, doubtful if the Marid moves tonight. It does have an incubus claw in its gizzard right now. Come..." Ink held out his hands like he expected Cal to leap into them.

My werewolf stared askance at Ink, then wrapped me up tight in a hug. Pressing his lips to my forehead, he whispered, "Don't do anything stupid."

"When do I ever...?" I started, only to be met with the slow growl of a wolf about to drag me to his den. "I'll save the stupidity for when you get back."

"Good. I lo—" Cal's words snapped to nothing as both he and Ink vanished back into the woods.

I stood with my arms still held up as if a man was in them and tried to calm my panicking heart.

"Shall we then?" Daniel asked, holding my spell book up for me.

I reached to take it, hoping that somehow I could touch him in that millisecond of time he touched my book. But my fingers passed straight on through. Nodding, I slapped a hand to my spells. "Let's burn the bastard."

Chapter Twenty-One

"Are you okay?"

The question wafted about the apartment and pinged off my giant 'when shit goes down' coffee mug. We'd been struggling through the book for hours. Daniel sat so close that, if he wasn't a ghost, I'd be on his knee. I'd forget he was leaning over my shoulder reading along until he'd whisper and ask me to turn the page.

I'd turn around and careen into those philosophically tragic eyes. Which would then end in me panicking as my body reminded me it couldn't feel anything. After five times, my knees were smacking into the armrest and I had nowhere to go.

"The hand's already healed," I said, waving my palm. All signs of the murderous water genie had been wiped away thanks to magic.

"That's not what I meant."

I looked up into the darkened room. Where Ink went, I couldn't say. He kept his own hours like an alley cat that always knew where to get the best belly rubs. I caught Daniel's worried gaze. "You…went through a lot tonight."

"I'm worried I'm getting used to it." I tried to deflect, but the sting of pain in his voice finally reached me. "What about you? Bryan… Or should I not say anything?" Silence fell, my body itching from every ringing second. "Do you feel bad about him selling you all out to a genie?"

A slow intake of breath was Daniel's response. I tucked up my legs into a cross and spun on the couch until I could stare directly into his face. Even after all of that, the mud from fighting in the river, the abrasions from cement shrapnel, he looked the exact same as the day I found him…except not. Under that dangerously handsome shell was a man who'd been blissfully unaware of his friend's betrayal and the cause of his death until I came along and ruined it all.

He spread his fingers out over his knees, straining each one as if he could reach back thirty years. "Bryan and that…creature posing as a cop, I remember now. Conway was who I'd found in Madison. It was why Bryan and I had a huge fight. His dealing with a dirty cop was going to get us all fucked. Or…just me. But he didn't deserve what that monster did to him."

I leaned forward and wrapped my hand around where his shoulder was. It clenched to nothing, but I had to try. "We'll get him, we'll stop him. Conway, or whatever he's called. The Marid is going to pay."

A doleful smile tugged at his lips. I couldn't stop staring in wonder at how they'd feel. Hard as his anger at the friend that betrayed him? Tender as the poetry he'd drop at a moment's notice? Or would they be as unforgettable as the man who played bass, wore grunge, and whispered classic literature in my ear?

The Marid had made certain I would never know.

Daniel's focus shifted and he turned his head. He paused at the side of my face, pursed his lips and blew. To my shock, a cool breeze barely stronger than a whisper brushed over my cheek. I touched my skin to find it tingling.

"Your hair had…" He shifted away, turtling his neck into his jacket. "It was down and I thought."

Absently, I pushed back the hair he was only able to make dance. But I'd felt him, at least his breath.

Daniel looked to the clock. "When will the werewolf be back?"

"Cal? I'm not sure. He's pretty deep into the woods, I think."

"And he's the boyfriend who's cool with the incubus." He tried to play it off like a clarification, but jealousy was banging pots together to be recognized.

"We have…an arrangement? I don't know, it's all very. I was going to say modern, but the way Ink talks about some ancient royal houses everyone screwing everyone without a care seems to always be popular."

"He's not what I expected. Some days, neither is your demon. Is it working? You and the demon and the werewolf?"

"Why?" I laughed with a girlish twirl like I didn't know how precarious this situation was. Like I wasn't both deeply in love with one lying to me, and lustfully mad about another that drove me up the wall.

"I just want to know you're happy."

I… God, I wanted to kiss him, run my fingers through his hair, caress his chest, take off his damn pants, and enjoy one night together. Shaking my head, I tried to purge the desire before we were interrupted. Either Ink was too far away to know, or he was mad at me too. The demon didn't arrive, but the knot of feelings rolling in my heart wouldn't abate.

You can't have him. You can't even touch him. And when you kill the genie, you'll lose him.

"We should get back to…" I turned the page on my spell book, and the next entry's handwriting leaped out at me. The wide e's, the unfinished k's, the loving attention feasted on the y. It was my mom's handwriting that I never thought to see again. Tears burned in my eyes and I tried to look away, but Daniel realized something was wrong.

He found my mother's name in the margins. "Was this…?"

With my hand slapped to my mouth, I could only nod.

Leaning closer, he took in the whole page. "She must have been an amazing person," he said after a time. I couldn't read her spell, the one she'd put down for me and whatever witch came after. My head ached and a haze of seafoam green washed over my vision.

"I saw her killer." It slipped from me and I jerked, pinching my mouth closed. But Daniel was already staring at me, needing an answer. "That goon, the one I touched. I stole his memories thinking he…"

"That he was the one who killed me."

"But he wasn't. Instead, he helped repaint and hide the SUV that killed her, to protect the man that…" My voice gave out to sobs racked with anger. A swirling, fiery vengeance boiled deep in my stomach. "I have to find him. I have to…"

Revenge. Every damn picture book, cartoon, after-school special, and more told me to abandon it. Vengeance was a rot on the soul and chasing it would only end in more pain. But I bet none of those creators had to lose their mother without a trace of justice.

Daniel leaned over my laptop. He'd figured out how to navigate the computer itself. No trackpad or mouse needed. "Do you know his name?"

"Terry. The guy kept saying Terry."

"Anything else?"

"The SUV, it was seafoam green. And the license plate, I remember the numbers." I'd barely looked, but the stolen memory had been burned deeper into my psyche than my own. I told them to Daniel even though the chances of finding anyone via such flimsy data seemed—

"Is this him?" he asked, shifting away.

I turned the screen and stared face to face with a picture of the same man who had pleaded for help in covering up a murder. His hair was thinner, his face even whiter, but I knew it. Clenching my fist, I scrolled down the page to find his address. It wasn't more than a couple of streets from here. All this time. Did I pass him while walking? Did I run into him in the store? Had I ever helped him?

My skin itched and tongue tasted of rotten garbage. He could have been laughing at me with every interaction, knowing he killed my family and gotten away with it.

"That man deserves worse than death." I swept a hand over my spell book.

Daniel suddenly turned wary. "Are you sure? Death isn't something you can erase."

I'd seen him, heard his voice. But the longer I stared at the still image, the flimsier my certainty became. "I'll find him, read his memory to prove to myself, to himself, what he did."

"And then?"

I had no idea. I'd marinated in revenge when I was younger. Imagined trapping my mom's killer in a pit of snakes. Drew pictures of him fed to lions. But I'd always been helpless, just another orphan dreaming the impossible. Now that it was in my grasp, I was lost.

"I'm going to need your help." No chance Cal would let me. He was too pure and sweet to even entertain the idea of vengeance. Ink might for a laugh, but he'd get in the way. No, I had to do it myself.

Daniel bowed his head and I faltered. "Or do you think I shouldn't?"

"I have spent thirty years in formless, voiceless limbo waiting for the opportunity to seek revenge on my murderer. Your mother deserves vengeance as much as me."

Tears pricked in my eyes that couldn't cease gazing at the only man on my side. I didn't even tell Cal or Ink about the vision. But I trusted Daniel to have my back almost instantly. "Thank you," I whispered, running my hand above his cheek. "This means everything to me."

"You're not alone, Layla."

* * * *

A gray dawn was greeted not by the crow of a rooster, but the mad barking of dogs. The street broke down into a series of potholes stretched together by crumbling concrete. Every color was swept away by ashy browns and rust-pitted reds. I could scoff at my mother's murderer winding up where a trailer park would be a luxury, but I'd lived in much the same. Some days it amazed me that I could afford my tiny apartment.

The stench of a packing plant rolled across the sluggish river winding just past the fifteen-foot chain-link fence. Unlike the crystal blues of the lake, this one reflected only the same dreary grays of lives forever stuck on hold. Another dog's rapid-fire barking drew me to look across the street as a screen door flew open.

Ratty hair the shade of snow found under tires, beady eyes sunken into a sallow face, and the lanky limbs of a man who hadn't had a full meal in a decade—it was him. The murderer slunk onto the porch where a couch had been left to die. He fished into the pocket on his work blues and dug out a lighter. When the cigarette caught, the only strike of color in the pale world, he fell onto the couch and stared at the sky.

I don't know what I expected to find. A man rolling in riches, ordering the peasant girl out of his foyer lest he release the hounds? A gangster snorting a briefcase worth of cocaine before shrieking that someone bring him his guns? I'd planned for anything but this pathetic life.

Except that was what he had—a life. It might be shit, but he still got to laugh, to sing, to savor a cigarette on a cold spring morning. He got to enjoy every single thing he took from my mother.

That wasn't going to happen again.

Easing around the junk left on the lawn, I kept one hand in my pocket clutching to my marker. The other I raised up and, in as civil a voice I could manage, called out, "Hello."

The cigarette shifted first, as if the man was surprised anyone cared enough to talk to him. As his head turned, my heart stopped. The vision played in my mind, that same man begging for Mac to fix his problem. *Mac wouldn't be helping you now.*

"Whatever you're selling, I don't want it," he said and turned away.

End it. You know it's him. You can feel it in your bones.
I clenched around the marker, the ward for fire burning
in my mind.

No, I had to be sure.

"I'm here to ask you a few questions," I said, getting
only a gruff snort for my bother. "I'm with the IRS."

That changed his tune. The murderer spun like a
cartoon character, his eyes bugging out and tongue
lolling. He caught his lagging cigarette and snuffed it
out. "Whatcha...?" The voice changed from dismissal
to sweetness. "What's the problem, ma'am?"

Shit. Why didn't I think to bring papers? I reached
into my purse and found a stack of syllabuses. "We've
been looking into your records, Mr. Hawkins."

He scratched his head with his middle finger, but
didn't throw me off his porch. "I...I doubt there's shit
to find in there. Been working at the plant for five years
now."

"This is in regards to your account fifteen years
prior," I said, staring him dead in the eye.

That cocky, flip-off-the-IRS attitude melted into
sweat dribbling down his face and his gaze darting
everywhere. "Wh...what do you care about...fif-fifteen
years ago? It's old history."

"Not to me," I snarled. "Or the IRS."

With hands trembling, he shook another cigarette
out of the pack despite the one still between his fingers.
It wasn't until he brought the second to the light that he
realized his mistake.

"Tell me, sir, about your vehicle and the night of
June twenty-fifth."

His jaw distended and he crammed his hand into it.
For a moment, I feared he might try to yank his tongue
off, but he went to town on his nails while muttering,
"Nothing. Nothing happened at all."

"Our records indicate otherwise."

"No!" he shrieked. "Nothing happened!"

Damn it. I needed to hear that confession. I needed to hear him admit that he killed her. He murdered a woman, drove away, and destroyed all evidence. That he took away the only person in the world who loved me.

Lashing out, I locked my hand around his upper arm. He stared at it, confusion crawling up his face, but it was too late. *Show me what he remembers. Now!*

Instead of white, blackness swarmed through my mind. The air thickened to tar and I struggled to breathe. A cough built in my lungs, and I bent over to hack it out, when light pierced the shadows. Another blared across my eyes and I looked away to avoid the pain.

Car parts and fast-food bags littered the front seat. I stared at the aqua-colored upholstery when the murderer turned his head. There was nothing but the sound.

I'd been expecting to see her face. She always kept her long hair in two braids twisted up into a bun. In my traitorous imagination, when he struck, her hair would fall. Her groceries would scatter across the pavement and she'd give out a single gasping cry.

None of that happened.

All I saw was a brown blur, then the thunk of one ton of metal meeting bone and flesh. *Oh god, what did I do? Why am I living this? I'm going to hear that sound every day for the rest of my life.*

The murderer's head slammed forward, the top smacking into his steering wheel. I felt his foot push on the brake, stopping the SUV, then the world streaked. His head bobbed like a boat in a storm. It turned not to the woman dying in the street, but the sound of another dashing over.

Someone had tried to help my mother?

I fought to get the bastard to focus on who this good Samaritan was. A knotted kerchief hid her hair. She wore a bulky coat, strange for a warm June. The murderer peered closer to watch the woman bend over the body in the road.

"Fuck!" he shouted.

This had to be when he left. When he realized what he'd done and peeled out like a coward. But the scene didn't shift. Terry stared in horror at the woman checking my mother's wrist then laying the hand back on her breast. The kerchief shook and I knew that was the exact moment she died.

At least she wasn't alone.

I couldn't cry but my head ached like I was bawling. I'd seen enough. I wanted out. He did it. He killed her. Spell!

The kerchief woman stood and she stared directly into the SUV.

No. That's not possible.

Eye as green as sea glass, hair a honey blonde I'd pretended was Rapunzel's, lips that thinned on the sides whenever I broke a vase. My mother stared back at me.

Light flooded from the dying woman. It engulfed my mother standing above, erasing her from my sight. Terry's eyes welled up even as he kept staring through the searing light. My mother was gone. In her place stood a woman with wider features, dark hair, and a cold smile.

That was a fucking magic spell. Did another witch kill my mom? I tried to unbuckle the seatbelt, but I had no control over Terry's hands. This was nothing more than a horror film that'd I never be able to escape.

The strange woman stared directly into my eyes and she upended my entire world. "You weren't supposed to see this," a stranger's lips said, but with the voice that'd sung me a thousand lullabies. The voice that'd chastise me when I'd vanish at a market. The voice was my mother's.

Because that woman standing there was Isabel Leeland. My mother changed her face to a dead woman's and vanished.

The witch raised her hand and, even trapped in Terry's head, I felt the world shifting for her magic. He screamed in fast bursts of air. Every staccato hit matched his actions of shifting the SUV into reverse and ramming on the accelerator. The woman my mother became faded out of his headlights. Still she stood there, a hand up, the magic rising.

Terry cranked the wheel so hard, the SUV drove up onto the sidewalk, and he rocketed away. I took one last look in the rearview mirror of a woman's foot vanishing into the night.

I fought against the magic yanking me to the present. No, something in there had to make sense. My mother wouldn't just...she wouldn't leave me. Abandon me. I was her fucking treasure.

Terry wasn't talking. He stared at the smog rising from the plant where he'd wasted his life. "The lady." His ragged voice cut through the morning air. "She changed her face. I see it, every time I try to sleep. I hit her, then I didn't. She was dead, but not dead. I didn't mean to, I swear. It was an accident."

I came here hoping for his tears. For the man to throw himself on my mercy so I could deny it to him. But he'd been used just as much as I had. My mom had used her magic so she could run away, so I'd have to mourn her. So I'd visit some random woman's grave every week with dollar-store flowers. She left me broken, walled off, and ignorant of this magical world I inherited. Why?

"Why?" Terry asked, then repeated two more times.

"I don't know." I rose from the couch to face the frostbitten sky. "But I'm going to find out."

The eyes I'd borrowed to learn the truth were blinking, tears trying to bead up and fall off his lashes. I didn't reach out to wipe them off, my charity dried to a husk, but I leaned closer to Terry. "You won't be bothered by me or anyone else from that day ever again."

He swung to me, his eyes wide. "You promise?"

How long had he lived in fear of the face-changing people coming for him? How much had that fucked up his life, people either laughing at him or calling him nuts? Pity and shame swarmed through me. I'd been more than prepared to end his life, now I just wanted to make it better.

Bending over, I spotted a stone left in the yard and drew a ward across its sheer surface. "Here, this will keep you safe." I passed it to him.

It meant nothing to the mortal — the ward was for keeping magical scroungers at bay. But Terry cradled the stone in his hands like it was his firstborn. I stumbled back, needing room to breathe, to think.

I'd woken up knowing my mother was dead. I'd yelled at Ink over it, ran from the first helpful witch I'd met over it. I'd suffered for years because of it. And, in the snap of a finger, it was all a lie.

My pocket jerked and I leaped to the side. It was my phone, someone calling instead of texting. *That can't be good.* Cal's worried voice blasted in my ear. "Layla, where are you?"

I stared at the broken man with a cigarette drooping on the side of his mouth, his hand wrapped around a magic stone. "Getting coffee," came to me without a moment's pause. "Why?"

"You need to get back here. Now."

Chapter Twenty-Two

I returned to male voices rebounding off each other until all I could hear was a battle of testosterone. Even if it was possible to make out who had which point, my energy to tease it out was long spent. I'd gone numb, not just emotionally but mentally. Thinking about what happened would only kick up a hornet's nest in my heart. With three very different men about to get in my face, I didn't have time to deal with that.

"You're back." Daniel was the first to recognize me. He'd placed his hands behind and raised his head. He didn't give the zip-up-the-lip move, but I knew he'd done as I'd asked—kept Ink distracted and hadn't told them where I went.

"Layla." Cal shoved the incubus, nearly flattening Ink against the wall, and reached for me. He was interrupted by three mildly warm cups in a drink carrier.

"Coffee?" I raised one up to him and he took it without looking at the receipt.

"Are you okay? Did you see anyone? Did anyone attack you?" Cal shot out fast, peering past me. Only the slow flicker of a dying CFL light in the hallway waited behind.

"I'm…" I paused in shrugging off my coat. Ink reached for the second cup that was the equivalent of a third grader making hot cocoa. He wasn't smiling. I didn't expect it from Cal. Daniel was in contemplative mode. But Ink…? My throat dried.

"What happened?" While asking, I flapped my trapped arm around like a wounded bird. It sent my elbow smacking into Cal's stomach, which did more damage to me than the steel eight-pack. He caught my panicked flailing and eased my wrist free, then pulled the rest of the jacket off like a gentleman. Why was I so flustered? Maybe because I'd learned my mom…

Nope. Not the time.

Cal laid my jacket over his arm while he hunted across my face. I risked looking up at him, certain he'd read everything I had just done. The bone-crushing arms of a panicked hug clasped around me. My jaw jarred against his collarbone, probably leaving a mark.

"You had me terrified." His voice sputtered on the air, the sound barely breaking above his breath.

Now you know how I felt.

I swept my hands up his back, my face turned to bury against his warm chest, and my whole body collapsed into his hug. I didn't realize how badly I needed to have him hold me until I was safe in his arms.

My mom left me. She faked her own death to abandon me. I'm that fucking unlovable.

"I'm sorry," I whispered. All I wanted was for my sometimes hairy boyfriend to take me to bed. To hold my face and trace the wide swoop of my cheeks. To kiss my forehead and swear it tasted like ice cream. To run his fingers between mine and tell me how lucky he was.

"We've been sent a message."

But I couldn't have any of that because my world was made up of monsters, and magic and a constant stream of things trying to kill me. I half-turned from Cal to Ink who remained in the kitchen by a box on my table.

"What is it?"

Ink hoisted up the box to reveal...

"Is that a...a dead fish?"

"A bass," Cal added, like any of us cared what kind of fish it was.

The scales were a speckle of black and silver, the beady eye milky white, and its mouth hung open. None of which mattered because someone sent me a dead fish. "Who the hell would...? Right, Marid. Trying to kill me. What does it mean?"

"A warning." Ink dropped the box back to the table and I heard the first sign of flies finding their next meal. Great, I'd have to trudge out to the alley to get rid of it. "He's telling us he knows where you live."

"Well, no fucking shit. I already knew he knew that. Anything else?"

Cal stared at Ink and the smart tongue of the incubus snapped quiet. "We know where he'll be tonight. At the Sunstar Canning factory down by the river."

The same place Terry worked. Hell of a coincidence, and I didn't believe anything was a coincidence with this watery genie. I glanced over my shoulder at Daniel who'd picked up my spell book to page through.

"How'd you figure that out? Did the fish tell you?"

Ink stepped forward and jerked his head to the side. "No, the messenger did after some *minor persuasion*."

I didn't ask them to torture someone for me. I didn't want them to. Cal spoke, "He gave that up far too easily."

"Yes, I suspect he was intended to be a sacrifice for the trap."

"You did not kill him in my apartment!" I darted around, trying to find blood stains or ripped off limbs scattered in my living room.

It was Cal who brushed a hand over my shoulder. "Don't worry."

"Your mutt stopped me, though I say the man deserved no less. Delivering a threatening piscine message before the noon meal? That would have gotten him strung up by his hamstrings in Venice."

"So there's a trap meant for me, maybe you too. I'm sure Conway wasn't happy about your interference." The words came so easy, my tone cool, assertive, not a hint of fear. What the hell was I becoming?

Cal shrugged and Ink beamed with pride at my assessment that they too had pissed off a Marid. I shouldn't have told Ink to join in. We could have kept him back, a surprise attack. But then Conway might have hurt Cal... No, I would not play the game where sacrificing pawns was an option.

"We might have found something. We? I mean me, of course. Those two have been gnashing teeth at each other for the past half-hour." Daniel jerked a dismissive hand at the whole mess.

"I'm sorry, little whisper, are you upset we didn't let you gently ruffle a single hair on the minion's head?"

"Ink..." I began, waving an exhausted finger at him.

The incubus shut up and leaned back into the shadow of my kitchen. Cal turned to look at him, both speaking with only their eyes. I ignored it all to try to read over Daniel's shoulder.

"These wards, they're a bit catch-all, but they could have potential."

"It's not a bad idea." Generic was an understatement, the wards working against all creatures of the nether realm. "Though there's a warning at the bottom about how the truly powerful could sneeze them away. Ink, you'll have to keep out of them."

Daniel snickered at that and I groaned. That wasn't what I meant.

"You may try to wound my ego, specter, but every punch of yours sails right through me."

Boys.

I focused on the plan. "If we do this, we'll have to find time to draw them before the Marid and his group arrive. That means a stakeout."

"You are not going," Cal boomed, taking my hands in his.

"I was thinking it'd just be you and Ink. Daniel and I stay back to find more spells, better ones to ensure we can actually win this."

I could only see the side of his icy eyes as Cal stared longer at Daniel and flexed his lips. "We can handle that, right, Ink?"

"I am but a humble servant to your random whims." He rolled his eyes and stuck a hand to his hip but I knew he'd follow through. Bitch about it the entire time, for sure, but Ink would watch the place like a hawk.

"Can I talk to you?" Cal whispered in my ear.

I nodded slowly. He swept his arm around the small of my back, half-guiding half-carrying me down my tiny hallway. We didn't go to the bedroom, but wound up partially standing in the bathroom. "Are you okay?"

A painful, acidic gurgle knotted in my throat. It was a cry for help and a dismissal in one non-answer. Patient Cal swept back my fallen hair and said, "Because I don't mind."

"Don't mind about what?" I sputtered, my body leaning away in shock. *I sure as hell minded that my mother's alive somewhere, that she's lied to me. Why wouldn't you?*

Because he doesn't know.

Cal glanced back out into the living room. "Ink told me about the...ghost situation. I thought about it on the ride, and what can you do with a ghost?"

"Not much," I muttered before my brain remembered it was my boyfriend doing the asking.

He laughed to himself. "One good reason why I'm not worried about him. If you're wanting to flirt with other guys, even the corporeal ones, just...let me know you're safe."

I should be ecstatic, he practically gave me carte blanche to have fun, but all those times of Daniel wondering what kind of man was fine with sharing me must have sunk in deeper. "Why don't you have an ego?"

Cal peered past me and I turned to find Daniel haphazardly standing alone with only my book for company. "I do. I can get jealous as hell over you."

There had to be a but. *Please let there be a but. I don't have time to clean blood stains off of...everything.*

My confounding boyfriend leaned closer and whispered in my ear. "I also know that no one out there, be it ghost, gargoyle or gorgon, is as good as me at making you howl." He caught my chin in his hand and pulled me right to his hard lips. I parted mine, giving in to his tongue.

Cal snagged the tip of his wolf fang right under my lip, pushing the full stretch of it up until he brought his top tooth against the straining flesh. I shivered in anticipation of the bite, the fangs strong enough to pierce my skin. When only a soft tap bounced against my lip, I opened my eyes, and he pinched my ass.

"Also I love you," he said with a toss of his head. The wolf in jeans vanished, Cal All-American boyfriend returning in his stead. "And you're the only girl I've ever...trusted."

Tell him. You have to tell him you saw the red wolf. Say it happened now. Or you were too upset to mention it before.

"There's something I need to, should've —"

"I found it!" Daniel shouted. He raised a hand and gestured me closer, but it was Ink who bobbed over and peered down at the book he couldn't read.

Cal bounced his hip into me. "We can talk about it later. After this fish mess is dealt with."

Yep. I will so have the spine to get into that fight later.

Never mind the fact I hadn't told them about my mother or how I left this morning to kill a man. I don't know why anyone could love me.

Turning the book to face me, Daniel pointed to a ward studded with five blackened candles. They formed a star of two crosses at a forty-five-degree angle to each other. Every segment held a symbol that didn't look too complicated to draw. I snagged my little notepad off the coffee table and began to copy it.

"What's it do?" I asked even while finishing the ward, then starting again. It was the best way to memorize it, especially if I had to draw fast while death was on my heels.

"With this, we can pin the Marid in place and force it to answer questions. It'll be incapable of lying."

"What purpose would this serve? Are we in a dreadful state fretting over what the djinn had for breakfast?" Ink prodded a finger over the book, though he pointed to a different spell.

"Because…" He knew about my mother. He had to. The man that helped Terry worked for the Marid. He knew my mother's name, my surname.

"He can point us in the direction of my murderer," Daniel said.

My mind churned with an insatiable need to trap Conway and get him to tell me why my mother left. What if he knew where she went? What if he knew where she was? I tapped the bottom of my pen so hard against my teeth, the end cracked. "Blech!" Wiping the spilled ink off my tongue with my palm, the dreadful taste clinging, I caught the concerned eye of Cal and Ink.

"What's wrong?" I asked. "Didn't you want to help discover his murderer so he could find peace?"

Ink's brow darkened. "Not if it risks your life."

"And yours."

"Yes, it would put me in a dangerous situation as well. But I would rather suffer a hundred years of a babbling spirit haunting this place than see you harmed."

Daniel folded his arms and huffed. "I do not babble."

I stared at Ink in confusion. He'd made it very clear that demons didn't do affection. But his comment felt like a love declaration in incubus terms. Absently scratching at my arm, I smeared more of the pen's blue ink across it. "If we catch it in this trap, then we can kill it too. Right? Probably?"

"I'd prefer a hard plan that does not involve probably nor maybe. Though, it seems moot either way as your book rat has yet to discern a viable path to dispatching a djinn."

Daniel glared harder at Ink. "I'm sorry, do you want to give it a try?" He held up the book, then scoffed. "As I assumed. Layla, we should get to work, preferably without interference from unhinged demons who don't understand buttons."

Ink's lip started to lift, his snarl strained to the breaking point. "I've changed my opinion upon the necessity of dispatching the spirit."

"We need to get to the plant." Cal grabbed Ink's arm and tried to tug the demon away. "They'll be getting in to work soon."

"They've already started," I said off-hand. "Probably."

"All the more reason to start the stakeout now. Got to see who comes and goes. Right?" He aimed that at Ink who was still grumbling. Cal, the quarterback of our plan, leaned over to kiss me on the cheek. "Keep your guard up. I wouldn't put it past the thing to try to attack now."

Pursing my lips tight, I nodded. There were lots of wards to protect the home...most of which required sheep's blood. I rather doubted the landlord would let me get away with that. What if I dragged a roast of mutton on the inside of the door?

Cal stomped to the door, tugging on the grumbling incubus to come with. At the threshold, my werewolf nodded like a soldier heading into battle. I turned to Daniel, prepared to get to work.

"Incidentally, if he becomes abhorrent," Ink added. "I've found that you can place his bone shard on the ledge and he is incapable of coming inside."

The door slammed shut in his face and all I could do was sigh.

Chapter Twenty-Three

Two hours passed with constant interruptions from Ink. I'd be sitting down at the table, jumbo mug of coffee at the ready, and he'd walk in with updates, information, potentially shady people, or just needing to pick up snacks. With the last one, I shoved an entire box of Whooseits into his arms. "For Cal, not you."

"Why must you wound me so, my bond? I do not sully my palate with such wretched confits." To finish his sentence, Ink grabbed a coffee pod from the counter, dumped the grounds in his mouth, then topped it off with a full spray of whipped cream.

"Yes, you're a true connoisseur." I shooed him out. Ink took a step to the side and no doubt appeared in the cold and lonely field outside the cannery. We still didn't have much by way of an attack plan beyond stop the monster, then try to murder it.

"Is he gone?" Daniel asked. Curled up on the couch, he looked like he belonged there. I scooped up my coffee and walked to him, only for a hand to appear from nowhere and wrap around my stomach.

A spell for fire sprung from my lips and fingers. I moved to plunge both into the attacking hand, when Ink whispered, "I'm always here."

"Ink!" I tried to call off the spell, but I set his sleeve on fire. The incubus cast a quick glance to the flames tearing up his shirt, then he pulled me in to kiss him. It'd probably be romantic if it weren't for the smoke getting in my eyes.

"Adieu," he said with a flourish of his hand that finally put out the fire before vanishing.

Only the lingering smoke from where I nearly burned his arm off remained. When did my life become a tale told by an idiot who huffed too much paint?

Fairly certain I was free for a time, I moved to join Daniel. He peered over the book, watching me sink into the couch then wish to keep going. If I was consumed by a sofa, I wouldn't have to fight a genie.

"Is he always like this?" Daniel's tone held more concern than I expected. "Or is it only because of me?"

"No, I'd say Ink's pretty much like this when he's bored...or worried? Can demons get worried?" Not the question we need to be answering. I took up the book, my eyes crossing at the language. The flowery stuff sent my dyslexia into a tailspin. If not for Daniel, I doubt I'd be able to read any of it.

"I've been ruminating on that passage we found earlier."

"Oh?"

"The tale of how another witch defeated a fire djinn. What was it called? Ifrit?"

I shrugged. It was all Latin to me. "I think you mean, you found. I've been no help."

"Don't be silly."

"It's true. It's like, I can see the words but by the time it hits my brain, they jumble. And I'm left trying to piece together this stupid puzzle while everyone else has turned the page. I hated it when I was a kid, and I really fucking hate it now!"

I slammed my hand against the book, but it wasn't enough. *Stupid. Slow. You know how* they *are.* And that came from the adults. Kids were ten times worse, sensing like blind mole rats that I was incapable of getting through day-to-day life, but not having a choice because my mother was dead. Was supposed to be dead.

"Ah!" I screamed, about to punch my book, when a wary sense washed over me. There was no eye, but I felt my spell book looking at me and giving a warning growl. It wouldn't put up with being hit again. Instead, I crumpled into my lap, working through my curls as if I could straighten them by willpower alone.

A cool sensation, like stepping onto a veranda overlooking a snowy mountain, glanced down my shoulder. I un-turtled just enough to see Daniel wafting his palm over me like he was trying to coax a feral dog out of hiding. "I'm guessing this is about...what happened with the man."

I whipped my head around, expecting for Ink to poke back in. But there was no demon, no werewolf. Just me and the ghost on my couch while I had a minor breakdown.

"Are you worried what the others will think about you taking vengeance?"

I hadn't cared in that moment. Even though I knew they'd fight me on it, especially Cal, it didn't matter. I had to put the man that killed my mom in the ground. More of that cooling sensation rolled over my arm and I leaned into Daniel. It didn't fix my boiling mass of anger, grief, confusion, and shame, but it felt nice.

"I've spent a good thirty years weighing what I would do to the man that shot me."

I pinched the bridge of my nose to chase the tears away. Still, my voice wobbled, as I said, "Let me guess, you'd find it in your heart to forgive him."

"I settled on removing his toes with a pair of gardening sheers, degloving both his hands and feet, tying his arms back with the skin, and watching him slowly die for hours in the freezing cold of the forest."

"Jesus Christ."

"Thirty years is a long time to hold a grudge. It is difficult for my heart to carry forgiveness when there's a bullet wedged inside."

"Yeah, but…" As if I hadn't thought the same while being passed from one foster home to the other. Nursing school brought some of the rage back. The human body could be surprisingly fragile if enough pressure or chemicals were applied. "What about acid?"

"I debated that, but I suspected being able to procure a high enough molarity to do the job would be difficult."

"Boiling oil? No, boiling sugar. Sit there and toss it at his naked body."

Daniel laughed. "Or there is the tried-and-true method of ants, hornets, any tiny insect the more burrowing the better. Death by a thousand cuts."

This was so macabre, but it was the first time I had felt awake. Being the busy student, the good girlfriend, the genial and happy twenty-five-year-old numbed my brain. It became nothing more than cotton balls bouncing back and forth between my skull. Letting it out, telling someone how badly I wanted to hurt the person that hurt me…except that wasn't Terry. He'd been just as fucked over as I was by my mom. She was the real villain.

"I didn't kill him." The confession fell out of me, my words so heavy they plopped from my mouth and landed in my lap.

"You're…a good person." After our discussion, Daniel was very careful in how he said that.

"No, I'm not. I would have, I almost did. I didn't kill him because I saw what happened that night. He didn't kill my mother, because she's still alive."

Daniel's eyes opened wide. "Well, that's…" He watched me, his voice downgrading from joy to that same careful tone. "That's wonderful news?"

I had mourned her for fifteen years. They took me to a trailer crammed with another three kids where I slept under a bunkbed. If not for the kick in the ass that got me into nursing school, I'd still be where that start got me.

But she was my mom. We'd make thumbprint cookies every Saturday and I'd eat half of them while they were still warm. When I'd cry about the thunder, she'd run in armed with flashlights and tell me we had to stop the fighting giants. I loved her, and I hated her.

"I don't know anymore. I don't think I know anything." I struggled to blink through the dry tears in my eyes.

"Yes, you do." Daniel placed his palm to my cheek. Only the slight tingle told me he was touching me. "You are brilliant, Ms. Leeland. In a matter of days, you've uncovered a deep conspiracy plot that's actually real. Who can say that?"

I laughed with embarrassment at that. "It'd mean more if we stop them before they take over slash destroy the world."

He added another hand to my face. I turned as if he could move my head and gazed deep into his eyes. Compassion swirled inside his brown irises, but so too did wonder, and a devotion that sent my heart racing. "If it weren't for you, Layla…"

"You'd have gone mad."

Daniel shook his head. "I wouldn't be torn to shreds over the idea of finally getting my revenge."

My heart skipped a beat and I crested my fingers over the top of his. God, I'd give anything to feel the warm skin, the thin bones that'd pluck strings to make music, just once.

"This djinn, this monster, he must be stopped at all costs. But I'm terrified at the prospect that in order to save you, I could lose you…forever."

Sweet words dripped from his lips and I lost my mind. Leaning forward, I shut my eyes tight and thought the witch's prayer. *Spells, magic, whatever you are, let me kiss him.*

It would have been poetic in that moment. If for only a second, god or fate took pity on me and let Daniel become corporeal. I didn't need a pottery wheel, I didn't need swelling orchestras, just a single kiss before we went off to war. But fate was a bitch and my lips met only cold air. My heart pounded faster and faster at the stupid move.

"I'm sorry." I stood up, my skin on fire. He tried to reach for me, but I was beyond reproach. *Why did I do that? Why'd I set myself up for nothing but heartbreak? Why'd I even need a man I couldn't touch? A man who listened, who stood by my side, who knew me better than I'd ever known?*

"Layla, wait." Daniel tried to catch me, his fingers falling through mine, when suddenly he didn't go all the way. My arm froze. I could feel it, but it was impossible to move. In a panic, I sat down and the rest of my body followed except for the arm.

"What did you do?" I sputtered, turning to the ghost who was partially inside of me.

His whole face went stricken and Daniel yanked his arm out. "I'm so, so, so-so sorry. I didn't mean to..."

Testing, I flexed my fingers in then out. Everything worked exactly as it had before. "It's like...you were controlling me."

"Layla, I swear, I had no intention to —"

"But I could feel it. I could feel my hand, and my hand could feel me."

Daniel stared from my face to me shaking my fingers back and forth as if any of that made sense. "You." He skirted his palm over the outside of my arm, only setting off a tingle that produced goosebumps. Daniel turned in his seat, his eyes sharp in surprise...then more.

He dipped his hand through me and, for a moment, I felt his fingers wrap around mine. As they held me, all control vanished. It was Daniel who guided my arm. I sat still, my breathing shallow while he tested my fingers wrapped around his. "You can feel this?" he asked, dotting the tips of my fingers up my other arm.

A smile rose at the playful dance and I nodded. Daniel reached my shoulder and worried my palm around it. The touch became a massage and I craned my neck to give him more room. My own fingers dug in tighter than I ever managed, eliciting a moan I'd been building up for a week.

Cool words in nothing but a whisper brushed in my ear. "Do you like this?" With only the tip of my index finger, Daniel gently tapped the side of my lip. A tingling followed his touch unlike anything from when I was the only driver. Giving in, a sigh slipped free, my mouth parting. Daniel began to sweep my finger around my lips, then back and forth over the bottom one while he watched me.

A glow burst against the deepening browns of his eyes, Daniel's focus on the tingle of pleasure causing me to clench my legs. More certain, he added two more of my fingers to the lip massage, tugging on the sensitive skin and letting one fall into my mouth. I reached out with my tongue and licked up my own finger. A moan escaped from Daniel and he started to chase my tongue with my finger.

I added my teeth, scraping against my skin and setting off another gasp of pleasure for both of us. "Layla," he begged, his gaze drifting down to my sweater. Daniel resumed rubbing my shoulder, my fingers drifting farther down my chest with each clasp of the palm.

The kiss of a ghost wasn't enough. I wanted more. "Daniel?" I got his attention and picked up the hem of my sweater. "Can you help?" He brought my other hand to the opposite side and together we worked it off. It was weird, like my whole hand had fallen asleep even though I could still feel it. But after tugging the trapped hair out and tossing my sweater aside, I could enjoy Daniel staring at me in wonder.

He clasped my hand to my chest like I was about to say the pledge of allegiance. My thumb kept drifting in a circle, finding its way under my bra, then back out. A nervous laugh broke from the man who'd had to abstain from touching a woman for thirty years. Pulling in a deep breath, I strained my chest and pressed my breast into my hand.

The uncertain chuckle became a gruff grunt and Daniel dove my fingers straight to my nipple. His gentle sweeping against the sensitive skin hardened my nip to a full point. I squirmed on my thighs, thrusting my chest out farther.

Daniel's mouth hung open in awe. I stared at the lips I couldn't kiss and he licked what was beyond me. "Should I—?"

"Keep going," I interrupted. My panties hadn't been this soaked from some second-base action since I had met Ink.

"Then, may I have your other hand?" he asked, holding his out like a gentleman about to sweep me off into a waltz. Smiling, I placed my palm above his. Daniel swung a leg over me to sit in my lap while his arm sunk into mine. For a moment, my fingers hung in the air, only the ring finger twitching as it learned about this new connection.

But he quickly gained control, sweeping my finger over my lips in his kiss while my other hand pinched tighter to my nipple. Every yelp I gave, Daniel would dot the tip of my finger over my tongue, then caress out to circle my mouth. It buzzed with an insatiable heat I'd never felt before.

I tried to chase my own finger, but Daniel pulled both hands away and reached behind my back. His nose crinkled and the awe quickly became consternation. He even stuck his tongue out and grunted before the bra band gave way. "This is much easier with my hands," he said, using mine to pull away the underwire trap.

At the full reveal, Daniel groaned. "'So long as men can breathe, or eyes can see. So long lives this, and this gives life to thee.'"

"What?" The words sounded familiar but my melting brain didn't stand a chance.

"It means…you're fucking beautiful and I'm losing my mind being able to touch them." He swept one of my palms down the side of my breast. "To touch you." Daniel curved my hands under my breasts, then began to knead.

He crooked the whole of my thumbs around my nipples and pinched them tight against my index finger. A yelp rose, but Daniel stared me dead in the eye. "Test yourself. I know the pleasure you find in pain. Dive for more."

Steadying my breath, I swallowed the cry. He pinched twice as hard and I lost all sense. Tossing my head back, my attempts to strangle the cry became a lone wail, but a wave of immense pleasure swept through me. Gently, Daniel trailed my fingers off my nipples and supported my breasts. The lone crack of wind stung against my flaming nips, but every breath was another strum of pleasure down a still-ringing power chord.

"That was..." My words, my voice, my mind sputtered. I wanted to shout from the hills how amazing that felt, but Daniel had his head quirked to the side.

I stared down at my lap with a ghost straddling it. My thighs were still clenched, trying to grind whatever pleasure it could to my clit. Why not keep going?

"Daniel, could you stand up?" I asked in a calm voice.

He nodded, not only retreating from my lap, but out of my arms as well. When he stood, so did I. Daniel began to drift away, but I leaned so close my lips could brush his ear. "I need you in my bed."

I kept waiting for the strangeness of the situation to hit me over the head. Even while trying to sashay to the bedroom alone, because my partner couldn't touch me, it didn't feel weird. Different, oh hell yes, but that extra challenge made me all the more curious what Daniel could do to me — with me.

Bouncing open the door with my ass, I walked backward into my bedroom while staring into his eyes. Straining my fingers for him, Daniel skirted the tips of his against mine. He didn't take control, only coolness tingling up my skin.

"What should I do?" I asked, stuck against my bed with no idea how to fuck a ghost.

A little chuckle slipped from Daniel and he brushed back his hair. It didn't work well, the blue tumbling over his eyes as he said, "Take off your pants."

"You don't..." Even as I wondered why he left it to me, I unbuttoned my jeans and wiggled out of them. Daniel floated behind, causing the 'I could be imagining all of this' feeling to creep back into my mind. Taking a deep breath, I hooked onto my panties when a hand slipped inside of mine.

"Wait." His voice was strained and breathy, causing me to shake. Daniel took control over my right hand. With it, he swept my palm over my hips. It'd been a while since I had any time to myself, what with an eternally horny incubus living on my couch. Daniel took his time tracing the curve of my hip down into the dip where it then rose to make my belly. For the first time in years, I shivered at the touch of my own body.

My finger slipped below my panties and I bit my lip. He tenderly stroked what he found, playing through the dark curls while I lost myself. "When I first met you, it was the sun piercing through a decade of clouds."

He dipped my finger right through the start of the cleft and I yelped. Staggering on my toes, I tried to guide my own finger to reach my clit, but Daniel held. "I couldn't cease thinking of you, the touch of your fingers, the silkiness of your kiss, the taste of your being."

"Oh, fuck!"

Daniel swept my finger over my clit. The small pulses of before swirled in pirouettes down through my throbbing lips and back up. I nearly gasped at the heat and lubrication waiting for me.

"Layla, my knight in a pointy hat." He pushed the whole of my hand down my panties and spread the thumb and finger wide. It opened my thighs and Daniel plunged two of my fingers inside. "Bend to me."

Cold snapped against the back of my legs and they began to move. Daniel lifted me onto the bed. He remained behind, his touch only inside my arm and legs. But as I bent to my knees, my thighs straddling wide, he retracted from them and took my other hand instead.

"These seem unnecessary now." With my hands, Daniel took my panties and tugged them down my thighs. They stopped at my knees and I began to shift my legs together to compensate, when he pushed them apart.

A groan at the force slipped from my tongue. I could barely keep upright, my balance straining and body about to tumble. But Daniel slipped my finger back to my clit and ran my other hand up my breast. I fought like hell to keep enraptured in that pleasure.

"Your smile gave me a reason to live through this death. Your laugh was an angel's song. And your body, the mere trace of it outlined against pulling cotton and tweed nearly sent me raving. Now…"

His voice drifted away and my hand abandoned my breast for my nightstand. He ran my palm over bottles, metal, leather, and finally found silicon. Clamping to it, Daniel brought one of my older toys to my face.

"A poor substitute for what I once had," he said, twirling the bottom of the toy one-handed. The pink head began to vibrate and I gulped. "But..." Daniel drew the trembling toy up my leg. "It'll do in a pinch."

A whimper slipped from my lips. My core screamed at me as I balanced on the one ab I had, but I struggled to widen my legs. He gripped the jiggly balls at the base and thrust the toy inside of me. In an instant, I remembered why it used to be my favorite.

Daniel pinched my nipple, the rest of my hand fondling and bouncing my breast. The other was busy thrusting the toy in and out. Heat snapped through me, sex sweat pooling at the back of my knees and dripping from my breasts. I tried to breathe, but he'd found *the* spot. Moaning, I began to thrust against him. I mean, against the toy.

The silicon balls twisted in his grip, suckering around my clit and spreading the dancing vibrations through the whole of my labia. I wanted to toss my head back and scream when I felt cold on my cheek. Opening my eyes, I caught Daniel resting on my shoulder. He peered past me to something.

"Look. Look at how fucking hot you are."

I followed his line of sight to my old mirror and the woman in it. She was nearly lost in the throes of self-pleasure, the ghost invisible in the glass. I grew disjointed knowing someone else teased my nipple and rammed a toy through me. But all I could see were my fingers pleasuring myself, the other Layla who had never become a witch. Who hadn't met a ghost, or werewolf or demon and welcomed them to root around in her panties.

I almost felt sorry for her.

"If I had to wait thirty years for this last chance," Daniel whispered, drawing me from what could have been. His eyes deepened to an inescapable black hole. Even if I wanted to look away, I couldn't. He pinched my nipple, hard, and I bit back the scream. Instead, I thrust down, swaying my hips to push the mad vibrations as deep as possible.

"Every lonely day, unending nights, empty weeks and eternal months...they were all worth it for you."

"Fuck!" The orgasm hit like a jumbo jet falling from the sky. As the pleasure overtook me, my straining stance crumbled and I fell back through Daniel. He slipped out of my hands, leaving me alone holding the toy in place for the last tremors. My other hand fell to my chest so I could feel my heart thundering across my palm.

Daniel sat beside me, his body not even denting my blanket. Slowly, he drew the tips of his fingers down my arm, leaving a chill in their wake. I struggled to breathe after that, more exhausted than after an incubus marathon. "That was..."

"Beautiful." His voice became winsome, the commanding, sexual heavyweight replaced by a wistful man.

Even though I wanted to sleep for a thousand years, I scrunched up to sit beside Daniel. Snuggling after was one of my favorite parts but it wasn't an option with Daniel. All I could do was be near him and talk. "If this works, if we kill the Marid and he was your murderer...?"

Daniel's head hung heavier than ever before. I wished I could give him a hug. Instead, I placed my palm up. He stared at it a moment, shaking slowly, before putting his against mine. We couldn't touch, but we could feel in our hearts.

"I cannot say that watching you...enraptured in bliss one time will be enough for me, but my afterlife would've been empty without the memory. Thank you."

I leaned over, brushing my head where Daniel's shoulder was. But in the mirror, I only saw a confused, broken woman trying to console herself.

Chapter Twenty-Four

"Just...humor me, okay." I pressed the instructions into Ink's hands. He gave me the same petulant stare this conversation had started with, but at least he didn't rip the paper up.

Wafting the sheet and extending it as if he needed bifocals, Ink said, "Is this a wise use of our resources?"

"You've already planted the other wards?"

Time was no longer on our side. The teleporting incubus had slipped into the factory with my chalk and drawn the wards that should hold the Marid in place...or so he claimed. I bounced on my heels, anxious to head out and join up with Cal.

"Yes, yes. The place is lousy with pink and green witch drawings. But this...?"

"Just, do it. Please?" I tried to plead with him.

"Oh, my bond." Ink patted my cheek and pulled me close. "You never need to beg, unless you want to." With that he vanished into the ether.

"I thought you were taking me!" I shouted to nothing. Guess I was driving. Laid out on the table

were the only weapons for this upcoming battle—
Sharpies, a mass of snacks for Cal, my spell book and a
stack of paper should I need to hand out spells. Ink
could draw all the wards I gave him, but it'd mean
nothing unless I sealed them. Though, if I drew one on
a paper and passed it on, he or Cal would be able to—
hopefully—burn the asshole to death.

I finished stuffing my bag with my elements of war
and turned to Daniel. We'd been quiet since the whole
whatever it was in the bedroom. Not out of discomfort,
but a shared awareness over where our lives were
leading and how neither of us could stop the train. The
Marid had to die and doing so would most likely
banish Daniel. No, it'd free him from this curse…which
was a good thing.

"Do you think this is going to work?" I asked.

Daniel, who'd found the passage on defeating the
other djinn, shrugged. "If the fire one could be
destroyed by water, then…"

It made sense, but it also seemed way too easy.
Didn't Ink say they were smart? Seemed like if his one
weakness was fire, he'd have found a way around that.

I didn't voice my concerns because there was no
point. We didn't have time to try to plan around it. All
we could do was act and hope.

"Layla."

Daniel knotted his fingers together and stared past
me, perhaps past the walls that couldn't stop him. "If
this ends the way I…I think it will, I want you to know
that." He pulled in a breath that shook his whole frame.
"That I am and will always—"

"Oops, nearly forgot." Ink appeared beside me and
wrapped a hand around my stomach. "Toot toot,
incubus express leaving the station."

"Wait, I…" There wasn't a rush of air, or even a fade to black. I went from standing in my kitchen listening to a ghost lay out his heart to stumbling down a small grassy hill. My knee buckled and curses rose, when a comforting hand pressed my shoulder.

I looked up into ice-blue eyes. Without pause, Cal wrapped me up in his arms. He drew his nose against my hair and breathed deep while I hung on for sanity.

"Are you ready for this?" he whispered.

"I don't have a choice." Was this going to be my life from now on, forever the target of monsters and hunters in a world that wasn't fond of witches? How many times would I have to hold on to my boyfriend not knowing if we'd see each other when the sun rose?

Cal placed his lips to my forehead and traced them against my skin. "I'll fight like fire for you."

"Hey," Ink interrupted. "We can save the maudlin declarations for the celebration after. They're changing the guards."

As one, we bent lower into the grass. Across the way, the bay doors for the cannery flew up. A single unmarked truck backed up to the loading dock. When the bed fell down, men leapt free. They carried boxes of what I guessed wasn't a load of walleye cheeks.

The once welcoming dawn behind the river had shifted to a muddy gray, clouds strangling the sunset. Soon the streetlights would be our only way of navigating the darkness, which the Marid seemed to prefer. I flared my fingers out, testing the fireball.

"You should refrain." Ink held my shoulder and I put out the flame. "You do not want to wear out your magic."

I could do that? I'd get exhausted after all the running and fearing for my life. But I'd never felt tired after using magic. Had I?

Cal twisted his head around. "Where's the ghost?"

"Give it a minute," Ink declared.

The air wobbled and Daniel stumbled through. He blinked a moment and stared up at the last of the sun before spotting me and smiling. Cal gave him a quick nod of the head, which Daniel cautiously returned. The ghost then gave me a curious look, probably wondering if I had told Cal what happened in the bedroom. That was a conversation I did not want to have. Besides, I had bigger ones waiting in the wings.

I shook off the flash of his red wolf memory and focused on the job. "How do we get in? I assume the front door is just as guarded as the back."

"Worse," Ink pouted. "It's locked."

"Sensors. It'd have the cops on us in a second."

"Which is the last thing we want," I said to Cal. Conway was one of them — doubtful they'd blink twice at him shooting a nursing student.

How could we break in? I furrowed my brow when Ink's laugh brushed against the back of my ear. "Do not fret so." He clamped down on my hand and I shifted from the cold wind of a spring night's hill to the freezing cement of a darkened factory.

"Ink?" I called, spinning around and realizing he had left me alone. My heart rate increased dramatically, my breath sputtering in short bursts while I stared around the silenced conveyor belts. Small clamps attached to a running metal bar hung above my head and the longer I looked up at it, the faster my panic set in. The last time I was in a place like this, I was nearly shot, Cal was nearly shot, and his brother...wasn't so lucky. Closing my eyes, instead of fish I saw Cal and Ink clamped to the hangers above.

Fingers traipsed down the side of my neck and I swung wide. The back of my hand smacked into Ink's cheek. For his part, he took the full blow without flinching. "Did you call me back for that?" he asked calmly.

"No. I..."

White light burst across the dark concrete, blinding my eyes. "I see you received my greeting," a voice boomed above. I blinked to find a line of men—who were all armed.

"Fuck!" I drew my hand in a circle and widened the bubble fast. As it expanded, I snatched onto Ink and pulled him back with me. Bullets flew, striking into the shield I threw around us. It hadn't been field tested much, just against a net. I had no idea if it could withstand a firefight. Sparks burst in the air where every bullet struck an invisible force and collapsed to the ground.

Pain sundered the back of my mind and weariness swept through me. My leg slipped while I tried to ease back from the firing squad. Waiting for them to run out of ammo didn't seem like an option. "Ink?" I turned to the demon by my side at the exact second the first round shot through my shield. The bullet struck deep into the middle of his chest.

Unimpressed, Ink stared down at where the friction had burned a hole in his shirt. He sighed loudly and tossed his shoulders back. Black wings of shadow stretched out, the left rising to cover me in darkness as he stepped up into the air.

With the heat off of me, I collapsed my shield and dove behind a boxing machine. I barely had time to tuck my legs up before the firing squad realized I'd moved. In the distance, I could hear an "Ooh," a shout of "What the fuck is that?" and the low chuckle of a demon who couldn't be killed by mortal weapons.

Where was Cal? He couldn't get in here with Ink distracted. What could he even do against guns? I yanked out a sheet of paper and drew a ward fast, then another. All the while, I heard the screams of men being dragged to their near-death by an incubus with a grudge.

A flutter of the air caused me to turn and come face to face with Daniel. "What's happening?"

"Ran into resistance early. Do you know where the wards are?"

He opened his mouth when he suddenly pivoted. "Behind you!"

I leapt to the right, putting myself back in the line of fire. A massive tentacle of water sliced clear through the sheet metal, exposing the wires. As it receded, it ripped out more, setting off sparks. The equipment above us jerked alive, belts running in various directions.

Spinning in place, I slammed my ward—another concrete shield—into the ground. While it rose to protect me from stray bullets, I stared at the monster rising from the grates in the floor. All pretense of humanity was long gone. Scales stretched over an entirely water form. It rippled below the illusion of arms and a torso. Conway's entire lower half looked like a snake, the conical end trailing back deeper into the factory.

"So nice of you to come," he said and slashed with his hand. It folded into a sphere of water, which came straight for my head. I reached my hand out when it collapsed around me, water gushing up my nose and down into my lungs.

Through the refraction, Daniel's wobbling face twisted in fear and he screamed, but I couldn't hear any of it trapped in my drowning fishbowl. Conway inched closer, but he didn't form his legs. If he kept that watery tail, all our plans were ruined.

"For being a warrior of the realm," the Marid chuckled, slithering until it was nearly on top of me, "you're not much of a challenge."

I flung my fingers out, igniting each tip, and slammed them through the water. Conway shrieked, steam quickly boiling off his hand. My face grew hotter, but I wouldn't break off. If I did, I'd die.

Glass shattered from a window lining the roof and a massive shadow leapt onto the moving conveyor belt above. Conway ripped his boiling hand off of me and I tumbled to the ground, sputtering water out of my nose and mouth. An angel in the form of a massive wolf ran for me. Conway raced to slap at Cal's ankles, but the wolf was too quick, dodging each one when he launched off the end, straight for Conway's head.

At the last second, Conway wrapped a tendril around Cal's midsection, pinning him in the air. "I'm exhausted with these beasts of yours," he snarled, and the bastard started to squeeze tighter. The yelp sent my heart reeling. Not caring that it was our Hail Mary, I yanked the Mason jar out of my bag, popped open the lid, and threw the mass of white beads straight at Conway's chest.

The scream from before was nothing to his heart-rending agony now. "Enjoy the anhydrous beads, you watery bastard!" I shouted, leaping to my feet. The Marid retracted all of its tentacles while the chemical ate apart the water supporting him. That left Cal, twisted on his back and falling.

I tried to run over and catch him, when Cal managed to twist just in time to land all four paws onto the drying surface. "Where's the ward?" I shouted at him.

He turned on his feet and took off to the right. Ducking down, I gave chase, my unzipped bag bouncing against my back. Daniel followed closely, warning me when Conway would try to hit again. His zings were much smaller than before. Without a river to feed him, he couldn't regenerate all the water I had stolen.

Stumbling on barely formed legs, the Marid gave chase. I made a full-on flamethrower with my hands and aimed it behind me. It struck anything in my way, cans of fish popping apart and splattering boiling tuna against the walls.

All the while, Cal kept his steady run. He'd gotten ahead and hooked his jaws around a tarp covering the ground. Ripping it away, cans of paint that'd held it down rolled across a giant pink trap ward. I spun around, walking backward as fast as I could. With both hands belching fire, I lost sight of Conway. He dared not draw too close, the fire boiling away his water. But he wasn't giving up either.

A sense of belonging washed over me and I knew I'd stepped into the ward. Bending down, I put out my fires and brushed my hand against the chalk.

"Layla, look out!"

Growling burst through the air and a box full of cans flew out of the smoke. "Shit!" I twisted, trying to leap out of the way. An edge slammed into my back, pushing me farther out of the ward.

Rising from the parting smoke, Conway appeared. His legs were solid, the feet pure gold to protect him from the flames. The metal carried up to his chest, where the scales electrified. Jagged lighting darted across the whole of his torso up to his snarling face.

Oh no! My knee scuffed the ward. It wasn't going to work like that. I fumbled for the chalk, my fingers still hot from the fire. The stench of burning plastic rose from my backpack, panic setting in until my arms shook.

"You've had your fun, witch. But I've grown quite tired with this little dance."

I slammed the end of the chalk into the ground, tracing the line I'd scuffed. It left me open, my entire arm exposed, and Conway winding up to attack. Not only with water, but the electricity crackling inside his body. Heavy paws landed on my back. Cal prepared to leap in place. No. If he jumped in front, it could kill him. He could get trapped.

Conway chuckled and flung his fist. "Goodnight, Goody Lee—"

"Can anyone step in?" Ink grabbed the tendril in both hands and held on. The whole of his body lit up like Christmas, sparks shooting from his elbows, knees, and off his hair that rose like a porcupine. But he didn't even wince at the snarling monster who couldn't tug back.

"You pesky sin of lust. What quarrel do you have in this fight?"

Ink stood just outside the ward. *This could work. Draw faster.* The chalk screamed as I swept it to close the inner circle, then traced the line. All that remained was the upside-down V.

"I could ask the same of you, Djinn of water. We're a long way from the nether realms."

"And I will send you back." Conway snarled and wound his arm up. It yanked Ink clear off the ground. The monster slammed him into the wall, then the conveyor belt above.

"My. Oof. Bond? Ooh. Have you —?"

"Yes!" I screamed, shoving the final line forward and leaping back. Ink let go the moment Conway snapped him, sending the incubus flying deeper into the cannery.

A demented chuckle rose from Conway, though it sounded like it came from hell itself. He swept around, his features bobbing from the back of his skull to the front and he glared down at me. Cal slid off my back and vanished into the shadows. Only Daniel stood beside me, the coolness of his touch radiating down my arm.

"Little witch has lost her friends," the Marid taunted. He took one step across the circle. I scrabbled back on my hands and feet, unable to look away. "Just like her...mother!" Conway threw a tentacle out for my neck, but in doing so, his back foot slid over the ward and the whole thing activated.

His hand slammed into an invisible wall, the water curling around the dome and back to him. "What is this?" he shrieked, punching twice more at nothing.

"It worked?" Ink asked, appearing behind me from wherever he'd been flung. Slowly, I staggered to my feet, watching the raging Marid like a zoo keeper observing a venomous snake. "How's it feel to be rendered impotent, djinn? Stings?"

"Finish him." Cal spoke behind me. I jerked in surprise to find him out of wolf form. He patted a hand over my back and jerked to the monster.

Conway's attacks stopped, his head twisting to the side. The monster was watching us. I opened my bag and pulled out the fire wards. Four of them — two quick starters and two slow burns — they'd boil away the last of Conway's water until there was nothing left. I touched the first, readying it for calling the spell to life. All I had to do was toss it into the bubble.

Just toss it in and…

The Marid's hand hung just inside. The bastard who was behind Daniel's death, who knew about my mother. What else was he hiding?

"Layla?" Cal began.

I clenched tighter to the wards and launched my hand inside the bubble. It folded around me, protecting me, letting me lock my palm around Conway's arm. *Let me know what this fucker knows!*

White swarmed my vision and I prepared myself for any eventuality. To wake up with blood on his hands, to watch him gun down Daniel myself. The white didn't fade. I shook my head… The unbroken eternity wasn't shattering.

Slowly, a single dark shadow formed in the distance. I tried to squint but it hurt, and a voice laughed all around me. "Did this witch think she could control the mind of a djinn? Oh child, you've brought a lighter to fight against a tidal wave."

Pain seared through my brain. I felt myself falling but couldn't see anything. With a chuckle, Conway pried open my skull and all I could do was fall.

Chapter Twenty-Five

"Tell me your name…"

The voice exploded in every corner of my mind, the cacophony both an indecipherable mess and one simple order. I struggled to cling to my sanity. There was nothing else to grip to. Moments from my past zipped back and forth across my vision, sounds blared in my ears, and neither matched up. I watched when I was five chasing after my mother in the Carpathian Mountains and heard the first time I was caught ditching school. The smells shifted too. Pizza from the joint Dana, Fariah, and I would hit up that did fried pickles. Rose water and incense my mother patted to her cheeks every night before bed. Ink's brimstone and Cal's earthy wood scent.

"Who are you?"

Jagged red lines stabbed through my memories. I felt my body buckling under the pressure though I couldn't see myself falling. What was happening outside of me? Had the world ceased to exist? Were Ink,

Cal and Daniel still out there fighting? Or did we already lose?

Another brash of ear-splitting noises stripped away my resolve. Tears rising in my eyes, I admitted, "Layla Leeland."

The voice screamed in rage. "That is not your name."

What?

"Tell me your name! Tell me who you are, witch, before I cut your soul in half and look for myself."

My memories rewound almost to the beginning. Hazy, half-spotted scenes of tiny hands reaching for my mom's long necklace played out. My mom's soft voice whispered in my ear, "Laylie Leeland, the littlest lady in the land."

I stared at her face so wide in my infant eyes that she filled my whole world. "Who are you?" the voice thundered, ripping the image of my mother to shreds.

Anger flared through me, chasing away the memory's scents. The stench of fish rooted me back to the cannery. But I could smell my boys too, waiting for me to return. I couldn't feel my fingers sliding over my thumb, but I kept snapping until I heard the sound. First a loud pop, then another, and finally the catch of fire.

"I am Layla fucking Leeland!" I directed all the fire forward and the voice screamed.

The cannery shattered back into view like someone ripped a blanket off my head. Pain rose up my arm and I realized I had it plunged through the Marid's chest. The water warped around my wrist, crushing the bones, but it couldn't finish the job as I pumped fire deeper into the depths. My flames petered without oxygen, but they did enough damage Conway couldn't throw me out.

"Layla!" Three men shouted my name at once. Two clung tightly to my waist, both trying to pull me free while the third stared wide-eyed from outside the barrier.

I'm sorry, Daniel. I couldn't read its mind. I didn't even get a chance to try. Maybe this was his killer, maybe this would be the end of his purgatory on Earth. Shaking my eyes to wipe away the tears, I clenched around the paper in my other hand. As it rolled into a ball, the rune glowed.

"Nighty night," I said, tossing the rising fire right at Conway's feet.

In one loud whoosh, the Marid clamped on my arm, then hurled me into the air. All I knew was bits of machinery smacking into my leg and back as I flew up, then the cement floor about to shatter my skull on the way down. Warm arms smelling of brimstone wrapped around me. Ink rolled into a ball and landed in a superhero pose with me draped across his knee.

"Did it get him?" I stumbled from his hold, my leg aching and side on fire. Turning, I hoped to find ten-foot flames sputtering inside my magic bubble. Smoke billowed from the invisible trap inside like a snow globe from hell. I couldn't see the Marid or tell if he was dead.

Cal ran up and grasped my hand tight in his. "Are you...? What happened in there?"

"Was it him?" Daniel asked quietly. He stared at his hands as if waiting for them to fade out of existence.

"I'm sorry." I shook my head, not knowing what would come next. "I don't—"

The magic bubble exploded, fire splattering through the air. It landed in clumps, flames eating through rubber and plastic above and below us. Smoke twirled in spouts, the gray and white haze hiding almost everything in the cannery. A massive silhouette rose from the ashes, its arms the size of a gorilla's, the head straining off a neck as wide as the shoulders.

"Foolish mortal!" the Marid boomed. "You thought that would hold me?"

"Run. Run!"

Water tentacles snapped out five at a time. Ink slashed at two, his hands elongating to full talons. But a third snuck in and wrapped around his leg to slam him to the ground. Cal transformed back into the wolf. His legs had barely changed when he clamped fangs onto the tentacle holding Ink. Another swung out of nowhere, racing to slam into his chest.

I twisted my fire, burning through the tentacle before it could touch Cal. Breath caught in my throat, my head pounding and vision constricting. I tried to take a step, only for my leg to collapse.

"Layla," Ink shouted, when another two tentacles wrapped around his ankles and hefted him up. As they went, the tentacles whacked him into the machinery. "Ru —" Ink's head bounced but he didn't even flinch "...un!"

"His body," Daniel said, the only one untouchable, the only one left to watch. "All the water returns to it."

He couldn't mean — a tentacle slammed into the ceiling above, breaking the conveyor belt. Cans of boiling hot fish rained down along with gears spitting from the sparking mechanisms. Reaching into my pocket, I fumbled for the piece of chalk I'd given Ink.

Quickly, I snapped it in half, and tossed the piece into a tentacle reaching for Cal.

Twisting on a paw, Cal leaped into the air to avoid its sting, but missed the incubus coming the other way. The two collided and slammed to the ground. I stood rooted, filling with a horror that one of them might not stand. Ink was the first to pop back up and he shouted at me, "Get going! Your mutt is fine." He raised Cal's concussed head, but his eyes were open and he shook his drooping tongue back in.

"Sorry, Djinn," Ink shouted, using arms and legs to attack the rising tentacles, "but you'll have to put in a request to join this three-way." Two wrapped around his ankles and yanked him into the sky. "To think some people spend coin for this."

"He's right," Daniel shouted. "This might be the only answer."

I slammed my palm to the ground, not wanting to accept the truth. Bursting off my feet, I ran away from the fight. "How do we know this will work? The nether realm trap sure as shit didn't."

Behind, I heard the sound of a body hitting the cement hard and I prayed it was the incubus who could take it and not the wolf who wouldn't. No time. I couldn't focus on that. Where the hell did Ink put it? We'd planned out every trap, but with this I just told him to get it done. Oh shit, what if he drew it behind the monster?

"Layla, I see something." Daniel pointed ahead to a stack of boxes. I didn't have time to stop and shove them aside. Instead, I barreled through them like the Kool-Aid man late to his wedding.

Five candles circled around a ring of chalk. Yes! "Thank you, you gorgeous demon," I shouted and leaped into the middle.

While bending down to finish the spell, I pulled out the broken bit of the chalk to finish the spell…and my mind blanked. "Ensnare? No, that's not it. En…there was an en. I know."

"Enshrine here!" Daniel shouted over the wind.

When did the wind pick up?

A droplet landed on the back of my hand and I stared up into massive clouds stretching over the whole ceiling of the factory. That couldn't be good.

"Enshrine here whosoever bears the mark of…" Another three drops struck me and I realized he was trying to wash the chalk marks away. "The mark of Calcar!"

Three massive tendrils launched from the clouds. One struck my hand, knocking the chalk piece to the ground. Another wrapped around my waist and hefted me off my feet toward the ceiling's murder storm. With a flick, I lifted five flames on the end of every finger and tossed them to the candles below. One at a time, the fire circled around the wicks until they formed the final piece of the spell.

Or what should be the final piece. Why wasn't it working? "Daniel, the chalk!" I shouted, pointing to the small chunk that had rolled out of the binding.

I tried to turn around to pump fire into the tentacle, but my hands couldn't reach. It held me right above the summoning circle and jerked me back and forth. All I could do was watch the last piece of the spell resting a mere centimeter from where it needed to be.

"Demon! Werewolf!" Daniel shouted, but they were in their own fight. I tried to dig my fingers through the water wrapped around my stomach, but it shook me harder. He stared up at me, his face stricken in horror. The Marid held all the cards. At this height, it could crack my skull open like an egg.

Dashing between the candles, Daniel fell to his hands and feet. With his lips next to the chalk, he started to blow as hard as possible. The piece didn't even shudder.

Maybe I could knock it to the side with a spell and…

"Fuck!" I screamed, the water around my midsection tightening. Pain ratcheted down my legs and up my chest. I couldn't breathe, my organs forced into my lungs as I scrabbled against the vise. All feeling in my legs vanished.

Conway intended to snap my spine while Daniel helplessly looked on. I stared down at his widening eyes. For a second, the sweet brown eyes caught in the candlelight and turned to flames. He slammed his cheek to the ground and blew.

The pain transformed into an unreachable agony. All I could do was grit my teeth and pray for it to end. Darkness seeped in tighter and tighter, the whole of my chest on fire, when gravity took hold. My scream barely had time to build from the bastard dropping me before I'd hit the ground.

I splayed my hands and feet out, hoping that would save me, when wet fur sprung out of nowhere to slip under my stomach. My hands latched on before my brain understood. Cal leapt the both of us clear over the circle and the whole sigil lit up in a blinding silver flash.

The very air inside the ward sparkled like a million snowflakes made out of broken glass. Each one danced in a swirling pattern up and down through the bubble, then they all zipped to the middle and the Marid stood in place.

He stared down at his feet locked to the center of the ward. Conway lifted a hand, his face knotted in concentration. With a snap of his wrist, he flung absolutely nothing at me. The water he'd possessed had been solidified to glass, leaving the monster in his full-scale glory. The shark head was gone, and his face had shrunk to a still monstrously wide grin full of golden dagger teeth. His eyes lost their glow, leaving only black dots on the sides of a wide nose.

I moved to slide off of Cal, only for my foot to buckle. A surprising hand caught mine, Ink taking all of my weight in his arms. "You're...I was afraid that the—" I brushed my fingers over his face, the shadows and his fallen hair hiding most of the terrible damage he took for me.

He caught my wrist. "You need not worry about me, my bond." Ink placed my knuckles to his lips and the movement caused his hair to slip to the side. A massive gash ran straight down the whole of his cheek, the skin blackened and burned. I swallowed deep, waiting for it to snap back into place. The redness seemed to be lightening, but this was going to take much longer than a handful of bullet wounds.

Ink, unconcerned about my concern, glanced at the djinn we had trapped in a large lamp. "Your spell seems to have worked after all."

"Oh ye of little faith."

"Faith is for the foolish and desperate," Ink said back, his tone snippy as if I had questioned his honor.

"Congratulations, little witch," the Marid spoke. His voice came through loud and clear like it was being projected while his movements were muffled. "You've

trapped me for a second dance. Shall you try again?"
He extended his hand and I full-body shuddered.

"What did he do to you?" Cal asked. I reached over
to wrap my other arm around my second protector's
shoulders. As he slid close, he bonked his forehead into
mine and brushed his eyelashes over my cheek.
Holding my two men, I stared over at Daniel who'd
stopped outside the bubble and held my open spell
book.

"I tried to see into his memories."

"We went over this," Cal ranted while Ink only
rolled his eyes and clucked his tongue.

"...but he dug into my mind instead." My voice was
barely a squeak, my brain a mess with long-lost
memories fracturing into each other.

"He did what?" Ink roared, striding closer.

"Whatever you do, don't break the circle!" Daniel
shouted. He waved a hand out as if that could stop a
rampaging incubus. Luckily, after the fight, Ink had
enough presence to stop from starting it all up again.

Cal ruffled through my hair, which was probably
crammed full of burnt tuna. "Are you okay?"

No. My hands shook, my legs ached, my back felt
about to collapse. But I wasn't going to stop now.
Raising my head, I stared the Marid in the eye. "Why
did you want to know my name?"

That caught Ink, who craned his head at an inhuman
angle to stare at me. A slow smile lifted up the blue-
gray lips of the Marid and he chuckled. "Names are
power, as your demon there knows."

At the mention, Ink's wings puffed out, the black
shadows straining into the still burning fires behind us.
"Did he take it?" he pressed on me. "Did he find your
name?"

There'd been so much rage, the voice's screams constant, flipping through my mind until I... "No," I said confidently. "I burned him away before he could."

That wasn't the full truth. He'd had me, combed through every second of life I could remember back to the time I was in a cradle, but he never found the truth...because I didn't know it. How could I not know my own name?

"This is bad," Cal whispered. "This sounds like beginning of the world magic. The old-school shit."

Names have power and there was no way his was Conway. "Marid," I shouted in my demanding voice, "what is your name?"

He smirked wider and shook his head...then a sliver of white moved into his black eyes. His trembling hands reached up for his throat and he began to crumble.

"I'm sorry, have you never seen a witch's truth circle before?"

The monster that'd been trying to kill us for the past hour collapsed to one knee with a loud thud. It shook the remaining tuna cans scattered on the ground. "You have to answer every question put to you, and if you try to lie..."

"Go to—" he started, when he tipped his head back and screamed.

"...all the book said was dire consequences. Not very descriptive, really. What exactly are you feeling? Ants under the skin? Acid down the throat? I'm curious."

He thought he could pry apart my mind like a teenager's diary? He'd tried to murder the man I loved and the man I...had complicated feelings for on a good day. Whoever he was, he'd learn that crossing Layla Leeland wasn't good for the body or soul.

The eyes started to roll back, the Marid thrashing on the ground. I turned to Daniel who must have read my mind. "He won't die. He can't. But he'll be in agonizing pain for every second he refuses to answer."

How long would this take? Minutes? Hours? Could I stomach watching even a murderous scaled water-monster writhing in pain? Ink nodded at me. Names were power. I needed his to keep my people safe. There wasn't another option on the table because he had taken them all away.

A blue tongue rolled out of the Marid's mouth and bounced on the ground. As it did, his voice — clear as a bell — said, "Samuke."

In an instant, the pain vanished. Samuke the Marid rose like he hadn't suffered at all. But I knew that look in his eyes. They burned with bone-deep hatred for me. *Welcome to my world.*

"Well, Samuke." That caused him to snarl like a rabid, backed-into-a-corner wolverine. This wasn't a fun game to him any longer. "Did you kill Daniel Lu?"

"No."

"Then —"

"Layla, wait." Daniel pointed to the ring of candles...three of which were only tendrils of smoke now. "They went out with each question. I think...I fear we only have two more."

"Then what?" I asked Daniel before slapping a hand to my mouth and looking at the wick on the fourth candle. Still burning. So I could ask others questions, just not ones of Samuke.

"We have to be very careful in how we frame a question. Straightforward, no room for doubt." Cal glared the Marid down while pressing his fingers into my side as if to remind me he was in my corner.

I tried to think, my mind a fog of pain. "He was involved in Daniel's death," I said.

"Was that question for me?" Samuke asked, smirking wildly at the ace up his sleeve.

"No." Still I checked on the candle. "It obviously wasn't. The trick is figuring out who killed Daniel." If I asked if he knew who had killed Daniel, he could take it to mean not as a friend, or not intimately. If I asked who had killed him, he might give me a name that'd been changed after the crime. Gah, there were so many pitfalls.

"Why would anyone even want Daniel dead?"

A candle's flame vanished into the air. Shit.

"It seems your ghostly friend observed a matter that my client found most distressing. Whatever you stumbled upon worried a seal-breaker, and that is not easily done. The bullet to your heart was meant to erase that secret. Rather hilarious that you'd become a ghost and a witch of death's make would find you."

Suddenly Samuke had gotten real chatty. I wrenched my hands at the whole thing, wanting to strangle him, but silence dropped around me. Cal glared at the floor, Daniel gazed dumbstruck through the wall, and Ink...he ceased holding me up and swiveled to look me dead in the eye.

"Why are we wasting time with this? Ask the creature how to kill it, then we do as it says."

Samuke put the full fifty-two-teeth smile on display as he swiveled to Ink. "Shall you be so cavalier when it's your turn in this, Sin?"

I expected Ink to fight back with some witty repartee, but he went stone silent. "That will never happen," I insisted to both Samuke and my incubus, but neither looked convinced.

"Layla, I think he's right." Cal massaged my back and I glared at him. "Not the…not the djinn. Maybe we should focus on stopping a threat to you before it gets worse."

"I assure you, moon child, the eternal torture you will see for every second left in this meager life until your death shall be nothing compared to what I do to your mate."

"Shut it, Samuke," I snapped back with. "Cal, you don't understand…"

"Is her life worth it?" he pleaded not to me but Daniel.

This was Daniel's one chance at slipping free to whatever afterlife awaited him. Otherwise, he faced an eternity of madness and fading to nothing. There was no chance a little threat to me could even compare to — slowly, Daniel shook his head.

"So it's agreed," Ink answered for us and the first cracks showed in Samuke's veneer.

"Wait! Witch of no name, isn't there something more pressing on your mind than my death?"

"You ordered the death of my…friend." I couldn't lift my eyes to look at him, my heart stewing. I wanted Samuke dead for so many reasons, but not at Daniel's expense.

"What of your mother?"

That caught me. I whipped my head up and stared at him in shock. "My…"

"I know where she went. The seal-breaker was most interested in her, which left me curious as well. Rare for one to try to interfere in a single witch's life."

I shook my head and raised my hand.

"More than that…" Samuke eased around the edge of the bubble, both hands splayed out to press to invisible glass. "I can tell you where she *is*."

I could find her? After all these years?

"Layla?" Cal stared at me — the orphan that had suddenly sprouted a parent.

I didn't want to see her again. She abandoned me.

Why the hell did she do it? Why couldn't she take me with her? What mother lets her kid think she died? I have to know, I have to…

My gaze skipped past Samuke's wheedling face to Daniel's. If not for him, I'd never have been able to read this spell to trap him and save myself. He deserved freedom, even if I'd have to lose him.

"Samuke." I stood up tall. One chance, one question, get it right. "Where can I find the man who killed Daniel Lu?"

"Are you serious?" He chuckled deep in his throat, water sloshing with the laughter. "After all of that wind-up…? Yes, yes, the pain." He wiped it away with a hand. "You'll find the young ghost's murderer at 6080 Adams Street. But you're not going to be happy about this."

"I — " Before I could say anything, the final candle snuffed out and the bubble collapsed. Light erupted from the middle of the sigil, blinding all of us. When I dropped my arm, Samuke was gone and with him went the last of the answers to my crumbling world.

"Well…that was a choice," Ink said with a sniff.

"Here." Cal wrapped his arms around me and hefted me off the ground. "We should get out of here." He looked to Daniel who stared forlornly where Samuke had been. "And get you your closure."

"Are you ready to be free?" I asked, reaching for Daniel.

He didn't answer, only drew the tips of his cool fingers against mine.

Chapter Twenty-Six

I'd parked my car outside the gate. After a long night of healing wounds, talking, and digging through my spell book for answers, the next morning felt brighter than usual. The unescapable winter drizzle had finally abated, leaving the grass a vibrant emerald and buds of pinks about to become blossoms on the trees. It was a beautiful spring morning, which felt completely out of place here.

Dashing up in far-too-long jogging shorts, Cal dodged around the other row of cars and the ominous hearse to reach me. He glanced to the back seat filled with Ink, and fell into the passenger seat beside me. Wiping the sweat off his brow, he said, "I couldn't spot anyone, but... I mean, he knew exactly where we'd go."

"Here." I picked up the thermos in my cup holder and sloshed it at him. He accepted the mixture, then frowned.

"What's exactly in this?"

My spell book was incredibly helpful in supplying a potion to protect us from Samuke once I learned his name. He could try to use his minions, but in the end, they were just human. I bit my tongue and said, "You don't want to know."

A steadying shudder fell from his lips and Cal tipped the thermos back. I caught the bottom, knowing he would try to stop the dreadful liquid filling his mouth. "Sonofa…" He sneered, whipping his head as if there was some way to escape the taste.

I handed him my other drink, this one full of sugar to try to fight against the cloying taste of skunk ass and burnt hair. Cal slammed both hands around it and guzzled down the cherry juice. A single dribble of red caught at the edge of his mouth and I reached over to wipe it off.

He jerked away from me, before sighing. "Sorry, still jumpy after…" Taking my fingers, Cal dabbed the tip of one to his mouth, then pressed each to his lips. "You are so heartbreaking sometimes." Pain fractured in his eyes, but he held tighter to my hand, not wanting to let go. "I mean, not that you try to hurt, only…"

"I get it. I told you it wasn't easy to be with me."

Cal hooked a hand behind my head and pulled me closer. "But worth it." He tugged me to him, his lips pursing, when his face turned green and he whipped away.

"Ah, the second round. Twice as pungent coming back up as it did going down." Ink clung to our headrests, pushing his face between the gap.

"You drank this too?" Cal asked, then slapped a hand over his mouth to keep the potion down.

"Of course. I always follow our witch's orders."

Unlike Cal's worrying or Daniel's... Ink was in a bright mood. He'd already eaten ten pancakes before dawn. I kept waiting for his chastising about how he knew my mother was alive, but it wouldn't come. If anything, he'd been attentive in his weird way.

"It's a beautiful spring morn and only one activity must be enjoyed as the world sheds its winter slumber."

"Shouldn't we be preparing for whatever that genie will try to throw at us?"

Ink laughed at Cal's fretting. "Do not knot yourself so, wolf. Is it a life worth guarding if it is never lived? And, if my understanding of package transportation is correct, that collar and leash should be arriving today."

Bright pink burned over Cal's face and he shook his head. "How do you...? That's not...? Are you reading my email?"

"Should I not?"

I stared out of the window at the man standing beside the recently laid sod over churned dirt. When we'd put the address Samuke gave us into Google, and realized why he'd said it was a heartbreak, Daniel insisted he wanted to do this alone. But I couldn't let him suffer so.

Opening my door, I checked once more with the funeral leaving the cemetery. Mourners piled into their cars, no doubt looking forward to a lunch of cold cuts and crackers in a basement. Out in that field was a stone bearing the name of a woman who cheated death, instead of the one buried below it. I clenched my fist at the thought, but this wasn't about me.

"Layla, decide this for us. Is it submission to only want one hand tied up?"

"I don't know. Tuesday," I said, shutting the door and leaving my werewolf and incubus to figure out what they'd surprise me with at home. On instinct, I moved to bundle my jacket tighter, but the sun cut through the sky, warming my witch bones.

Crossing the well-worn gravel road, I veered away from the machinery burying another coffin in the ground. Most of the stones here were the tall expensive ones made out of marble. Daniel stood next to the only grave with a placeholder marker, not that it was needed. The plot was covered with flowers, balloons, and pictures.

I didn't recognize him, not from any of the newspapers, police bulletins or news segments. It wasn't until my browser helpfully pointed me to a 'related article' about the cemetery that I stared directly into the lost councilman's eyes — and the wine-colored birthmark on his neck. It was the same man who'd been fleeing from a murderous water genie when I was working at Bellpeppers, the one the whole city was looking for until his body was found.

Daniel stood with both feet firmly planted at the head of the grave, staring down at the outpouring of love for the man that killed him. A breeze picked up from the south, scattering ribbons and petals, but not moving a hair on Daniel's head. "This is how it all ends, my bones left by a river, his…"

Shaking his head, he stared up at the sun. I winced at the bright rays, but the ghost didn't even blink. Digging into my pocket, I fished out the old article I found on the lost councilman's past. "He'd had a pretty bad start, but one day — like a miracle — everything turned around."

"Let me guess, that day was June twenty-fifth."

I nodded grimly even though Daniel's back was to me. "Seems as if he made a deal with the water devil for everything he could want. And thirty years later, he paid the price." If only I'd known that wild man who ran shrieking through my store that night was the lost councilman. Daniel could have gotten the peace he deserved.

"How are you...? Stupid question, you can't possibly be anything but angry."

A slow breath raised his ghostly shoulders. "I am beyond reproach for my life having been nothing but a stepping stone to a man who carried my murder to power and wealth. But I'm also...relieved." He abandoned the sun to look at me. Light off the mylar balloons reflected in his eyes, causing small glints of silver to rise in them.

"You must be even more enraged," Daniel said. "Why...? You could have saved yourself from this creature, saved so many others, or found your mother. Why did you waste that last question on me?"

"Because." I didn't know. If I asked where my mother was, then I'd have to find her. I'd have to learn why she thought I was worth abandoning. And if I asked how to kill a Marid, then I could no longer pretend my witchcraft was a source of good. It wouldn't be killing in self-defense anymore... It'd be straight-up murder.

But there was more. "I guess I just...I wanted you to be happy. To give you one last good thing in this shit world. Instead, you're saddled with no escape. The bastard took that from you too."

Daniel smiled even with his face twisted in pain. "Layla, you've shown me kindness, life...love, more than anything I've known in decades. Even before my death. A part of me didn't want you to find my murderer, and a part of me is glad he's already dead."

He reached his hand out to me and I brushed my fingers under his palm. The chill of his body fought against the spring sun and I strained for it. "I didn't want you to leave either. I don't want you to. But if it means you'll be trapped —"

Daniel slipped his hand into mine, and placed my finger to my lips. "It means nothing to me. The future is an unending desert with white sands and a gray sky. With you, the present is every color and I will fight with everything in my power to protect you, to shield you from the monster I brought into your life."

He brushed my finger around my lips, softly tingling the skin with his ghost kiss. With a voice overrun in pain and joy, Daniel said, "I love you, Layla. No matter what fate or madness may await me in the unending march of time, nothing and no one can take that from me. No one will take this spark you planted."

I cupped the locket around my neck and held it safe. "Daniel, I..." Tears burned in my eyes and I tried to shake them away. It'd been an unending week of stretching my emotions to the breaking point. I couldn't trust myself to admit I liked pizza, never mind reciprocate his confession of love. But one thought wouldn't leave me and I had to say it aloud. "Stay with me. Haunt me. Please."

He leaned closer, the cold of his forehead brushing through mine.

"My bond?"

"Layla?"

A slow laugh rolled in my throat and I turned to watch Cal and Ink climbing the hill side by side. Ink caught up to me first. He wiped away my tears without pause and kissed my lips. For a moment, his gaze darted to the fingers Daniel controlled, but he didn't say anything. Cal brushed back my hair and whispered in my ear, "We're thinking pizza for lunch. How does that sound?"

"Ah," Ink interrupted.

"Your bottomless pit wants donuts on top of the pizza. I'm leaning toward pepperoni myself. I'm guessing mushrooms and pineapple for you."

Ink stuck his tongue out at that. "Pineapple? Are you mad?"

"A lot of monsters probably think so," I admitted before turning to Daniel. "Do you want to join me? Join all of this?"

He only stared at Ink and Cal a second before beaming into my eyes. "With everything in my heart."

A werewolf, a demon and a ghost at my beck and call—what would people say?

That I was the luckiest damn witch in the world.

"Let's get out of here," I said. "I'd like to not set foot in another graveyard for a long time."

"Seconded," Daniel added.

"So that's one half pepperoni, one half mushroom and pineapple?" Cal asked, typing on his phone to place the order.

"What of my request?"

"One third mushroom and pineapple, one third pepperoni and one third abomination," I said with a laugh.

Ink wrapped a hand around my waist and buried his lips against my neck. "I have it on good authority that you quite enjoy my abomination in all its incarnations."

"Hey," Cal interrupted, "pizza first, then the...thing we talked about in the car."

The two boys resumed their minor bickering while Ink stared over Cal's shoulders at his phone. Only the ghost remained standing in place. I turned back to Daniel who closed his eyes and breathed. "I'm not certain if I should follow you to your apartment. A warm pizza with dripping cheese and fighting for your affections sounds like an afternoon for the living."

"About that." I reached over to catch his fingers. He took control of mine, Daniel holding my hand with his. "I've been thinking that my book is full of wondrous magic. There has to be a solution to bring you back."

"You believe so?"

I couldn't explain it, but I felt it was possible, even if I had no idea how. "I do. And I will move heaven and earth to bring you back whole."

"Then I can..." He smiled wide. "I will finally be able to kiss you."

I leaned up closer to whisper in his ear. "We'll do a hell of a lot more than just kiss."

"That's an afterlife worth waiting for."

Together we walked away from the graveyard, looking forward to a future growing brighter with every day.

Epilogue

A mass of mourners stumbled right in front of his view. They cried on about their beloved aunt as if he should care. Unless their devoted sister and grand-dame had some involvement in the ongoing war against magical creatures running rampant, he didn't have time for it.

"Yes, sorry, so sad. She was quite genuine," slipped from his tongue. He adjusted the long black overcoat, wishing he could abandon it. When did the weather perk up so? At least their headquarters was as cold as the grave.

"I'm getting reports of an inextinguishable fire at the cannery. Can anyone confirm?" Dispatch chirped in his ear. No doubt one of the others would deal with it. He had far bigger fish to fry.

Dead leaves clung to deader vines plunging in and out of the chain-link fence. He didn't want to draw close and risk being seen, but he needed visual confirmation. Reaching his fingers between the clumped snarls of brown foliage, he staggered up onto his toes and peeked inside the graveyard.

To the world, it looked like a woman of average height and an impressive figure—not that he'd put such down in a report—walked through the cemetery on the arms of two gentlemen. He plucked his glasses out of his coat pocket and placed them on his nose. Another man appeared beside her, his face phasing in and out with the tree behind. Black shadows strained from the back of the dark-haired man and claws sprouted off the blond. But it was the woman he focused on, her body electric with the inescapable pulse of dangerous magic.

"This is Detective Stone," he said to his organization's leaders. "I've found the witch."

Want to see more from this author? Here's a taster for you to enjoy!

Happily Ever Austen:
Pride and Pancakes
Ellen Mint

Excerpt

Why isn't the car spinning out in the snow? Nothing dramatic that'd require an ambulance or the jaws of life, just a minor hiccup in her travel plans. Anything to delay her from this coming storm. But, no, Beth couldn't be that lucky.

Wringing her hands over the rented Civic's steering wheel, she glared out at the stark white landscape. It'd started muddy and drab, dawn hours away when she'd left New York City. Six hours later, deep in Vermont's snow-capped mountains, the azure skies did nothing to evaporate the dread in her heart.

The road was little more than dirt and snow packed down by wide wheels, increasing the throbbing headache Beth knew wouldn't vanish once she reached her destination. At the sign for the Honeymoon Cabin — *charming* — she turned right to follow an even thinner trail. The tiny car barely made it into the ruts dug out by a monstrous SUV, Beth listening to every *chunk-chunk* of snow splatting out of the wheel wells.

As a twist of smoke pierced the snow-peaked horizon, her editor's parting words rang through her skull. *'Land this damn interview, Cho. If you don't…'*

He didn't need to finish his threat—everyone in journalism was well aware of the always-looming cutbacks. It didn't matter how much money their website pulled in, it was never enough for investors. And the easiest way to line their pockets was by sending yet another reporter to the breadlines.

While the six-hour-plus drive in inclement leaning to suicidal weather didn't endear her, it was the subject of the interview that had Beth chewing glass. If it had been a fickle actor known for being handsy, she'd have brought her friend Bruno as an assistant. If it had been a mealy-mouthed politician—not that her employer cared about politics beyond if one was caught without pants—she'd have kept a slew of previous soundbites at the ready.

But this? This was…

Her thought snapped away when the ever-rising ground finally leveled out and she emerged before a picturesque cabin. It looked like a Victorian Christmas card had come to life. The cabin of massive red logs boasted a single chimney puffing perfect clouds of smoke into the air over snow-capped shingles. Quaint green shutters hung off the three windows she could make out. There was clearly a picture window for the living room, but it was frosted over from the encroaching cold. Pine trees lined the driveway, each one dusted in white snow as if a designer had painted them.

It'd be a lovely place to vacation or hide away in for a week while trying to hammer a book out. But that wasn't what awaited her inside.

Pulling a cleansing breath into her lungs, Beth snatched up her purse and laptop and struck out into the cold. Her leg sunk a foot into the snow, the freezing air punching into her chest and a gasp escaping her mouth. Cruel, frozen water tumbled into her shoes.

Damn it! Damn it! Damn it!

With each step she took to the cabin, more plummeting snow filled her ankle-high boots. They were cute for the city in winter but pointless this deep into the wilderness. It was doubtful anything short of a whole bearskin would keep someone warm up here. Thanks to her having turned up the heat in the car, the snow quickly melted to slush, seeping up her socks and leaving her crankier.

Despite dreading what awaited her inside, Beth dashed for the cabin. At least it'd be warm and snow-free. She grabbed onto the wooden railings with their woodland animal carvings and leaped up the three front steps. The door was a firehouse red with a wreath of cedar and holly hanging from it. Breathing in the smell of hamster bedding, she pushed on the handle and let herself in.

A flash of lightbulbs from by the fireplace interrupted Beth's entrances. Orange flames danced inside the stones there, three stockings without names dangling off plastic greenery above the fire. And standing beside it, an arm lazily draped over the mantel, was what had had her grinding her teeth for six hours.

"Tristan?" the photographer called the stone man glaring through space. "Can you turn and raise your chin?"

If he raised it any higher, all her shots would be directly up his nose.

Tristan Harty. Once a teenage heartthrob sporting floppy hair that dusted over those striking blue eyes, he'd climbed the charts with a handful of songs plucked out on his guitar. The trajectory of his career followed the majority of those who began in the same way. He'd grown older, teenage girls had moved on, his star had faded. Now, he was trying a comeback thanks to the rise in '90s nostalgia and his PR team had finagled an exclusive interview with her magazine.

Instead of the leather jacket overtop an expertly distressed T-shirt, they'd dressed him like Father Christmas. A black suit coat, tailored tight to his thin frame, lay unbuttoned over a crimson vest. A pocket watch, of all things, dangled off the vest. *Does he intend to recite some Dickens to the photographer as well?* Time had thinned the soulful mane of his younger years. Locks shorn to an inch revealed more of his forehead than any had seen in a decade.

While most men his age would have wrinkles piling up across that vast brow, the cold demeanor of Tristan Harty kept his face nearly as preserved as if he were a botoxed socialite. Somehow, his record company had convinced an entire generation of fifteen-year-olds that he was the deepest, most soulful man in existence. Beth wanted to laugh at the thought when the man in question focused away from his photographer to where she stood dripping at the front door.

Eyes bluer than a sapphire burned into her soul. She tried to swallow, but her throat constricted. Even turning her head was proving impossible as ten thousand watts bore down upon her.

"You!" a voice shouted, evaporating the confounding spell. Beth blinked, glancing back at the once bewitching man. With the glare broken, he transformed back into a snooty aristocrat hoisting up a guitar.

From the mess of photography equipment that claimed the cabin's entire living room bustled a wide man. He wasn't fat, at least not in that lovable oaf way, but his rectangular build easily fit into a doorway. He was the comedic opposite of the thin man pretending to play a song for the camera.

"Who are you?" he shouted at Beth.

She flexed her lips in a not smile. "The interviewer."

What had to be the manager scoffed. "You're late. What took you so damn long?"

"I'm afraid transporters haven't been invented yet, so I had to rely upon the old-fashioned horseless carriage," Beth snapped, in no mood to be shouted down by the reason she was in this mess. There were a dozen more interesting concerts and art house movies she could be reviewing at home instead of wasting an entire weekend in Vermont.

The manager pinged his beady eyes skyward. "What? You never heard of airplanes?"

She chewed on her tongue, keeping the caustic comment at bay. There was no chance of her company splurging on an airline ticket, seeing as how they couldn't ship their reporters as freight.

"Barry...?" A voice of reason stepped into the fray as the very subject of the interview spoke up. "Let it be," Tristan whispered. His speaking voice was soft and drifted in the tenor range, a surprise for anyone who knew his songs.

Barry the manager was in no mood to do such a thing. He was clearly incensed there was no underpaid intern to boss around and had to take all that anger out on someone. "Listen here..." Whatever derogatory term floated in his brain remained there, though he stared twice as hard at her eyes. "We ain't got time to waste here. So get this little Q&A session done fast. Got it?"

"Mr. Barry." Beth unlatched her purse, picking up her phone. "This little 'Q&A session' is part of the deal. I have full access to your…talent, and we host a release for his album." She should have been surprised at having to remind him of the back-scratching contract, but it was a wonder sometimes that most managers had the wherewithal to work a bed.

His annoyance at her tripled in strength. Beth internally smiled at her barbs when Barry pointed toward an open room. "Fine! Set up in there. I'll send Tristan in once he's finished."

"Thank you ever so much." She hefted her bag closer to her side. Just before she turned her back on the primping and posturing, another cobalt glare burned across her sights. For a foolish breath, her cheeks burned.

So I'm to work in the bedroom? While grateful she wasn't being forced to conduct her interview in the bathroom, she'd done worse. Once, she'd had to question a football player while crammed inside a food truck while an untended open fire singed an inch off her hair. Though, as she gazed around the room, a new unease settled in her gut.

While the living room and small adjacent kitchen were rustic and woodland themed, this was where the honeymoon adjective came from. The bed was gigantic, with four posters painted like birch trees, and a damn canopy, of all things. Red and pink silks hung off the posts and a shimmery duvet covered the bed itself. Perched between the ordinary pillows was one in the shape of a heart. There were no bottles of wine in a bucket on the nightstand, but a remote sat there instead. Beth was both curious and terrified to see what it was for.

She glanced at the oval-shaped mirror set in the vanity, finding in the glass an exhausted woman who'd been awake since three a.m., driven up a mountain and still had to crack this damn introvert. At least she'd thought to check in at the hotel first, knowing she'd be exhausted by the time this was over. A warm bath and a night of typing in her terrycloth pajamas was as good a reward as she could count on.

Unbuttoning her blazer, Beth set to work. There wasn't much in the way of seating in the bedroom, so she picked up the vanity's chair and placed it in the center. Hopefully, Tristan would feel just comfortable enough to be uncomfortable. Laying out her tools of the trade the way a warrior would before battle, Beth inspected the batteries' lives. Her phone was holding strong — she'd learned to keep her apps to a minimum lest she miss a vital picture or be unable to record a pivotal quote. The laptop was at seventy percent. Not great, but she'd only crack into it once she was back at the hotel.

The room felt too bright and cheerful. For some subjects, that'd be perfect. The candy-coated-sprinkle types loved nothing more than to bake cupcakes and divulge all their secrets while frosting. But not Tristan Harty. He'd been in the spotlight for over fifteen years, then out for eight. In all that time, the most people'd gotten out of him was his name, date of birth and current hit song. He was a black hole of personal information, and in order to keep her job, Beth had to get this vacuum to sing.

Cracking her knuckles, she took one last look at her reflection. Instead of the fretting thirty-year-old reporter, she saw a little girl. With her neon-pink unicorn notebook in hand, that girl in pigtails had been prepared to ask dictators and humanitarians alike the hard questions, and wouldn't stop until she got them. This Beth could handle some has-been musician.

About the Author

Ellen Mint adores the adorkable heroes who charm with their shy smiles and heroines that pack a punch. She has a needy black lab named after Granny Weatherwax from Discworld. Sadly, her dog is more of a Magrat.

When she's not writing imposing incubi or saucy aliens, she does silly things like make a tiny library full of her books. Her background is in genetics and she married a food scientist so the two of them nerd out over things like gut bacteria. She also loves gaming, particularly some of the bigger RPG titles. If you want to get her talking for hours, just bring up Dragon Age.

Ellen loves to hear from readers. You can find her contact information, website details and author profile page at https://www.totallybound.com

Home of Erotic Romance

Sign up for our newsletter and find out about all our romance book releases, eBook sales and promotions, sneak peeks and FREE romance books!